The man came out of nowhere.

One second the passenger seat beside Allison was empty, and the next second, there he was, all huffing six feet of him.

"Just drive," he barked at her. "I mean it. Drive! I—I have a gun!"

Stay calm, stay calm, stay calm, she chanted over and over in her head.

He certainly didn't *look* like a criminal. No prison pallor, for one thing. And you could hardly call those deep blue eyes shifty. With that tousled black hair and sexy cleft in his chin, it was easier to picture his face on a movie screen than on a Wanted poster.

But just because he was good-looking didn't mean he wasn't dangerous. He had an air of desperation about him; he was breathing more rapidly than *she* was, for heaven's sake.

Just who was in trouble here, anyway?

Dear Reader,

Welcome to the Silhouette **Special Edition**
experience! With your search for consistently
satisfying reading in mind, every month the
authors and editors of Silhouette **Special Edition**
aim to offer you a stimulating blend of deep
emotions and high romance.

The name Silhouette **Special Edition** and the
distinctive arch on the cover represent a
commitment—a commitment to bring you six
sensitive, substantial novels each month. In the
pages of a Silhouette **Special Edition**, compelling
true-to-life characters face riveting emotional
issues—and come out winners. Both celebrated
authors and newcomers to the series strive for
depth and dimension, vividness and warmth, in
writing these stories of living and loving in today's
world.

The result, we hope, is romance you can believe in.
Deeply emotional, richly romantic, infinitely
rewarding—that's the Silhouette **Special Edition**
experience. Come share it with us—six times a
month!

From all the authors and editors of Silhouette
Special Edition,

Best wishes,

Leslie Kazanjian,
Senior Editor

KAYLA DANIELS
Father Knows Best

Silhouette Special Edition

Published by Silhouette Books New York

America's Publisher of Contemporary Romance

For Jenny-Bear,
who makes life
a merry-go-round

SILHOUETTE BOOKS
300 East 42nd St., New York, N.Y. 10017

Copyright © 1990 by Kayla Daniels

ISBN: 0-373-09578-3

First Silhouette Books printing February 1990

Printed in the U.S.A.

Books by Kayla Daniels

Silhouette Special Edition

Spitting Image #474
Father Knows Best #578

KAYLA DANIELS

has three great passions: travel, ballroom dancing and
Norwegian cuisine. She is currently working her way
from Afghanistan to Zimbabwe by reading one book
about every country in the world. She takes breaks
from writing to study piano and to play baritone horn
with the local college band.

DAD AND ME IN CALIFORNIA

1 - Dad and me met this weird lady in Los Angeles and went in her car. Dad drove.

2 - I wanted to go to the zoo, but Dad wouldn't stop driving.

3 - Dad had stuff to do, and Allison bought us corn dogs.

4 - Dad told Allison to buy stuff. She got a piñata, but it was empty.

5 - We drove *forever*, then stopped at night. The next day we went to the beach. I think Dad likes Allison.

6 - I ran away from Allison so I could see the sea lions. Dad got real mad. Then all our stuff got stoled, and I got real sick.

7 - After I got better we went to see all the people at Fisherman's Wharf. Then the bad man found us again, and we had to run away on the trolley car.

8 - I like Allison a lot. We all went to Fresno. I don't know why, but Dad took us there, and I guess he knows best....

Chapter One

Nick Caldwell switched on the ignition, then froze.

Across the palm tree-lined residential street sat a nondescript brown late-model American car. A bit below standard for this wealthy Pacific Palisades, California neighborhood, but other than that, nothing unusual.

It wasn't the car that interested Nick, however. It was the driver.

Pretending to search for something in the glove compartment of his pickup truck, Nick scrutinized the man.

Although the driver was slumped down behind the steering wheel pretending to doze, Nick got a good look at him. Glasses perched on a hawk-like nose, long hair on one side combed over his head to cover a bald spot. Damn! Nick could swear it was the same guy who'd followed him in El Paso. And if not...well, he wasn't about to take any chances.

Flicking off the ignition, Nick opened the door and stepped into the street. The man in the brown car sat up a little straighter. Forcing himself to move slowly, calmly, Nick walked back up the driveway of the house where he'd spent the morning laying down a flagstone patio.

You've forgotten something in the backyard, he told himself. *No need to hurry—you're just going to retrieve a tool and then come back to the truck. Nothing urgent.*

Yet it took every ounce of his considerable willpower to move slowly. Sweat trickled down the back of his neck, even though the late May sunshine wasn't that hot. He sensed watchful eyes boring into his back, urging him to break loose and run.

Not yet, he said silently.

Just a few more yards, a few more feet, and he would be out of sight. And then Nick *did* break into a run, dashing across the backyard and the newly finished patio, scrambling over the high brick wall and launching himself into the next backyard.

He jogged across the grass, dodging the swimming pool and praying whoever owned this house didn't own Doberman pinschers as well. Sweat dripped in his eyes, blinding him; adrenaline pumped through his veins. Over the deafening thud of his own heart, he strained to hear any sound of pursuit.

Hunched over, Nick skirted the house and stumbled onto the front sidewalk. Which way now? He raked his fingers through dark, sweat-damp hair, bouncing nervously on the balls of his feet, trying to decide which direction to run.

Behind him, he heard a faint scrabbling sound, as if someone were trying to follow him over the brick wall.

Nick's heaving chest was compressed by an iron band, as a flicker of panic knifed through his guts. He had to get out of here, had to escape or else . . .

For a moment his ragged panting filled the quiet cul-de-sac. Then a blue Volkswagen van skidded around the corner.

Allison Reed was trying to read a map and drive at the same time. Where the heck was Vesuvius Drive, anyway? She peered at the map book balanced on the steering wheel, then looked up just in time to avoid grazing a fire hydrant.

She pushed a loose strand of auburn hair from her eyes and squinted at the map again. Let's see, she'd turned left off Sunset Boulevard, so one of these streets—

She veered sharply back into her lane as an oncoming garbage truck bore down on her, horn blasting angrily.

Damn! As if she didn't have enough to worry about, without getting lost in the wilds of Pacific Palisades! This catering job could mean a new account, if Allison could wow Mrs. Van Doren and her garden club with her shrimp puffs and pasta salad. Being late for the club's monthly meeting and luncheon was definitely *not* part of Allison's strategy to impress the ladies.

Not that Allison and her partner, Marilyn, were desperate for new business. Incredible Edibles was doing quite well in its fifth year of operation.

But every little bit helps, Allison thought. *Or should I say, every little bite?* She giggled, inordinately pleased with her own bad joke.

Now if she could only find Mrs. Van Doren's house! Why couldn't this luncheon be someplace like Santa Monica or West Los Angeles, where streets ran in nice perpendicular grids as they were meant to? For some reason, the wealthy seemed compelled to build their homes on convoluted, curvy streets that required a degree in geography to navigate.

Oops, was this her turn? Allison swung left suddenly. Rats! Not only was this street not Vesuvius Drive, but she'd managed to wind up in another dead end!

She zoomed down the block to where the cul-de-sac opened into a large circle, then realized she hadn't turned sharply enough to complete the maneuver. Double rats! She jammed the transmission into reverse, remembering to slow down as she backed up. The rear of the van was outfitted with built-in warming compartments and a refrigerator. *Mustn't let Mrs. Van Doren's Swedish meatballs go tumbling all over the floor,* Allison scolded herself.

She shifted the van into first gear, and that's when the passenger door flew open.

The man came out of nowhere. One second the seat beside Allison was empty, and the next second, there he was, all huffing six feet of him.

"Hey, what do you think you're—"

"Just drive," he barked at her. When Allison refused to budge, staring at him in open-mouthed astonishment, he said, "I mean it. Drive! I—I have a gun!"

With his hand stuffed in the pocket of his navy-blue sweatshirt jacket, he brandished a hidden weapon at her. Allison gulped. Her green eyes darted up and down the street. Deserted. No one to help her. Slowly, she depressed the accelerator.

"Faster!" he demanded. He seemed almost as terrified as she was.

Allison sped up reluctantly, but the corner stop sign soon forced her to stop—thank goodness. She wasn't about to drive this maniac to some dark, secluded warehouse where he could assault her without being disturbed. This might be her last chance to escape.

In a blur of motion, Allison yanked back the door handle, ready to fling herself out onto the pavement, into the path of oncoming cars, in front of a steamroller—she didn't care what. Anything was preferable to the fate awaiting her at the hands of this madman.

The door refused to open. In one sinking instant Allison realized that her door was locked, and wouldn't open until she pulled up the knob. It figured. She'd left the passenger side conveniently unlocked so some escaped felon could jump in, but locked her own side so she couldn't escape.

Like lightning, she twisted to unlock the door, but her captor grabbed her arm before she could reach the knob. "None of that," he warned. "Now let's get out of here." He waved the concealed gun at her. "Now!"

Gulping, Allison started to drive. *Stay calm Stay calm Stay calm,* she chanted over and over in her head. She had to think clearly to be able to outwit him. "Wh-where do you want me to go?" she squeaked. God, her throat felt like sandpaper!

"Turn left at this corner. Then right." He directed her through a maze of streets until she was hopelessly confused. As if she weren't lost enough to begin with!

"Look, I'm sorry about this," he said. "I promise not to hurt you if you just drive where I tell you." He licked his lips. "I don't *want* to hurt you," he continued, sounding as if he were pleading with her.

Well, Allison would be happy to oblige him. It seemed they both wanted the same thing.

As they turned onto Sunset Boulevard, Allison spotted a police car prowling slowly ahead of them in the right lane. Hope rose in her heart like a helium balloon. She switched lanes and prepared to pull up alongside the cruiser.

Taking a deep breath, Allison got ready to attract attention by swerving the catering van from side to side, maybe even bashing into the police car if she was lucky. With a flash of regret, she remembered all the food stored neatly in the back. Not for long.

Then a hand fell on her wrist, causing her to veer slightly. "Uh-uh," he said. "Don't do it."

Allison cleared her throat as hope congealed in her stomach like cold oatmeal. "Do what?" she asked innocently.

"You know what I'm talking about."

So, another plan shot down in flames. What now? She'd seen lots of hostage situations on TV. Didn't they always try to reason with the bad guy, keep him talking?

Allison forced herself to look sideways at him. He met Allison's gaze, then looked away guiltily. Maybe she had a chance after all.

"You don't have to threaten me, you know," she said. "I'll drive you wherever you want to go, if you need to get there that badly."

She felt the man studying her. "I doubt that," he said finally. "If I were you, I'd try all the things *you've* tried so far to escape." Something about his voice made Allison relax a tiny fraction. Her abductor seemed strangely sympathetic to her plight.

"Would you mind telling me where we're going?" she asked casually.

"Turn left here." He directed her out of Pacific Palisades, down into the winding roads of Santa Monica Canyon. "I promise as soon as we get there, I'll let you go." One hand was still in his pocket; he rubbed his square jaw with the other. "I just want you to know, I've never done anything like this before," he said.

"Well, let me assure you, you're doing a swell job for a novice."

He stared at Allison for a second, then burst out laughing. The rich, vibrant sound filled the van, bringing a wobbly smile to Allison's lips. "You have a pretty good sense of humor," he said.

"Thank you. It comes in handy during situations like this."

He arched his dark eyebrows. "Don't tell me this has happened to you before!"

"No, no... I'm as new at this as you are." Allison spared him another glance. He certainly didn't *look* like a criminal. No prison pallor, for one thing. Well-tanned and muscular, he looked as if he was used to working outdoors. And you could hardly call those deep blue eyes shifty. Worried, maybe, but not shifty. With that tousled black hair and sexy cleft in his chin, it was easier to picture his face on a movie screen than on a wanted poster.

Yet here he was, threatening her with a gun. Well, he hadn't exactly *threatened* her, had he? In fact, he seemed particularly anxious *not* to hurt her.

And how did she know he really had a gun, anyway? Why did he hide it in his sweatshirt pocket? Maybe she should call his bluff....

No way. Just because he was good-looking didn't mean he wasn't dangerous. He had an air of desperation about him; he was breathing more rapidly than *she* was, for heaven's sake. Just who was in trouble here, anyway?

"Pull over, please."

The van coasted to a stop in front of an elementary school. They were in Santa Monica, only about a mile from Allison's house, as a matter of fact. The knowledge was somehow comforting.

"You can go now," he said.

Allison stared at him. "You mean that's it?"

He nodded almost apologetically.

"You hijack me at gunpoint to drive you around in circles for fifteen minutes and then drop you off less than five miles away? What's the matter, did you leave the house without bus fare this morning?"

Now that the danger was apparently past, anger rose in Allison's chest, replacing the fear that had so recently lodged there. *Shut up, Allison,* a little voice warned. How many times before had speaking or acting impulsively gotten her in trouble?

Yet relief was like a drug in her bloodstream, stimulating her, making her reckless. The tremendous pressure she'd just been subjected to demanded some release. She was back in control, and she was furious.

"You've got a lot of nerve, mister, waving a gun in my face, scaring me half to death and then dismissing me like a taxicab driver! What the hell did you think—"

"I don't have a gun," he muttered.

Allison paused. "What?"

"I said, I don't have a gun." With a sheepish grin, he pulled his hand from his pocket and dangled a bunch of keys in front of her eyes. "See?"

Allison nearly choked with indignation. "Of all the—"

"Look, would it have made you feel better if I really had a gun?" he asked. "I apologize. I told you. I'm new at this. Next time I'll know better."

Allison collapsed against the seat. She shook her head, burying her face in her hands. After a moment she looked up. "I don't believe this," she said with a laugh. "We're on *Candid Camera*, right?"

Her former captor tried to smile. "I can't tell you how sorry I am about this," he said. "I wish I could make it up to you, but I don't suppose I'll ever have the chance."

"Not if I see you coming first," Allison retorted. Then her lips curved into a reluctant smile. This whole situation was so ridiculous, how could she stay angry?

But when he reached for her hand, she recoiled instinctively, still wary. He clasped her slender fingers between his large, callused hands for a moment. His touch was strong yet gentle. An odd thrill shimmered down Allison's spine. The man's eyes glowed with some unfathomable yearning.

His face could have been chiseled from a block of granite, all solid lines and forceful angles. He looked like a man who had suffered a lot, but learned to endure. He really was exceptionally handsome, Allison reflected. Too bad he was a lunatic.

"I've got to go," he said softly, as if bidding her goodbye after a pleasant evening. "Thanks again. I wish I could tell you how much you've helped me." Reluctantly, he released her hand.

Then he was gone, loping across the street with athletic grace and vanishing into an alley that ran between two apartment buildings.

Allison watched him disappear, intrigued in spite of herself by his broad, sweatshirt-clad shoulders and the snug-fitting jeans that hugged his long, lean legs.

Blinking, she thumped the side of her head with the heel of her hand. Had she dreamed the whole adventure? When she woke up, she was definitely swearing off the blue-cheese-and-pepperoni pizza before bedtime.

"Omigosh!" Allison yelped. "Mrs. Van Doren's luncheon!"

She wavered for an instant. Shouldn't she call the police or something? After all, she'd just been the victim of a kidnapping, no matter how offbeat.

Glancing at her watch, Allison made a quick decision. If she really stepped on it, she could still make it to Vesuvius Drive in time to salvage the luncheon. Maybe she would call the police later. After all, no harm done, right? A person needed a good scare now and then. It kept you on your toes, she reasoned.

Satisfied with her rationalization, Allison started the engine and swooped into a screeching U-turn.

As the catering van roared off, Nick Caldwell stepped out of the alley. He crossed the street, then jogged up the front steps of the elementary school and disappeared inside.

"Have you lost your mind?" Marilyn Grant asked.

"More coffee?" replied Allison. "It's the last of the Blue Mountain Jamaica. You might as well finish it—the stuff's as expensive as diamonds."

"You haven't answered my question," Marilyn said, but she extended her cup for a refill.

The two women were perched on tall counter stools back in the kitchen of their downtown Santa Monica storefront. Fifteen minutes earlier, Marilyn had locked the front door to signal the close of another business day. Once the two women were alone and wouldn't be interrupted by customers, Allison poured out the story of the handsome hijacker.

She'd been dying to tell Marilyn about it ever since returning from Mrs. Van Doren's that afternoon. The luncheon had been a success despite the caterer's delayed appearance, and Allison was confident that Incredible Edibles had just found another regular customer.

But that wasn't what Allison wanted to talk about as she and Marilyn sipped coffee and rested their feet after closing.

Unfortunately, Marilyn wasn't as enchanted with Allison's narrow escape as Allison was.

"How many times have I warned you about keeping the van locked up?" she scolded. "If you'd listened to me, none of this would have happened."

Allison rolled her eyes. Marilyn was forty-five, sixteen years older than she was. Sometimes she acted more like a mother than a business partner, but Allison was extremely fond of her anyway. It's just that Allison already *had* a perfectly good mother back in Minnesota. "Okay, okay, you're right, I should have kept both doors locked. But doesn't it sound exciting?"

"That kind of excitement I can do without. What I don't understand is why you didn't call the police right away."

Allison shrugged. "Well, I don't know...I kind of felt sorry for the guy. I hated to sic the cops on him."

"You're amazing." Marilyn shook her head. "What you really mean is that you didn't call the police because you were attracted to the guy."

Allison chewed her lower lip. "Well...maybe I was. But that's not why I didn't call them. No, really!" she insisted as Marilyn raised a skeptical eyebrow. "What would have been the point? By the time they arrived, he would have been long gone. They'd never have found him. Besides, he didn't hurt me or anything."

"He threatened you with a gun!" Marilyn exclaimed.

"No, he threatened me with a set of keys," Allison pointed out.

Marilyn threw up her hands. "I give up! If you intend to make a habit of consorting with criminals, it's your life. Just promise you won't tell *me* about it." She patted her short, brown, elegantly coiffed hair. "I have enough gray hairs already."

"But they're very becoming gray hairs," Allison teased.

"You're changing the subject," Marilyn said, sliding off the stool. "But I'm going to let you get away with it, because it's your night to clean up and I'm exhausted and I'm going home now. So there."

Allison walked Marilyn to the back door and, on impulse, gave her partner a quick hug. "Thanks for worrying about me," she said.

Marilyn reddened, brushing Allison's thanks aside. Gruffly, she said, "Well, *someone* has to look out for you. Since you're so rotten at it."

"Gee, thanks," Allison laughed. She waved goodbye as Marilyn got into her car. "See you tomorrow!" she called.

Then she was alone in the kitchen, savoring the delicious coffee and baking smells, and wondering how a mismatched pair like Marilyn and her had ever wound up together.

As she swept the floor and loaded the dishwasher, Allison mused about their differences. Marilyn, at five feet ten inches, towered over Allison by half a foot. Marilyn's baby-fine hair was always perfectly in place, while Allison's long, unruly auburn locks defied restraint. Marilyn wore expensive skirt suits with ruffled blouses, while Allison's favorite garb was jeans and a pullover sweater.

So much for physical comparisons. Their personality contrasts were equally stark. Marilyn was sensible and down-to-earth, while Allison had her head in the clouds. Marilyn was skeptical and a bit cynical, the result of an ugly divorce seven years ago. Allison's love life had been a comedy of errors so far, but through the series of disasters, she'd managed to retain her idealism and her sense of romance.

Yet their business partnership had flourished. Allison totted up the day's receipts with satisfaction. They weren't rich yet, but someday...

And despite their differences, the two women were genuinely fond of each other. Didn't Marilyn's little lecture earlier prove that she was concerned about Allison's well-being?

Guilt nibbled at Allison. She hadn't told Marilyn *everything* about the handsome hijacker. For instance, she'd neglected to mention finding his keys wedged in the passenger seat of the van this afternoon.

Allison switched off the lights, let herself outside and locked the back door. As she set the burglar alarm, she wondered what Marilyn would say if she knew there was an excellent chance Allison would be seeing her abductor again. Soon.

And this time, he would have some explaining to do.

"Dad, where are we going?"

Good question, Nick thought. *I wish I had the slightest idea.*

Danny had been delighted to be pulled out of class, especially since the first grade was in the middle of a spelling test. Nick wasn't sure the teacher had believed his flimsy story that he'd just remembered Danny had a dental appointment at noon, but it probably didn't matter.

Neither Nick nor Danny would ever see the teacher again.

"How come we're riding the bus?" Danny asked. "Where's the car?"

"At home, sport," Nick replied absently, ruffling his son's fine blond hair. He was trying to figure out the safest plan for getting in and out of their apartment. Would someone be watching it? He didn't think so. Otherwise that private detective would simply have waited there for Nick to show up with Danny. He wouldn't have been spying on Nick in Pacific Palisades unless he still didn't know where they lived.

But now that their pursuer was this close, it wouldn't take him long to discover the Caldwells' address.

Nick wouldn't even risk going back to the apartment, except the car was there, along with several thousand dollars he'd stashed in one of the sofa cushions. There wasn't time to pack; they would have to leave everything else behind, including the pickup truck Nick used for work.

It didn't matter. As long as the one thing in the world he cared about was safe.

Nick gazed at his son, resisting the nearly overwhelming urge to grab him in his arms and smother him with hugs. Seven-year-old boys weren't too keen on public displays of affection—especially seven-year-olds who wanted to be Mickey Mantle when they grew up.

Danny surveyed the passing scenery, swinging his thin legs back and forth. He was obviously happy to be out of school, and seemed completely unconcerned about whatever lay ahead. For that, Nick was grateful.

But he dreaded telling Danny they had to go on the run again. Danny had made a few friends here in Santa Monica, and even found some kids to play baseball with after school. That pale, haunted look in his face had faded, along with the dark rings that used to circle his enormous blue eyes. His bruises—physical and emotional—were healing, and Nick hated like hell to uproot him again.

But the alternative was worse.

Warm exhaust fumes enveloped them as they hopped off the bus two stops past their apartment. Nick wasn't taking any chances in case someone was watching for them. They took a roundabout route home, Danny happily swinging his Dodgers lunch box back and forth, banging it against his knees.

Every time a car approached, Nick tensed, ready to snatch Danny up and run like hell. As they drew closer to home, Nick's caution increased. He led Danny up the alley and into the laundry room of the apartment building next door to theirs.

The room was empty, except for the smell of detergent and fabric softener. None of the machines was running. Luck was with Nick for the first time that day. Well, for the second time, he amended, remembering the catering van and its gorgeous driver.

Closing the door behind him, Nick knelt in front of Danny and held his son by the shoulders. Looking him squarely in the eye, Nick said, "Danny, I have something very important to tell you. It's bad news, but if you and I work together, everything will be okay."

Danny blinked, and his eyes seemed to expand to fill his whole face. "Do we hafta run away again, Dad?"

Nick squeezed his thin shoulders. "I'm afraid so, Shortstop. But we're gonna stick together, you and me, and we'll be all right."

"Did that bad man find us?" Danny's thumb crept toward his mouth; then he apparently remembered he'd given up that childish habit, and dropped his hand to his side.

Nick nodded. "He isn't exactly a bad man, Danny. But we can't let him find us."

"He wants to take me away, doesn't he?" Danny's eyes glittered with tears.

Nick shuddered with repressed violence. He could kill them all—Sheila, the judge, the detective—for the terrified look on his son's face.

This time he *did* hug his son, and for a moment Nick couldn't speak, as his own throat clogged with tears.

Then he held Danny at arm's length and tweaked his nose. "Now I want you to listen very carefully and do exactly what I say, okay, kiddo?"

Danny sniffled and nodded his head.

"I'm going to go home and grab a few of our things. I want you to wait here for me. After I leave, you turn this little button in the doorknob and lock the door." Nick didn't know if the building's tenants had keys to this room or not, since apparently it was normally unlocked. But at least a locked door would slow them down a bit. And more than that, it would keep anyone else out.

"Don't open the door for anyone but me. You can peek out the curtain and see who it is first, okay? I won't be gone long."

As Nick rose to his feet, Danny said, "Dad?"

"Uh-huh?"

"Can you bring my baseball?"

His autographed baseball, signed by the great Ted Williams. Nick had passed it on to his son years ago, in another lifetime. It was Danny's most prized possession, just as it had once been Nick's.

"Sure," he said. "I'll bring your baseball."

With one final hug, Nick slipped out the door, waiting until Danny locked the door behind him. He ran a few steps down the alley, then cautiously edged along the walkway of their apartment building.

They lived in one of the middle apartments on the second floor, and as Nick bounded up the stairs two at a time, his senses were alert for any unusual sights or sounds. At the same time his brain was frantically planning ahead, deciding what to take, figuring he would drive the car down the alley and pull up just outside the laundry room so Danny wouldn't be out in the open for more than a second.

At the head of the stairs Nick hesitated. No sign of trouble.

As he walked swiftly to their apartment, Nick reached into his sweatshirt pocket for his keys. Frowning, he dug into his jeans pockets, then patted the rear pocket where he kept his wallet.

Cursing, Nick pounded the front door once with his fist, then slumped against it in despair. His wallet was there, all right.

But his keys were missing.

Chapter Two

Two years on the run had sharpened Nick's powers of observation. More than once, his acute awareness and eye for detail had gotten Danny and him out of a tight spot.

Earlier, when he'd commandeered that catering truck and its lovely driver, he'd noticed a stack of advertising brochures on the floor of the van. So he knew that Incredible Edibles was owned by Marilyn Grant and Allison Reed.

But which one was the pretty driver?

Nick dropped a quarter in a pay phone at Santa Monica Place shopping mall, where he and Danny were hiding out until dark. They had less chance of being spotted at night. Besides, Nick wanted to give Marilyn or Allison time to get home from work before he went after his keys.

Nick had broken a bathroom window to get into his apartment, where he'd stuffed a few of Danny's clothes—and his Ted Williams autographed baseball—into the boy's backpack. Then he'd retrieved the cash from the sofa cushion and stuffed it into the bottom of a battered suitcase, hastily covering it with some of his own clothes.

Unfortunately, two years on the run had *not* taught Nick how to hot-wire a car, so his Toyota was still in its parking space back at the apartment building. He would have to get his keys back first, before he and Danny could be on their way.

In desperation, Nick had left Danny in the shopping mall while he jogged the three blocks to Incredible Edibles. He'd found the catering van parked out back, but couldn't spot his keys through the windows.

Then Nick discovered one of the doors was unlocked. He hesitated for an instant, then slipped inside the van. After all, they were *his* keys, weren't they? He found it hard to believe the driver hadn't learned her lesson and started locking her doors, but he wasn't about to argue with this unexpected stroke of luck. Unfortunately, his good luck was short-lived, because the keys weren't there.

Nick was positive he'd dropped them in the van. Which meant that his former captive had found them. His keys were probably in some police evidence locker already, but Nick had to be sure. Without the car, he and Danny were *really* in a fix.

So after searching the van, Nick had come back to the mall and picked up Danny at the pet store, where he'd left his son making friends with a basset hound puppy. As Nick punched out the number on the pay phone, he kept an eye on Danny, who sat on a nearby bench, guarding the suitcase.

The phone rang at the other end of the line. The abrupt "Hello?" wasn't enough to tell Nick if this was the van's driver.

"May I please speak to Marilyn Grant?" he asked, making his voice as deep as possible so she wouldn't recognize it.

"This is Marilyn Grant," she replied. "Who's this?"

It wasn't her. "I'm very sorry, I wanted someone else named Marilyn Grant. I must have the wrong number."

A horrible thought struck Nick as he hung up. What if the van driver wasn't either Marilyn Grant or Allison Reed, but one of their employees? He would never have time to track her down.

He dialed Allison Reed's number, and his knees went weak with relief when a familiar voice answered. He would recognize that voice anywhere. Without saying a word, Nick gently replaced the receiver. He'd already checked the phone book, and had both women's addresses. Now he knew that Allison Reed was the one he wanted.

The mall was getting ready to close. "Come on, sport," he said to Danny. "Time to go."

Allison Reed lived in a small Spanish-style bungalow about a ten-minute bus ride from the mall. The front of the tan stucco house was partially concealed by bushes, where Nick was able to find a temporary hiding place for Danny.

"I'll only be a minute," Nick whispered. "You guard the suitcase."

Danny nodded solemnly, and Nick gave his son's baseball cap a playful tug before gliding silently over the lawn, trying to stay in the shadows cast by the yellow porch light. He skirted the house, peering into each window, not knowing what to expect. What if Allison had roommates, or worse—some big, beefy husband who would pound the stuffing out of Nick when Allison screamed at the sight of him.

He was also worried the detective might show up. If the guy had spotted Nick getting into Allison's catering van that morning, it wouldn't take him long to track her down.

Nick edged up the driveway, past a beat-up green Volvo, and found Allison in the kitchen. She had a radio tuned to a rock station and was prancing around to the rhythmic beat in front of her open refrigerator, a jar of peanut butter in her hand.

Nick stepped to the back door and rapped sharply on the glass window. "Hey, lady, is dis your car out here?" he yelled sharply on the glass window. "Hey, lady, is dis your car out here?" he yelled in his best Brooklyn accent.

The door flew open. "Yes, what's the mat—oh, no, *you* again!" she exclaimed. She tried to slam the door shut, but Nick got his foot partway inside. This was a highly overrated method of gaining entrance, he decided, grimacing from the sharp pain in his foot.

"Please, don't yell, all right? I just want ten seconds of your time, that's all. Please. I swear I won't hurt you. I need your help. Please, Allison, let me in."

Startled, Allison studied him through the six-inch gap in the doorway. How did he know her name? Curiosity finally convinced her to let him in. That and the knowledge that he was perfectly capable of forcing the door all the way open whether or not she let him in willingly. The fact that he hadn't done so seemed evidence that he really didn't mean her any harm.

Warily, Allison stood aside as he limped into her kitchen. "I really appreciate this," he said. "I won't take up much of your time, but I—I—" He paused, then lowered his voice. "Say, your, uh, boyfriend's not around or anything, is he?"

Allison folded her arms. "Just my rottweiler, Max. He's in the other room. One command from me, and he'll rip your throat out."

"Oh." His hand moved instinctively toward his neck. "Well, see, I left something in your van earlier today, something very important, and I need to get it back."

"Oh?" Allison's green eyes widened innocently. "And what might that be?"

"A set of keys."

"Gee, are you sure?" she asked. Whoever this guy was, he was sure cute when he was ill at ease. Definitely cute. "They must still be in the van, I guess."

He mumbled something.

"I beg your pardon?"

He sighed, then met her gaze straight on. "I said, they're *not* still in the van."

"Oh?" This was getting more interesting by the moment. "And just how do you know that?"

"Because I searched the van before I came over here," he said. He raked his long, tanned fingers through his black hair. "I'm sorry. I didn't like trespassing, but it's absolutely imperative that I find those keys."

Allison had no intention of informing her unexpected guest that the keys he was so desperate to get his hands on were at that very moment in a drawer less than four feet from him.

She planned to keep that news flash a secret—until she knew what he was up to.

"You snuck into my van?" Allison exclaimed, trying to sound more indignant than she really felt. "Why, I ought to call the—" At that moment, a frenzied yapping came from somewhere near the front of the house.

Allison groaned. "There's that damn dog again."

Nick followed her through the living room, puzzled. That high-pitched yipping certainly didn't sound like a rottweiler....

When Allison flung open the door and stalked down the front steps, Nick realized with a stab of fear that the racket came from outside, from where he had left Danny.

Nick raced past Allison, trying to get to his son first and prevent Allison from discovering Danny hiding in the bushes.

Some kind of miniature terrier, its shaggy hair tied up on top of its head with a ribbon, was barking madly at a spot behind the shrubbery.

"It's the neighbors' little beast," Allison said. "They let it run loose all the time, and I won't disgust you with descriptions of what it does to other people's lawns." Reaching down, she scooped up the creature, holding it at arm's length so its sharp little teeth were out of range.

"Beat it, mutt," she growled, carrying it to the low hedge that separated her yard from the neighbor's, and depositing the dog on the other side.

It continued its maddening yaps, until Allison stamped her foot and clapped at it. Then it beat a hasty retreat with a few more defiant yips.

Allison dusted her hands together. "Good riddance," she said with satisfaction. "I hope the little mongrel gets fleas. The next time he—hey, wait a second!"

Nick, having ascertained with a quick glance that Danny was unscathed, had stepped in front of the bushes to block him from Allison's view. But some movement or reflection must have caught her attention, because she strode quickly forward now, trying to peer around Nick.

"Hey, there's a *kid* behind you!" To Danny, she said, "Aren't you one of the Lindquist boys from down the block? What are you doing outside after dark? Your mother's going to be furious—"

Then something in the way Danny was watching Nick, fidgeting, swallowing nervously, clued her in. "Wait a minute. He's with *you*, isn't he?"

Nick nodded, figuring things had gone too far to deny it.

Allison reached behind him, taking Danny by the wrist and pulling him to his feet. She dragged him a few steps forward, so the porch light illuminated him.

"It's just a little boy," she said in wonder. Then she scowled at Nick. "You hid a little boy behind my bushes? You left him outside all alone in the dark?" Her voice rose to an indignant squeak.

Nick grabbed Danny's other hand. "Look, I'm sorry I bothered you. Since you don't have my keys, we'll just be going now—"

"Don't be ridiculous. You're both coming inside with me right now. And you'd better have a good explanation for all this." She patted Danny's head. "It's pretty chilly out here. I bet you'd like some hot chocolate, wouldn't you?"

He looked up at his father. "Can I, Dad?"

"Dad?" Allison repeated, raising her eyebrows.

Nick looked at Allison, then down at Danny. "Okay, Shortstop. Let's have some hot chocolate." He knew when he was outnumbered.

As they sipped cocoa at the table in Allison's cheery kitchen, she had her first chance to take a long, appraising look at the man who'd barged so abruptly into her life.

She guessed his age to be about thirty-three or thirty-four, although he had a haunted, intense look in his vivid blue eyes that made him seem older, as if he'd already seen a lifetime's worth of tragedy.

His lean body was solid muscle, radiating a powerful masculinity that Allison found quite seductive. He wore the same clothes as before, with the sleeves of his sweatshirt pushed up. Allison's eyes kept straying to his bronze, corded forearms.

He was smiling at Danny now, his even teeth flashing white above the sexy cleft in his chin. His strong fingers enveloped the mug of cocoa, reminding Allison of the way they'd clasped her hand earlier today. She propped her chin in her palm and watched the two of them.

"Is he really your father?" she asked Danny.

Danny bobbed his head up and down. "He's my dad."

"Hmm. You sure don't look much like each other. I mean, your dad's got black hair, and you've got blond, for example."

Danny looked uncertain, and Allison had to repress the urge not to smile at the chocolate mustache above his lip. "Want another marshmallow in that cocoa?" she asked. As she reached into the plastic bag and dropped the white confection into Danny's mug, she said to Nick, "You two seem like you're in quite a hurry to get someplace."

Nick cleared his throat. He would have to tell Allison *something*. But not in front of Danny. "Hey, Shortstop, how'd you like to watch TV for a while? If that's okay," he added, looking at Allison.

"Sure." She took Danny's hand and led him into the living room. "You sit there on the couch, and I'll turn on the TV. I think there might even be a baseball game on. That is, if you like baseball," she said, hiding a grin.

Danny's eyes lit up. "Sure!" he said. "I *love* baseball."

Leaving Danny happily engrossed in the Dodgers versus the Mets, Allison returned to the kitchen. Leaning back against the counter, she glared at Nick. "Okay. Talk."

Nick sighed. "I really don't have time to explain everything. You were right. Danny and I *are* in a hurry."

"Yes, I want to talk to you about that." She traced a random pattern on the counter with the tip of her finger. "How do I know Danny's really your son? How do I know you're not some . . . kidnapper or something?"

She'd unintentionally hit close to home, and Nick winced. "Look, he told you I was his father, didn't he?"

"Yes, but . . ." Allison continued her invisible doodling. "You read in the newspapers all the time about kidnappers who convince their victims of that. Maybe you stole him when he was a baby, and he doesn't remember who his real parents are."

Nick drummed his fingers on the table. "I'd be happy to submit to one of those paternity blood tests, but there isn't time."

"It's just that . . . well, you have to admit, there isn't much of a family resemblance."

"His mother has light blond hair," Nick said through clenched teeth.

Allison looked at him. "And that's another thing. Where *is* his mother?"

Nick rose to his feet. "It's a long story, and we don't have much time."

"I notice you keep staring at the window, as if you expect someone to show up. The police, maybe?"

Nick made a quick decision. If he couldn't satisfy Allison with an explanation, she would have no choice but to call the cops. He supposed he would do the same thing in her place. And while as far as he knew the police weren't a direct threat, they could detain him and Danny long enough for the private detective to catch up with them.

Nick took a deep breath. "Okay, here goes. The whole story, *Reader's Digest* condensed version."

"Maybe I'd better sit down."

"Good idea." They both sat down at the table again.

"Danny *is* my son," Nick began. "Two years ago, his mother and I were divorced. The judge awarded full custody of Danny to my ex-wife."

The truth hit Allison like a bulldozer. She jumped to her feet. "You're a child snatcher!" she cried. "I've read about people like you! Just because you didn't get your way, you stole Danny from his mother!" Her eyes blazed with indignation. "My God, how could you? Can you imagine what that poor woman's going through?"

Nick closed his eyes, suddenly very tired. "You haven't heard the whole story."

"I've heard as much as I want to hear." Allison grabbed the phone receiver off the wall.

In two long strides, Nick was next to her, his hand gripping her wrist. "Hear me out. Please. Then if you still want to, you can call the police."

Their bodies were inches apart. Nick could feel the warmth of Allison's skin and see the soft flush across her face and neck. Her bulky angora sweater did little to conceal her full breasts and narrow waist. Nick inhaled the faint fragrance of floral shampoo, and, for an instant, forgot who and where he was. His fingers itched to bury themselves in her lush, reddish-brown hair; his tongue yearned to taste her pink, trembling lips.

A shudder racked his body, shaking him back to reality. No matter how much Nick wanted her, the fact remained that Allison Reed posed a very real danger to him and his son.

He guided her hand to replace the phone receiver. She stared up at him, swallowing, as if she, too, had felt the electric current pass between their bodies. "All right," she said softly. "I'll listen to your story."

Nick led her back to the table. Absently, she sipped her cocoa, then made a face. "Ugh. This stuff's cold. How about some brandy?"

As she poured them each a drink, Nick began again. "You're right. I did steal Danny from his mother. But I think you'll agree I had a good reason. You see..." He tightened his fingers around the brandy snifter. "Danny's mother abused him."

Allison set her glass down with a loud *clink*. "What do you mean, *abused* him?"

"She hit him."

"You mean . . . she spanked him?"

"No, you don't understand. She *hit* him. Slapped him around. Locked him in the closet."

Allison's eyes widened in horror. "Those are *terrible* accusations! Do you have any proof?"

"I'll say I have proof." Nick drained his brandy in one gulp. "Bruises. Bloody noses. She broke his arm once, for God's sake!" He leaned forward. "That woman beat the hell out of that kid, understand?"

Allison's mouth moved, but no sound came out. Good heavens, if what he was saying was true...

Nick slumped back in his chair. He rubbed his forehead. "You see, we had another son whom we...lost. Our eldest son, Kevin, was killed by a drunk driver four years ago. Sheila, my ex-wife, just fell apart." He combed his fingers through his hair, staring at the table. "God knows, I wasn't in much better shape myself, but Sheila started drinking. She was in such pain, and she started taking it out on Danny and me. She just shut us both out, even when what we really needed then was to stick together."

"I'm so sorry," Allison said softly.

Nick managed a half smile. "It was a pretty rough time. As the months went by, Sheila got worse instead of better. She was drunk almost all the time now, and lashing out at Danny and me every chance she had. I could take it—I understood the pain she was going through. But Danny—God, he was only three years old! How do you think he felt when Sheila constantly scolded him, demanding to know why he couldn't be more like Kevin? Why wasn't he as smart as Kevin? Why wasn't he as well-behaved as Kevin?" Nick paused. "Could I have another drink?"

Wordlessly, Allison poured him more brandy. She couldn't begin to imagine the hell that Nick and Danny had been through.

"After about a year of this," Nick continued, "I packed up and left, taking Danny with me. Sheila refused to get professional help, and God knows, she certainly wasn't letting *me* help her. Our marriage was in shambles, and I had to do something to get Danny out of that awful environment. It was destroying him. Poor kid. He hardly talked anymore, and he flinched whenever anyone tried to talk to him. He hid in his room all day, and at night, he'd wake up screaming with these terrible nightmares."

"Dear God," Allison whispered.

"Danny and I moved into a house in another part of Boston. I'd drop him off once a week to visit Sheila—I didn't think it was right to cut Danny completely off from his mother, no matter how she treated him. It was after a couple of months of these visits that I began to suspect that Sheila's verbal abuse had become physical as well. Danny would come home with these mysterious bruises, and his nightmares came back. I couldn't believe it at first—I didn't *want* to believe that Sheila was capable of such violence. Then when Danny wound up with a broken arm after one of his visits, I confronted Sheila. She denied everything, of course. She said Danny fell down a lot. Said he'd broken his arm by falling out of a tree in the backyard. 'He's so clumsy,' she said. 'Not like Kevin.'" A shadow crossed Nick's face. "As she said it, I could smell the alcohol on her breath. Even the pores of her skin seemed to exude it. That was when I decided to file for divorce."

Just then the front doorbell rang, making them both jump. A ferocious barking came from the living room. Nick's chair clattered to the floor as he bounded from the kitchen. He'd forgotten about Allison's dog; Danny must be terrified.

Allison flew after Nick. "It's okay, it's okay, it's just a recording!"

Danny was cowering at one end of the sofa, frightened and bewildered. The barking continued, but there was no dog in sight. Nick sat down and put his arm around Danny, as Allison went to the front door. "Down, Max, down!" she yelled. Then Nick spotted a white box that looked like an intercom, right next to the door. Allison pushed a button, and the barking stopped.

"It's hooked up to start playing when someone rings the doorbell," she whispered.

Nick started to laugh, then leaped up and crossed the room. "Don't answer the door yet." He peered through the peephole set into the door. His heart plummeted to his stomach. It was the detective.

Allison heard Nick inhale sharply, saw his whole body coil like a spring. Even before she saw the tense, trapped look on his face, she knew something was wrong. And it didn't take her long to figure out what. Not after the story he'd just told her.

Nick scooped Danny up from the sofa. Facing Allison, he said in a low voice, "Please. I'm begging you. For Danny's sake, don't tell him we're here." His face was haggard, shaded by dark hollows. His eyes pleaded with her silently. In his arms, Danny trembled with fear. All the color had drained from the little boy's face, making him look like a ghost.

Before Allison could respond one way or the other, the doorbell rang again, setting off the recorded barking. She turned, distracted and confused, and when she looked back, Nick and Danny were retreating through the kitchen, into the relative safety of her bedroom.

Allison gave a halfhearted "Down, Max" before turning the recording off. She took a deep breath. "Who's there?"

"My name is Raymond Kellogg," came the muffled voice. "I'm a private investigator. I'd like to ask you a few questions, Ms. Reed."

How do all these total strangers know my name? Allison wondered as she pushed her hair back and opened the door a crack.

"What kind of questions?" she asked.

"Well, I'm looking for, uh—may I come inside? I think it would be easier."

Reluctantly, Allison stood aside and let him in. The man wore an expensive three-piece suit, and the watch on his wrist didn't come from the drugstore. Snappy dresser. But why did some balding men insist on growing their hair long on one side and then plastering it over the tops of their heads? Did they really think it hid their baldness, rather than drawing attention to it?

"Would you like to sit down?" Allison didn't want to appear too eager to get rid of him. Then he'd suspect she was hiding something. Or someone.

"Thank you." He withdrew a notepad from his inside pocket and made a note with a gold pen. "Ms. Reed, you are one of the owners of a catering establishment called Incredible Edibles, is that correct?" When she nodded, he continued, "Shortly before noon today, a man was seen getting into one of your catering vans. He was in rather a hurry."

Allison frowned. "I'm afraid I don't know what you're referring to."

Kellogg cleared his throat. "Ms. Reed, I've already spoken to your business partner, Marilyn Grant. She informed me that earlier today you told her quite an exciting story about being hijacked by a man with a gun."

"Oh, him!" Allison said with a laugh. "Yes, that was quite an experience. I thought you were talking about someone I *knew*."

"Hmm, yes." Kellogg peered at her over gold-rimmed glasses. "So you're saying you didn't know this man."

"Never saw him before in my life."

"Why didn't you call the police? After all, he committed a criminal act."

"Well . . . I guess I *should* have called the police. But he didn't hurt me, and I was in kind of a hurry myself. I was late for a big catering job."

"I see." He tapped his pen against the notepad, regarding her with open skepticism. "Tell me, where did you take this man?"

"I dropped him off...somewhere in West L.A. Up on Wilshire Boulevard, by the veterans' hospital."

"And where did he go after you dropped him off?"

"Let's see—he, uh, he ran off into the hospital grounds and disappeared. That's another reason I didn't call the police. I figured he might be a little...you know, shell-shocked." She tapped the side of her head with her index finger. "What do they call it—post-Vietnam stress syndrome or something? I figured the poor guy could use a break."

Kellogg seemed a bit dazed. He blinked his eyes slowly, like a middle-aged tortoise. "And you haven't seen this man since?"

Allison shook her head vehemently, her auburn locks streaming from side to side. "Nope. He's probably back in the psycho ward by now."

Two photographs were paper-clipped to the cover of his notepad. He passed one of them to Allison. "Is this the man who jumped into your van today?"

Looking at the picture gave Allison a queer feeling in her stomach. It was him, all right, looking the same, yet so different. He was dressed in a tuxedo and white tie, very elegant and self-assured. His hair was shorter than it was now, and he looked younger, happier. His arm was around a beautiful blonde wearing a glittering evening gown. Both were smiling into the camera unselfconsciously. Behind them were several other figures, chatting and holding champagne glasses. Some fancy ball or reception. The kind Allison catered on occasion.

"Is that the man?" Kellogg asked.

Allison's forehead furrowed. "Well, it *might* be. I can't be sure."

Kellogg glanced at her sharply, then handed her the other picture. "Have you ever seen this little boy?" he asked.

Allison studied the picture of Danny, who beamed at the camera, looking so different from the timid, haunted child who was hiding in her bedroom at this very moment. He wore a Boston Red Sox uniform, and on a picnic table behind him, she could see crumpled wrapping paper and what looked like the remains of a chocolate cake. It must have been a birthday party.

"This picture was taken several years ago, so naturally the child would look older now," Kellogg said helpfully.

Allison shook her head, handing him back both pictures. "Nope. I've never seen the little boy before."

Kellogg made a clicking noise in his throat as he clipped the photos back onto his notepad. He glanced longingly toward the kitchen, as if he would love to search the rest of the house for fugitives. But he had no legal authority. Sighing, he fished a business card out of his expensive-looking wallet and scribbled something on the back. Rising to his feet, he extended the card toward Allison between two fingers. "Here's the name and phone number of my firm back in Boston. I've written the man's and boy's names on the back. If you see either one of them, or hear anything more about them, or remember something else that might be helpful, please call this number. Collect, of course. My office will know how to get in touch with me."

As Kellogg walked out to his car, Allison called after him, "Say, what's this guy done, anyway?"

Kellogg paused, halfway inside the car. "He's a kidnapper." Then he slammed the door, started the engine and drove off.

Allison closed the door thoughtfully. Then it suddenly occurred to her that she didn't even know the name of the man hiding in her bedroom. Turning over the business card, she studied the neat handwriting.

"Nick," she said softly, trying the name out on her tongue. "Nick Caldwell."

She found her purse behind the couch and tucked the card into her wallet.

A moment later, she tapped on her bedroom door. "The coast is clear," she called.

The door opened a crack, and then Nick emerged, putting his finger to his lips. "Danny's asleep," he whispered. "The poor little guy was exhausted." Closing the door behind him, he took Allison by the elbow and led her halfway down the hall. "What happened?" he asked, his eyes studying her intently.

"Obviously you know who it was at the door." His grip tightened on her elbow. "He asked about this morning. I told him I'd never seen you before, and that I dropped you off over in West L.A. I told him I hadn't seen you since."

Nick's eyes closed, as his whole body relaxed. When he opened his eyes, Allison was startled by their intensity. "Thank you," he said in a low, husky voice. "Oh God, Allison, thank you."

Before she knew what was happening, he pulled her to him, crushing her breasts against him, and pressed his lips to hers with a hard, searing kiss. Instinctively, Allison put her hands up to ward him off, then found herself clutching his jacket, hanging on for dear life as her legs went weak.

She savored the taste of Nick's brandy-flavored mouth, the feel of his lean, iron-hard body against hers. She could feel his heart pounding in his chest, echoing the impassioned rhythm of her own.

There was a desperate quality to his kiss, like a drowning man clinging to a rope. Allison arched her back, pressing close to Nick, longing to reassure him, yet not understanding what he was afraid of. He tightened his arms around her, as a low moan escaped his throat. His lips moved over hers, questing, seeking, sending a ripple of sensuous pleasure throughout her entire body.

It was all over in an instant. Just as the hall began to spin around Allison, Nick drew back, releasing her. He licked his lips, then wiped the back of his wrist across his forehead. Stuffing his hands in his pockets, he gave Allison a crooked grin. "Sorry about that," he said. "It's just that I...really appreciate what you did for us."

Allison leaned against the wall, trying to catch her breath. "No problem," she gasped.

Nick scuffed his toe on the floor, then shrugged. "Aw, hell. That's not true. I mean, I really can't thank you enough for what you did. But the fact is, I've been wanting to do that all day."

"I see." Allison was starting to feel giddy again. "Well, as long as we're telling the truth, I've been sort of wanting the same thing."

Nick's eyes darkened. He stepped toward her. "Allison—"

"Dad?" The muffled call from the bedroom stopped him. He met Allison's gaze, and they both smiled sheepishly.

As Allison followed Nick into the bedroom, she decided it was for the best that Danny had interrupted them. Goodness knows where another kiss might lead, and the last thing Allison wanted was to get involved with a fugitive. She wasn't one hundred percent convinced that Nick was justified in keeping Danny from his mother. After all, Allison had only heard one side of the story. She kept hearing the contempt in Kellogg's voice when he called Nick a kidnapper.

Danny could hardly keep his eyes open as Nick murmured comforting words to him in the semidarkness. Allison stood aside, her mind whirling furiously. If she confessed to Nick that she had his car keys, he and Danny could be on their way.

But something made her hold back. She tried to tell herself it was only concern for Danny. What if the tragic story Nick had told her was a pack of lies? Maybe Danny's mother was a good, decent woman who cried herself to sleep every night because her child had been stolen from her.

If Allison let them escape, she would never know whether Nick was a scoundrel or the loving father he appeared to be. She would be tortured with doubt, never knowing whether or not she'd done the right thing in letting Nick get away with Danny.

But a tiny part of her had another reason for not allowing the Caldwells to slip away just yet. Allison brushed her fingertips across her mouth, where the memory of Nick's brief kiss still lingered. Something was happening between her and Nick—something sweet and powerful and irresistible. She'd never experienced this instant chemistry with any man before, and she was reluctant to let him get away without exploring this strange new world further.

Before Allison could change her mind, her words spilled out with a will of their own. "You're both exhausted, and Danny's practically asleep anyway. Why don't you both stay here tonight?"

Chapter Three

Allison woke up on her couch with a crick in her neck, feeling like a pretzel. Her sleep-swaddled brain searched for some explanation. Had she fallen asleep watching TV? No, the set was off. Then why—?

She sat bolt upright, clutching the blanket to her chest as yesterday's events flooded her memory. What had she been thinking of, inviting two strangers to spend the night?

And what had she been thinking of, insisting that Nick share her bed with Danny, while she bunked on the hard, too-short sofa?

She staggered to the kitchen, eyelids at half-mast, filled the tea kettle with water, then clunked it on the stove. She caught sight of the kitchen clock and groaned. Six-thirty in the morning! The crack of dawn. She hadn't been up this early in years. No wonder she felt like a zombie.

Yawning, she plodded barefoot to the half-bathroom off the hallway. Her morning shower would have to wait until later, since she had no intention of parading past Nick and Danny to reach the other bathroom off her bedroom.

She splashed water on her face, then stuck her tongue out at her reflection. Not a pretty sight in the morning, she decided. She found a piece of yarn and tied back her unruly tangle of long auburn hair. At least she'd had the presence of mind last night to retrieve her flannel night-shirt and bathrobe before turning her bedroom over to Nick and Danny. Danny had already been asleep on her bed, and it seemed cruel to move the poor kid. Besides, Nick's six feet of solid masculinity would have been even more cramped on Allison's couch than she herself had been.

Well, anyway, it seemed logical at the time, she thought, stretching her arms and legs to get the kinks out. She tightened the belt of her blue chenille robe, yawned again and stumbled back to the kitchen. The grating whir of the coffee grinder made her wince, but as she poured water through a paper filter containing the Guatemalan coffee, she hoped the noise had woken Nick up. They had a lot to talk about, and she wasn't quite bold enough to barge into the bedroom and shake him awake.

Her plan worked. She looked up from making the coffee and there he was, leaning against the arched doorway, buttoning a shirt that must have been in the suitcase he'd fetched from behind the bushes last night. Allison's heart gave a queer lurch at the sight of his par-tially bared chest, covered with a pelt of curly black hair that tapered off into his jeans. She found herself fascinated by his large fingers as they easily manipulated the small buttons of his plaid shirt.

"Coffee ready?" he asked, as if they were used to having breakfast together every morning.

"Can you wait a minute till it's ready to drink, or would you prefer an immediate injection directly into the bloodstream?"

Nick chuckled, his voice gravelly with sleep. "I guess I can wait." He pulled out a chair and sat down at the butcher-block table.

"Is Danny still asleep?" she asked, pouring two mugs of coffee.

"Yes. He didn't sleep too well last night, so I suppose he'll be out for a while. I wish I didn't have to wake him up so soon. Thanks." As he took the coffee mug from her hand, their fingertips touched, and for some reason, Allison blushed.

Their eyes met across the table, and Allison was powerless to look away, held by a dreamy spell Nick seemed to cast over her. His thoughts were sketched plainly in every angle and line of his face. He was reliving last night's kiss, and bidding Allison to remember it, too—that brief moment of insanity when they both forgot who they were and where they were, aware only of their urgent need and desire.

Nick ran his tongue across his lips, and Allison could see that his desire still burned . . . as did hers. It coursed through her body like a power surge of electricity, and she wouldn't have been the least surprised to see sparks fly from her fingertips.

This was dangerous. She had to keep a clear head where Nick was concerned. But how could she, when these erotic fantasies kept intruding? Somehow Allison tore her gaze from Nick's and forced herself to swallow hot coffee and concentrate on the problem at hand.

It took three or four gulps of steaming liquid to give Allison the nerve to ask her next question. "What are your plans?"

Nick eyed her over the brim of his mug, plainly not sure how much he should tell her. "We've got to get out of town as soon as possible. Within the hour, if I can figure out some kind of transportation."

Allison started to speak, then bit her tongue. She'd nearly told Nick that his car keys were right here in the same room! Not yet, she thought. "Where will you go?" she asked.

Nick leaned forward, resting his weight on his forearms. "You don't really expect me to tell you that, do you?"

Allison traced the rim of her mug with one finger. "I don't see why not. After all, I could have turned you over to Kellogg last night, but I didn't."

"Who?" Nick looked at her in confusion, then nodded his head in understanding. "Oh, you mean that private eye. So that's his name, huh?"

Allison's eyes widened in surprise. "You mean you don't even know the name of the man chasing you?"

"Nope." Nick stretched his long arm to the stove, grasped the coffee pot and refilled his mug. "Would you like some more?"

"Not yet."

He replaced the pot on the stove. "The first time I laid eyes on the guy was back in El Paso."

"El Paso? As in Texas?"

Nick nodded.

"What were you doing there? I thought you were from Boston."

"Originally, yes. But Danny and I have moved around a lot. I got suspicious in El Paso one day when the same car kept showing up every place I went. After I deliberately led him on a merry chase and he was still following me, I knew it must be someone Sheila and her father hired. I got one good look at the guy before I managed to ditch him. Then Danny and I got the hell out of town."

"Just like you're planning now."

Nick sensed the disapproval in her voice. "Do you have any other suggestions?"

"Couldn't you—I don't know, leave Danny with a relative or something while you go back to Boston and try to straighten things out?"

"My only relative is my Aunt Lydia. She lives in Boston, too, and they're probably watching her house, just hoping Danny and I will show up someday."

"Aren't you being a little paranoid?"

Nick shook his head. "You don't know Sheila's family. Ever hear of Hammond Industries?"

"Sure. They're one of those big, multinational conglomerates, right? They're into everything—publishing, entertainment, finance."

"Right. Well, Sheila's maiden name is Hammond. Her father is Lawrence Hammond, chairman of the board."

Allison emitted a low whistle.

Nick grimaced. "I really know how to pick my adversaries, don't I?"

That explained the white-tie affair in the photo Kellogg had shown Allison. Nick's in-laws—*former* in-laws, she corrected herself—were rich. Filthy rich. *Obscenely* rich. Nick must have been used to hobnobbing with high

society at one time. Good heavens, he *was* high society
at one time!

But in the end, his ex-wife's fortune turned out to be
a double-edged sword. Because now, the vast resources
of the Hammond empire had been turned against Nick.
Millions of dollars, political influence, powerful connections... all dedicated to tracking down and capturing one frightened little boy.

It was amazing—and a tribute to Nick's ingenuity—
that he and Danny had been able to hide for as long as
they had.

"There's something I don't understand," Allison said
slowly. "How could the judge award custody to your ex-
wife, after the way she abused Danny?"

Nick gave Allison a bitter smile. "Sheila was given
custody for a number of reasons," he said. "First, she's
Danny's mother. The mother is usually awarded custody."

"But if she abused Danny..."

Nick turned his palms up in a resigned gesture. "You
have to understand—Danny didn't admit right away that
his mother mistreated him. He was frightened and confused—he didn't want his mother to go to jail."

"That poor little boy," Allison whispered.

"It took months before I could pry the truth out of
him. Naturally, I was ready to kill Sheila."

"But you...didn't."

Nick glanced sharply at Allison. "Don't worry," he
said. "You're not drinking coffee with a murderer, if
that's what you're thinking."

"I wasn't thinking that at all," she protested.

"Mmm. Anyway, I was the only person who believed
Danny. The social workers who got involved, the
judge—they all decided Danny was just making a bid for

attention, that he was traumatized by his brother's death and his parents' divorce. The bruises on his body were simply the result of normal childhood spills. Danny was only five years old at the time, remember. I guess that was a convenient excuse for ignoring his cry for help."

"Dear God," Allison breathed. "I can't believe with all the publicity these days about child abuse, no one took him seriously."

"Don't forget, we're talking about the Hammond family. Who would associate the sordid stories of child abuse you read about in the papers with a family like the Hammonds? Wealthy, prominent, morally upright. Child abuse isn't very socially acceptable. And if there's one thing the Hammonds are, it's socially acceptable."

"But still, a judge—"

"The other thing the Hammonds are is well-connected politically. I could never prove it, but I suspect they were able to influence the judge, put a little political pressure on him, just as extra insurance."

"Dad?" At that moment Danny wandered into the kitchen, rubbing the sleep from his eyes.

Nick put an arm around his son and pulled him close. When he kissed the top of Danny's head, Danny squirmed, as if embarrassed by this mushy display. "How'd you sleep, Shortstop?"

Danny shrugged. "I had some bad dreams." He looked shyly at Allison. "I'm hungry, Dad."

"We'll stop and get something on the road—your choice, how about that? You go get dressed and pack up your pajamas, and we'll get going."

Allison bounced up. "I've got a better idea. Why don't I fix all of us some breakfast right now?"

Danny's face brightened, but Nick frowned. "We have to be on our way, so there really isn't time—"

"Don't be silly. You can't start a trip on an empty stomach. I'll bet you didn't eat much for supper last night, did you, Danny?"

Danny slanted a guilty glance at his father. "We had corn dogs at the mall."

Allison rolled her eyes. "Corn dogs, huh? Well, those are real nutritious, aren't they?"

"We don't want to put you to any trouble," Nick said.

"Hey, I'm a caterer, remember? I could whip up breakfast in my sleep." She opened the refrigerator door. "Let's see, what have I got in here...how about liver pâté and artichoke hearts for breakfast, Danny? Doesn't that sound yummy?"

Danny squinched up his face and made a noise that sounded like "Ugh!"

Allison cocked her head sideways. "No, huh? Well, okay. How about...scrambled eggs and bacon and toast with jelly?"

Danny bobbed his head up and down with enthusiasm.

"Bacon and eggs it is, then."

As Allison ferried food from the refrigerator to the counter, Nick said, "Danny, go get dressed and pack your stuff. We'll be leaving right after breakfast."

After Danny left the room, Allison said, "I have to tell you, I'm not too thrilled with this situation."

"What do you mean?"

"Well, how do I know you've told me the whole truth?" She scrambled the eggs furiously. "Even if everything you've told me is true, I'm not totally convinced you're doing the right thing."

At first her comment was met with silence. Then, "You don't have to be convinced. It's none of your business."

Allison whirled around, brandishing a spatula. "Oh, yes it is, Nick Caldwell. You made it my business when you hijacked my van yesterday, and then showed up here last night." She flipped the sizzling bacon. "I'm involved whether you like it or not. And I can't just let you and Danny disappear until I'm convinced you have no other choice."

"Come with us, then."

Allison dropped a fork on the floor with a loud clatter. She put her hands on her hips and stared at Nick. "Are you crazy?"

He swallowed the last of his coffee. "Maybe."

"What possible purpose could there be for my coming with you?"

Nick rose, walked over to the yellow-curtained window and peered out. "I don't mean you have to join forces with us permanently. Just come with us for a few days." He sniffed the air. "Your toast is burning."

"Oh, darn it!" Allison popped the charred toast up, burning her fingers as she transferred it to the trash.

Nick came and stood next to her at the stove. Allison was suddenly aware that she wasn't wearing much under her bathrobe. For some reason, the vivid memory of Nick's kiss flashed through her mind again.

"You could go with us," Nick continued. "After a few days, if you aren't convinced that I'm doing what's best for Danny...you can call Kellogg and tell him where we are. He *did* leave you his phone number, didn't he?"

Allison nodded guiltily.

"Well, then, you can call him whenever you want to. All I ask is that you tell me when you're going to do it. That's fair, isn't it? After all, I could walk out of here with Danny right now. I'm doing you a favor by giving you a chance to soothe your conscience."

"*You're* doing *me* a favor?" Allison asked, incredulous.

Nick grinned, shrugging. "Well, let's say if you come with us, it'll be mutually beneficial. Danny and I could use someone to fix us breakfast, for example. Although, if you don't mind my saying so, you're not doing a very good job of it this morning." He pointed at the frying pan where the scrambled eggs were now a scorched mess.

Allison cursed as she snatched the pan off the burner.

"I thought you said you could make breakfast in your sleep," he teased.

"I *can* do it in my sleep," she retorted. "It's when I'm awake that I have trouble." Especially when a tall, sexy male was hovering at her shoulder and making ridiculous proposals, she thought.

"Well, what do you say?" Nick asked, watching her break fresh eggs into the skillet.

"I—I can't possibly go with you. I have a business to run, for one thing."

"You have a partner, don't you? What happens when one of you is sick? Surely she could cover for you for a few days."

Allison could just picture Marilyn's reaction to the news that Allison was taking a few days off work to go on the lam with the guy who'd hijacked her at keypoint.

"It isn't just that. I—the whole idea's insane! I don't even know you!"

"That's the whole point, isn't it?" Nick leaned closer, so close Allison could feel the warmth radiating from his body. "The whole idea is for you to get to know me better. So you can see that Danny is better off with me, even if we have to live like criminals."

"Well..." Nick's breath was tickling the hairs at the nape of her neck.

"I want you to have a clear conscience, Allison. I owe you that much, after what I put you through yesterday. But we have to get out of town. Now. Are you coming with us?"

Nick caught her glance and held it. Allison was confused, lost in the probing intensity of his gaze. Warning alarms sounded in the sensible part of her brain, reminding her of all the times her impulsive actions had gotten her in trouble before.

Yet part of her desperately wanted to go with Nick and his son, and not just to prove to herself that everything Nick had told her was true. She was drawn to Nick like a compass needle to the north pole. She longed to follow him, to solve the mystery of this man who'd entered her life so unexpectedly and touched her emotions in a way that left her breathless.

She'd known him less than twenty-four hours, yet already Allison knew that she would never forget the determined set of his jaw...the solid, dark streak of his brows above those fiery azure eyes...the insistent press of his mouth on hers....

Unconsciously, Allison swayed toward Nick, seeing his eyes light up and his lips part in welcome invitation. Then she caught sight of movement behind him, and quickly returned to her senses. "I'll think about it during breakfast," she mumbled, forking bacon onto a plate. A chair scraped against the floor as Danny seated himself at the table. Nick squeezed Allison's arm, and she sensed the promise of something more...if she were willing to take the risk, that is.

"Here you go, Danny. What kind of jelly would you like with your toast?" Allison dodged out of Nick's way, certain that even *considering* his wild suggestion was courting trouble.

Nick wolfed down his breakfast like a man starved. And starving he was ... but not just for food. He found the domesticity of the present setting strangely appealing. How long had it been since a woman had made breakfast for him, anyway?

Chewing a piece of bacon, he couldn't even think of a previous occasion. Certainly Sheila had never made the effort, not with a full-time cook at her disposal. The family breakfasts Nick had shared with his ex-wife had been more formal productions. Covered silver platters of eggs Benedict or French omelets, carried in by Mrs. Benson, the cook. Crystal champagne flutes filled with mimosas, linen napkins, coffee brewed in a special European glass coffee maker. Nick would sit at one end of the long mahogany dining table, Sheila at the other, the boys sitting across from each other, legs dangling from the high, cushioned chairs.

At the thought of Kevin, Nick's heart twisted with that familiar pain he'd learned to accept, but would never grow accustomed to. He missed his elder son. And that loss only made Danny more precious to him.

Now, seated around the butcher-block table in Allison's cozy kitchen, Nick felt strangely at home, as if, somehow, this place was where he and Danny belonged. Maybe it was some distant memory of his own childhood, when he'd sat at the kitchen table with Mom and Pop, eating scrambled eggs and smearing jelly on his face just as Danny was doing now.

Or maybe it had more to do with the woman across from him. Allison, looking somehow even more desirable, with the remnants of sleep softening her face, than she had last night. Her long, tousled hair was escaping from the confines of the yarn that held it and curling softly around her face.

Sharing this moment—the three of them—seemed so... so *right* to Nick. If only this could be the first of many, many mornings to follow....

That was impossible, of course. Nick had nothing to offer Allison or any other woman. Living like a criminal, barely eking out a living whenever he could get construction work or some handyman job, constantly watching over his shoulder and jumping at shadows.

How could he ask any woman to share his life, when that life was so uncertain? Nick never knew from one day to the next when he would have to pull up stakes, grab Danny and hit the road. He had no way to predict where he would be living a week from now, let alone a month, or a year.

So why had he asked Allison to go with them?

Logically, it was to prevent her from calling Kellogg the minute he and Danny slipped out her back door. But logic had very little to do with Nick's reactions to Allison Reed.

He sensed that he and Allison had the potential for something special, something different from any relationship he'd known before. He longed to push aside her loosely belted robe and explore her soft, lush curves; his fingers itched to entwine themselves in her thick, curly hair and raise her head to his, until their lips melded in an explosive, passionate union.

But Nick's attraction to Allison ran far deeper than mere physical yearnings. He was drawn to the sparkle in her eye, her sense of humor, her spunk. How many women would invite two wayward strangers to spend the night, and then whip up breakfast for them in the morning?

Nick knew he was being unfair, asking Allison to go with them. Any future for them was impossible. But he wasn't ready to leave her behind just yet. The hard, quick kiss they'd shared last night had only whetted his appetite for more. Nick knew that bringing Allison along would probably complicate matters considerably.

But just this once, Nick was willing to take the risk.

Back in Allison's bedroom, he stuffed yesterday's clothes in his suitcase, made the bed and grabbed Danny's backpack. Giving the room one final scan for anything they might have left behind, he noticed the montage of family photographs that covered one wall. Solid, down-to-earth folk; conservative, settled. Parents, brothers and sisters, children. Some of the shots had snow-covered backgrounds; Allison's family must live somewhere in the Midwest, or maybe back East.

Nick felt that old familiar emptiness, that longing for family, for tradition, for roots. He'd sought those things in his marriage to Sheila, and never found them. Not the kind he was looking for, anyway.

Now he and Danny had no one but each other. But that was enough. It had to be.

Allison was drying the breakfast dishes when Nick returned, having settled Danny in front of *Sesame Street*. He was tempted to sneak up behind her and slide his arms around her narrow waist, like any old married couple. But he refrained. Allison would probably clobber him with a wet frying pan.

The faint, leftover smells of bacon, toast and coffee mingled in the air. Nick parted the curtain and scanned the driveway for any sign of Kellogg. He was sure the detective would be back to question Allison further, after his other leads reached dead ends. It was time to go.

"Well?" he said. "Have you decided?"

Allison's face, when she turned from the sink, was a portrait of conflict. "If only I could be sure of—of—"

"Of me?"

She bit her lower lip, nodding.

"There's only one way to be sure...find out for yourself."

Allison twisted the dish towel in her hands. "How are you—I mean, what would we use for transportation?"

"Well, there's always *your* car," Nick replied, bracing himself for the response he knew was coming.

Allison flung the towel onto the counter, her eyes emitting green sparks. "So that's it!" she said. "That's what all this 'come with us' business is all about! You just want to use my Volvo as a getaway car!" She glared at Nick, hands planted firmly on her hips.

"Not at all," he said soothingly. "For one thing— look, no offense, but that bucket of bolts out there isn't exactly the car I'd choose as an escape vehicle."

"It beats walking, which is your only alternative, as far as I can see!"

Nick shrugged. "Actually, we'd probably be better off catching a bus or train. Either one would be more anonymous. You can bet that Kellogg jotted down your license plate number when he was here last night."

"Why should he care about *my* car?"

"Allison, Sheila and her father don't hire amateurs. That guy is undoubtedly the best private investigator Boston has to offer. He's thorough. He probably suspects you weren't telling him the truth about not seeing me again."

"Then I can't see why you'd want to use my car anyway, if he's likely to trace it."

"I was thinking of you, actually."

Allison raised a skeptical eyebrow. "Of *me*?"

"If you come with us, you'll need some way to get back to Los Angeles. Your own car would be more convenient than public transportation, right?"

"Well...yes, I suppose so."

"So, what do you say? Are you coming with us?"

Nick held his breath, awaiting her reply. As far as eluding Kellogg, it didn't make much difference if Allison called him right now and tipped him off. Nick and Danny would be gone by the time he arrived, and Kellogg wouldn't really learn anything he hadn't already suspected.

But Nick still wanted Allison to say yes. Badly.

In her face, he could see mind and heart battling for the final decision. He could tell that Allison's mind was dead set against this crazy escapade. He could only hope that something in her heart would overrule common sense.

She hung up the damp dish towel, then slammed the open silverware drawer shut. Tilting her chin up, she looked Nick straight in the eye and said, "Okay. I'm coming with you."

Happiness and relief flooded him, but he was careful not to let it show. "Fine," he said. "Go get dressed and pack your things. We've got to get out of here."

"Giving orders already, I see," she retorted, but she was smiling.

Nick closed the distance between them and put his hands on her shoulders. "This isn't a vacation, Allison. This is very serious. Danny's whole future is at stake. While we're together, I'm afraid you'll have to get used to taking orders once in a while."

He could tell from the pink flush that suffused Allison's cheeks that his last statement wasn't going down too well. But all she said was, "I have to make a phone call first. Will you excuse me?"

Nick's grip on her shoulders tightened.

"Not to Kellogg, to Marilyn. My partner. I have to tell her I'll be gone for a few days."

Nick released her. "Sorry."

As Allison picked up the phone, she said, "You know, you're going to have to learn to trust me, Nick."

"I could say the same thing."

"Mmm." She regarded him thoughtfully until the phone was answered. "Marilyn? It's me."

"Allison? I was just going to call you. Some private detective showed up at my house last night, asking questions about that guy who hijacked the van."

Allison squeezed her eyes shut. This was going to complicate things. "Yeah, he came here, too. I couldn't tell him much."

"He told me the man's a kidnapper, can you believe that? You're lucky you escaped without being hurt."

"I didn't *escape*, Marilyn. The man let me go. But that's not why I called you."

"What's up?"

"I'm, uh, going to be taking a few days off."

"Are you sick?"

"Well, um, sort of. I mean, I just feel like I need a rest."

"Poor kid." Allison could hear Marilyn's maternal instincts kick into high gear. "You've been working pretty hard lately, haven't you? Tell you what—after I close up the shop today, I'll bring over a pizza and a bottle of wine. I'll rent a couple of videotapes and we can watch old movies. It'll be fun!"

Allison groaned silently. She wanted to stay as vague as possible about her whereabouts for the next few days.

Especially since she herself had no idea where she would be. "Marilyn, that's really sweet of you, but as a matter of fact, I'm . . . going to be out of town."

"Oh?" Marilyn paused. "This sounds like serious relaxation. Where are you going?"

"Uh . . . here and there. Wherever the road takes us." Allison winced, instantly regretting her choice of words.

"Us?" Marilyn said. "Who are you going with?"

"Just a friend, that's all. Look, he's waiting for me, I've really got to go—"

"Allison Reed, just what exactly are you up to?"

"Why, nothing. What do you mean?" she asked innocently.

"There's something funny going on here." Allison could hear Marilyn's long, red-lacquered nails clicking on the table.

"I don't know what you're talking about, Marilyn."

"This doesn't have anything to do with that lunatic you ran into yesterday, does it?"

Allison's tongue felt stuck to the roof of her mouth. "Of course not. Don't be silly."

"You are the world's worst liar! This *does* have something to do with him, doesn't it? Allison, what have you gotten yourself into this time?"

"Marilyn, I have to go," Allison said desperately. "You can take care of the shop for a few days, can't you?"

"It's not the shop I'm worried about, it's you! Allison, for God's sake, the man's a criminal!"

"Marilyn, I'll see you in a few days. Thanks for taking care of things."

"Allison—"

"Bye, now!" Allison replaced the receiver with Marilyn's outraged voice still echoing in her ears.

Nick leaned against the doorway, thumbs hooked into his belt. "She knows, doesn't she?"

"She *suspects*, that's all." Allison fiddled with the belt of her robe. "You overheard me—I didn't tell her anything. She just knows me so well, damn it."

"It doesn't matter. She doesn't know where we're heading."

"That makes two of us," Allison muttered.

Nick arched one eyebrow, but didn't volunteer any information. They regarded each other in silence, volumes of unspoken words hovering in the air between them.

Brrrnnnggg!

Allison jumped, her hand flying to her heart. She studied the telephone without moving. Then she turned to Nick. "One guess who that is," she said with a sigh. "Now we don't just have Kellogg on our trail. We have to worry about Marilyn showing up."

"In that case, I suggest a rapid departure is in order." Nick was secretly pleased with the way Allison said "*our* trail." It showed she'd made an important mental adjustment and now considered herself allied with Nick and Danny.

"Right, chief." Allison threw Nick a mock salute, then hurried to her bedroom. The persistent ring of the phone followed her down the hall.

She threw open her closet and scanned it with indecision. What did one take when one went on the run? She wanted to be properly attired for life as a fugitive. As she stuffed a few random items into an airline flight bag, Allison wondered about Nick's keys. Should she admit to having them?

She wasn't too thrilled about making their escape in *her* car, but as Nick had pointed out, that would make her return trip easier.

Besides, she couldn't muffle the sneaking suspicion that Nick had asked her along only because she could provide transportation. Maybe if he could drive his own car, he would leave Allison behind.

For some reason, she found that a very disturbing prospect. Because of Danny, of course. She wanted to make sure that the boy would be better off with Nick than returned to his mother in Boston.

This crazy attraction she felt for Nick was irrelevant. Well, maybe not completely.

She struggled with the zipper, trying to close the overstuffed bag.

"Having trouble?" Nick had entered the room silently and stood right behind her.

As Allison whirled in surprise, she came face-to-face with him. They were mere inches apart. She could see the crinkles at the corners of his eyes, the curved lines etched at the sides of his mouth as he smiled slightly. His eyes were bright embers glowing with promise. A stray lock of dark hair fell across his forehead. Allison could see the even row of white teeth behind his slightly parted lips; she smelled the faint trace of shaving gel on his smooth skin. Strength and masculinity emanated from him, enveloping Allison, drawing her closer to him, drowning out all sound but a singing rush in her ears.

Then Nick took her in his arms and *did* draw her close, pulling her against his hard chest, bringing her face up to meet his.

Their lips met in a crash of cymbals, an explosion of fireworks. His kiss was different from before; less urgent, more tender. He moved his mouth gently over hers, while sliding his fingers beneath her thick mane of hair and stroking the bare skin at the nape of her neck.

Nick slid his tongue between Allison's parted teeth, gliding eagerly into the moist corners of her mouth. Allison responded in kind, languidly stroking the hard, velvety intruder, as a tiny moan welled up in her throat.

His arousal pressed hard against her, and something deep inside Allison melted. Her knees went weak, and she clung to him, her hands splayed against his broad back, hugging him as if she would never let him go.

After an eternity that was all too brief, Nick eased his lips away from hers. He brushed his nose playfully against Allison's and smiled. When he spoke, he was so close she could feel his warm breath in her mouth.

"I'm glad you're coming with us," he murmured.

Dizzy and drained, Allison tried to detach herself from Nick's embrace. The edge of the bed pushed against the back of her knees; she was trapped. "We—we'd better get going," she said, unaccustomed to the huskiness in her voice.

Nick released her with obvious reluctance. "You're right," he said. Stepping back, he combed his fingers through his hair and shook his head, as if to clear it. "I almost forgot about leaving." With a rueful grin, he added, "You're quite a distraction, you know."

Any more distractions like this and she'd be incapable of going anywhere, Allison thought.

Moments later, Danny and Nick were safely ensconced in her car, and Allison was locking her back door, wondering what she would be feeling the next time she unlocked it.

Nick had told her he was glad she was going with them.

Allison could only hope that after a few days around sexy, mysterious Nick Caldwell, she would feel the same way.

Chapter Four

It wasn't too hard to figure out where they were going. After all, the reason they called Interstate 5 the San Diego Freeway was that it went to San Diego.

So even though Nick had barely spoken two words since they'd left her house, Allison had his whole escape plan worked out. Only it wasn't much of an escape plan, in her opinion. San Diego was only a two-hour drive from Los Angeles. From a man who'd fled Boston to Seattle to El Paso to Los Angeles, Allison would have expected something a little more dramatic. A marathon drive across the continent to New York, for example. Or up the coast to Alaska.

It was just as well that Nick had no such grandiose plans in mind. Allison didn't think her faithful old car could make it that far. And she wasn't sure how far *she* could make it, either. What crazed logic had seized possession of her brain, convincing her that joining Nick and Danny in their flight was the solution to her dilemma?

Going on the run with them was a lot more likely to create problems than to solve them. Especially if this maddening attraction to Nick persisted.

Without moving her head, Allison shifted her gaze from the sparkling shoreline to Nick. His profile hadn't changed in the last hour—jaw still clamped in a square angle, eyes riveted to the road, dark brows slanted with determination. To the casual observer, his body might appear relaxed, but Allison's observations were far from casual. She noticed Nick's white-knuckled grip on the steering wheel, the slight hunch to his wide shoulders, the way his left foot tapped the floorboard impatiently. He was like a spring waiting to explode.

Allison glanced at the speedometer. Nick was maintaining a constant speed exactly one mile per hour below the speed limit. No doubt he wished that both the traffic laws and the condition of Allison's Volvo would permit him to crank the car up to ninety miles an hour.

Nick must have sensed Allison's scrutiny, for he slanted a sideways glance at her. She looked quickly away, but not quickly enough. She'd seen the grin starting to twitch at the corner of his mouth.

"Still mad at me 'cause I wouldn't let you drive?" he asked.

"Who, me? I'm not mad," she replied indignantly. "Whatever gave you that idea?"

He lifted one shoulder. "Well, you've been giving me the silent treatment ever since I insisted on driving."

"*I've* been giving *you* the silent treatment? You're the one who's been tight-mouthed as a clam ever since we left," she retorted. "Besides, I *let* you drive."

"It's just that I'm the one who knows where we're going. And if I spot someone following us, it might require some rather drastic driving action to shake him off our tail." Nick's eyes twinkled. "And I've seen how you drive."

Allison's mouth fell open. "*You* try driving with a gun pointed at you, and see how well *you* do, buddy—" Then she saw the mirth in his face. "Very funny," she mumbled, folding her arms and staring straight ahead through the windshield.

Nick laid his hand on her knee. "I'm sorry I teased you. And you're right—I haven't been very good company. I apologize for that, too. It's just that I have a lot on my mind at the moment." He squeezed her knee. "Do you forgive me?"

How could Allison resist those pleading blue eyes, that humble expression?

How could she ignore the ripples of pleasure that radiated through her body from the touch of his hand, melting her annoyance and making her wonder what it would feel like if Nick slid his hand farther up her leg...?

"You're forgiven," she replied, hoping Nick didn't notice the faint quaver in her voice.

"Good." He threw her a dazzling smile. She would have forgiven him anything.

"Where are we going, Dad?" Danny's voice so close to her ear made Allison jump. Nick hastily pulled his hand from her knee.

"We'll know when we get there, Shortstop." He reached over and ruffled his son's hair. "I thought you were asleep back there."

"I was, but you guys woke me up."

"Oops." Allison pressed her hand to her mouth.

Nick winked at her. "Look out the window, Danny. See the ocean?"

"Hey, yeah, that's neat!" Danny crawled to the window. "There's surfers out there, Dad."

"How about fastening your seat belt, okay?"

"Sure." The faint clink of metal reached the front seat. "Dad, when are we going to stop?"

"Not for a while, kiddo."

"Okay." Danny turned his attention to the surfers, his nose almost touching the window.

"You've got a great kid there," Allison said quietly.

"I know." Nick's forearms flexed as he gripped the steering wheel. "And I intend to keep him." His features, so recently relaxed with amusement, were once again set in stony determination.

Allison longed to discuss Nick's statement further, to explore possible alternatives to this reckless flight. But she couldn't very well raise the subject with Danny in the car. Instead, she joined him in watching the scenery go by.

"Look, Danny, there's a billboard for the San Diego Zoo! Have you ever been to a zoo?"

"Dad took me once. Dad, where was that zoo where we saw the lions and tigers and I got to ride on an elephant?"

"That was in El Paso."

"Oh, yeah, that's right, I remember now. It was in El Paso," he told Allison.

She smothered a smile. "Maybe your dad will take us to the zoo while we're in San Diego."

"Hey, yeah! Dad, can we go to the zoo? Please? Can we?"

"We're not going to stay in San Diego, Danny. The zoo will have to wait till some other time." The frown

Nick cast at Allison told her she'd made a mistake. She hadn't meant to raise Danny's hopes, but she'd been so certain Nick planned to hole up in San Diego for a while....

"Where exactly are we going, then?" she asked quietly.

Nick's expression was indecipherable. Was he angry at her? Or did he simply not trust her? "We'll know when we get there," he said, echoing his earlier words to Danny.

Allison opened her mouth to demand a less vague reply, then pressed her lips together. She wouldn't give Nick the satisfaction of begging for crumbs of information. If he insisted on playing this close to his chest, fine. Let him think he was James Bond or something. Allison had agreed to let Nick run the show, and by golly, she wouldn't break her promise.

For about the hundredth time that morning, she wondered what she'd gotten herself into.

Her apprehension increased as they sped through San Diego. After Nick's announcement that they wouldn't be staying there, Allison had assumed he meant to change to Interstate 8 and head for Phoenix or Tucson. But when they passed the interchange without a flicker of interest on Nick's part, Allison's eyes widened in horror.

"You're heading for the Mexican border, aren't you?" she whispered, mindful of Danny in the back seat.

Nick spared her a neutral look. "What if I am?"

"Are you insane? Dragging Danny all over the country is bad enough, but transporting a kidnap victim across an international border is something else altogether! It's got to be some kind of federal offense. Do you want to get us all thrown into a Mexican jail to rot forever?''

"Are you quite finished?'' Nick's voice was level, but there was no mistaking his exasperation. "First of all, Danny is not a kidnap victim, he's my son. Secondly, the Mexican police would hardly be interested in an American custody case. Thirdly, you agreed to go along with my decisions, so would you please pipe down and take it easy?''

Nick jerked his head toward the back seat, reminding Allison of Danny's presence and stifling the hot retort she was ready to fling at Nick. She slumped in her seat, fuming. It was true that Nick had warned her she would have to take orders from him once in a while. But she hadn't bargained on him turning into Captain Bligh! She drilled her fingers on the door handle, feeling especially mutinous.

"I'm sorry.'' Nick's voice was so low, Allison wasn't sure she'd really heard it. When she glanced at him, his mouth was curved in a wobbly smile. "I didn't mean to fly off the handle like that. I'm not used to having someone along who questions my every move.''

"Maybe we should call this whole thing off. I'll go back to Los Angeles and you and Danny can go your merry way.''

"No, no, that isn't what I meant!'' Alarm flared in Nick's face. "I mean, I'd hate for you to leave without being sure that I'm doing the right thing with Danny.''

"You're just afraid if you let me out of your sight for a minute, I'll call that detective and tell him where you are.'' Allison wasn't sure if she believed that or not, but something prodded her to provoke Nick and get his reaction.

He surprised her. "That's part of it," he admitted. "But there's more to it than that. For some reason that I can't even begin to understand—" He shifted his eyes to her for a minute, then shook his head in wonder. "For some strange reason, it's very important to me that you believe what I'm doing is best for Danny." He shrugged. "Not that I've ever given a damn what people thought of me, as long as I knew I was right. But in your case..." He rubbed his chin slowly. "I want a chance to convince you that I have no other choice where Danny's concerned. I can't take him back. I just can't. And I don't want you to leave until I can make you understand that." He threw Allison a sheepish grin. "End of speech."

She gazed out the window, considering what Nick had said. She was flattered that he cared so much about her opinion of him. Maybe he cared a little bit about her, too. Maybe this irresistible attraction they seemed to have for each other was based on something a little more substantial than hormones—like mutual respect, for example.

Or maybe Nick was selling her a bill of goods because he wanted to keep using her car.

Allison studied him from the corner of her eye. She wanted to trust Nick; she *almost* trusted him—but not completely. She'd fallen victim too many times in the past to handsome sweet-talkers with a sexy smile and a truckload of charm. They'd always turned out to be all surface and no substance. Allison sensed Nick wasn't like the others. She'd noticed the muted suffering in his secretive blue eyes, and witnessed his undeniable love and concern for Danny. Her instincts cried that Nick was no slick con man—but her instincts had been wrong before. She couldn't take a chance on being wrong again, because more was at stake this time than her own happiness. At risk was the well-being and entire future of an adorable seven-year-old boy.

"I'll stick around for a while," she mumbled.

"What did you say?"

"I said you're not getting rid of me yet. Not for a while, anyway."

Nick loosened his grip on the steering wheel. "Look, if you're worried about getting into trouble with the law, you can claim that I kidnapped you."

"Don't be ridiculous."

"No, I mean it. I won't dispute your story."

"It's out of the question. Besides, I'd look pretty stupid if I admitted to being kidnapped twice by the same person."

"Whatever you think best." Nick's lips quivered suspiciously, as if he were trying to stifle a smile.

Allison began to revise her earlier assessment that Nick was no con man.

After a few minutes, he said quietly, "You don't have to worry about being arrested as my accomplice or anything. The police have no authority to interfere with us."

"What are you talking about?"

Nick sighed and turned his head quickly to make sure Danny was still engrossed by the view. "As I understand it, states don't have jurisdiction over other states' custody cases. In other words, the only state where we'd have anything to fear from the police is Massachusetts."

"But that's terrible!" Allison exclaimed. "So a parent can swipe a child, and once they've crossed the state line, the law can't do anything about it?"

"That's about the size of it."

"How awful! It makes it too easy for people to steal children."

His chin jutted forward. "It's certainly worked to my advantage in this case. It's also worked to Danny's benefit. But I would have taken him even if it meant dodging the FBI for the rest of my life." The angry, determined force behind his words was unmistakable.

Allison sank back in confusion. Surely it was tragic that there was no legal machinery to track down children stolen by their own parents... but here she was, face-to-face with a case where the justice system had apparently broken down.

What was the right answer for Nick and Danny? *Was* there a right answer?

"That's why Sheila and her father hired a private detective," Nick said. "The police couldn't help them, but if a private detective tracked us down, Sheila could come and snatch Danny back. That's about the only solution in these cases, unfortunately."

Allison shook her head sadly. "That must be awfully traumatic for the poor children involved."

Nick glared at her. "I'm not exactly in love with the situation," he said through clenched teeth. "But I don't see a better alternative."

Allison's hand flew to his shoulder. "I didn't mean that the way it sounded, Nick," she said. "I understand the terrible position you're in."

"Do you?" The harsh lines of his face softened. Slowly he expelled a deep breath. "I *want* you to understand. It's so hard sometimes, having to bottle all this inside me, never being able to talk about it with anyone." He placed his left hand on his shoulder over hers. Squeezing her fingers, he said, "I'm kind of glad you stumbled onto our secret after all."

Swallowing, Allison squeezed back. His fingers felt nice, strong and callused with short clipped nails. She shivered as an unbidden image rose to her mind—an image of Nick's fingers caressing her bare flesh, trailing across her body... leaving desire in their wake. The sensation was so eerily vivid that Allison's skin flushed hot, then cold. She jerked her hand from Nick's.

When he looked at her in surprise, she rolled her eyes toward the back seat, using Danny as an excuse for her sudden retreat.

"Oh," he muttered, winking at her. "Good point."

Allison didn't have much chance to sort out the jumble of feelings Nick had inadvertently aroused. Moments later he steered the car off the freeway and began cruising the dusty streets, searching for a parking space.

"Where are we, anyway?" Allison asked. She'd been too distracted lately to notice any signs.

"San Ysidro," Nick replied over his shoulder as he skillfully maneuvered the Volvo into a parking space barely big enough for a motorcycle.

"I repeat, where are we?"

"At the border. Almost."

Ahead Allison could see a row of low buildings and a long line of cars. The border of Mexico.

"Why are we stopping here?" The potholed street was crowded with a questionable assortment of pedestrians, none of whom Allison would care to meet in a dark alley at night—or in broad daylight, for that matter. Seedy storefronts lined the block, displaying a mixture of signs in both English and Spanish.

"To buy Mexican auto insurance. American insurance is no good in Mexico."

"Then we *are* going to cross the—okay, okay, I won't say another word." Allison slumped back in her seat, watching Nick lope across the street to a ramshackle building whose gaudy orange-and-white sign advertised Mexican Car Insurance! Cheapest Rates! No Waiting!

She stretched across the front seat and locked the door.

"Where'd my dad go?"

Allison twisted so she could talk to Danny in the back seat. "He'll be right back, honey. He had to buy something, but it shouldn't take him very long." *I hope,* she amended silently.

"Is he buying something to eat? I'm getting hungry." Danny's eyes didn't quite meet Allison's, as if he didn't know exactly what to make of this stranger who'd so abruptly entered their lives.

"Are you hungry? So am I. We'll have to talk your dad into stopping for lunch soon."

Danny's attention had drifted out the window. "Why is that man drinking out of a paper bag?" he asked innocently.

Allison's head whipped around. "Oh, er... why, I guess he just came from the market where he bought that bottle of—uh, soda pop, only he was too thirsty to wait until he got home." She sighed. What on earth was keeping Nick, anyway?

Moments later—although it seemed much longer to Allison—Nick was rattling the door handle. Allison unlocked the door, then took an envelope he handed her. "Stick that in the glove compartment, would you, please?"

"What took you so long?" she asked.

Nick started the car. "I got into a conversation with the man selling insurance. I asked him to recommend some places in Mexico where we might stay tonight."

Allison frowned. "Do you think that's wise? After all, if anyone traces us this far, he'll be able to tell them where we're heading."

"That's the idea."

Now what did he mean by that? The expression on Nick's face warned Allison against asking any more questions, so she kept her mouth shut—for the time being. As soon as they reached their immediate destination—wherever that might be—she intended to pry some answers from Nick. He might be in charge of this show, but Allison had never agreed to be kept in the dark about every aspect of their "trip."

Allison's heart was in her throat as they joined the line of cars waiting to cross the border, but after a couple of perfunctory questions, the official waved them through. Nick seemed perfectly unruffled, as if they really *were* a normal family intending to spend the day poking around the shopping bazaars of Tijuana for piñatas and cheap pottery.

I suppose after two years as a fugitive, he's used to this sort of thing, Allison thought. She shuddered. She'd just seen for herself what a cool liar Nick could be. Had he lied to her as well?

Every mile they drove could be carrying Allison deeper into danger. What if Nick only wanted her car after all, and decided to abandon her in the middle of the desert, stranding her among the cacti and rattlesnakes?

Yet Allison couldn't reconcile that dastardly scenario with the reality of her own perceptions. Nick's love and concern for Danny was no act. Surely she had nothing to fear from a man capable of such emotions.

Besides, Allison sensed that somehow she was special to Nick. She wasn't sure why, and she had no idea where it might lead. But sitting next to Nick, secretly observing the firm set of his chin and his confident grip on the steering wheel, Allison felt perfectly safe and secure. She wasn't used to blindly following another person's decisions; she was far too independent—okay, stubborn—for that. But as long as another person had to be in charge, Allison was glad it was Nick. Even if she occasionally rebelled against him.

Nick projected an undeniable air of competence and reliability. Allison's heart told her to trust him. But the logical part of her brain still whispered warnings.

A bone-crunching jolt rudely interrupted her musings.

"Sorry about that," Nick said. "I couldn't avoid that pothole without running into another car."

"No problem," Allison replied, rubbing the top of her head, which had bumped into the roof of the car.

"You okay, Shortstop?" Nick threw a glance toward the back seat.

"Just hungry, Dad."

"We'll stop soon, I promise."

Allison studied the streets of Tijuana with interest. She'd come here once before with Marilyn for an afternoon of shopping, but the shabbiness and pandemonium of the bustling city still fascinated her. The buckled sidewalks lining the crowded streets were jammed with a motley spectrum of humanity—old women wrapped in black shawls, street vendors, mothers with children, mangy dogs, hucksters selling everything imaginable...and plenty of things unimaginable as well. As they crossed over a narrow bridge, Allison saw hundreds of corrugated-tin shacks strewn along the ravine below. Her own dilemma shrank to insignificance in the face of such numbing poverty.

Was this where Nick planned to hide out with Danny? Before Allison's eyes flashed the photograph the detective had shown her—the picture of Nick in a tuxedo, sipping expensive champagne and hobnobbing among the potted palms with the wealthy upper crust of Boston.

The stark contrast with their present surroundings drove home to Allison the magnitude of what Nick had sacrificed for his son.

Nick parked the Volvo in front of a building covered with peeling turquoise plaster. Before Allison could say a word, he was out of the car. "Be right back."

She recognized the word *Banco* over the door where he'd disappeared. What now? Well, if Nick planned to rob the place, he would certainly have left the engine running.

Danny's face had a pinched, worried look as he watched the building intently. Allison's heart went out to the boy. Poor kid—he had to be confused by all this. Lord knows, she herself had no idea what Nick was up to.

Smiling at Danny, she said, "Hey, I'm starved! What d'ya say we go find something to eat, huh?"

"I dunno...maybe we better wait for my dad." He gave Allison a doubtful look.

"We could starve to death by then. Come on, we won't go far."

"Well..."

"We'll bring back something for your dad to eat. I bet he's hungry, too."

That convinced Danny. At least, he put up no resistance when Allison opened the car door and took his hand. "Look, there's a place just up the block."

They paused in front of a pushcart vendor with an enormous Pancho Villa mustache. "What would you like, Danny? A taco? Enchilada? Tamale?"

When he continued to stare in bewilderment, Allison said gently, "How about a tamale?"

Danny nodded, his eyes huge.

"*Dos tamales, por favor.* No, no—*tres tamales,*" she told the vendor. The man leered at her with a gap-toothed smile that Allison ignored. "Drat, I forgot—all I have is American money. *Dinero americano?*" she asked, showing him a five-dollar bill.

"*Sí, sí,*" he replied, bobbing his head eagerly.

Allison handed Danny a tamale. "Wow, you speak Mexican?" he said.

Unable to resist his momentary admiration, Allison shrugged modestly. "I know a few words." Which was, in fact, the truth. She picked up the other tamales. "Mmm, don't these smell good? If your dad doesn't come back quick, his tamale's going to be gone."

As if he'd been waiting in the wings for his cue, Nick stepped out of the bank. When he saw the empty car, he started to run. Then he spotted them. "You should have waited for me in the car," he said, frowning.

"Don't be such a grouch. Here, have a tamale. Maybe it'll improve your disposition."

Nick studied the tamale Allison had stuffed into his hand. "Is this safe to eat?" he asked doubtfully.

"As long as you don't eat the aluminum foil it's wrapped in."

"Ha, ha."

They leaned against the car, wolfing down their lunch. "Mmm, this *is* pretty good," Nick admitted. "Although I suppose a tamale is quite an assault on your rarefied taste buds."

Allison swallowed a bite of cornmeal. "Huh?"

"Well, being a caterer, you're probably used to cuisine that's a little more haute."

"Not really." She took another bite. "I don't eat much of the stuff I cook. To tell you the truth, I'd pick a chili dog over pâté de foie gras any day."

"Me, too!" Danny chimed in.

Allison and Nick laughed. Ruffling Danny's hair, Allison said, "I'll bet you don't even know what pâté de foie gras is!"

Danny wrinkled his nose. "I don't like the way it sounds."

"I guess that's as good a reason as any," Allison smiled. "You must like the way tamale sounds, the way you gobbled that one down."

"It was pretty good."

"Good, 'cause I guess we'll be eating lots of Mexican food for a while." She slanted a glance at Nick, but he refused to confirm or deny her statement.

Nick finished the last bite of tamale and balled up the aluminum foil. "Time to hit the road." As Danny scrambled into the back seat, Nick's eyes met Allison's.

Before she could react, he raised his hand to her face and stroked his thumb across the corner of her mouth. Spellbound, she gazed into his eyes, mesmerized by something she saw there—something suggestive... inviting... wistful.

"You had a dab of hot sauce right there," he said softly.

Allison licked her lips. "There wasn't any hot sauce on that tamale," she said. Her voice sounded far away.

"I guess I was mistaken, then." Nick held her chin between his thumb and forefinger, grazing the sensitive skin in the arch of her neck. His lips twitched slightly, as if he were imagining them moving over Allison's.

Her face flushed pink, as warmth flooded her limbs. Thank goodness she was leaning against the car, or she would surely have toppled to the ground by now! She swayed instinctively toward Nick, igniting an eager glint in his eyes.

Simultaneously, they remembered where they were and who might be watching them. Nick gripped Allison's shoulder, both to steady her and to keep her at arm's length. In his face she saw a reflection of her own regret that the tantalizing promise of this moment had to be cut short.

Clearing his throat, Nick gave Allison's shoulder a final parting squeeze. "We'd better get going," he said. "I want to put as much distance as possible between us and Kellogg."

"Do you really think he could have tracked us this far?" Allison slid into the front seat.

"I'm counting on it," Nick replied grimly.

Completely unenlightened by his cryptic response, Allison kept her mouth closed. She was tired of pestering Nick for information. Besides, she didn't want to fight with him in front of Danny. Once they'd stopped for the night and Danny was asleep, maybe she could pry more details out of Nick.

Allison's stomach gave a queer lurch. She hadn't considered sleeping arrangements before; what did Nick have in mind for tonight? Did his pretense that they were a normal family on vacation include sharing the same hotel room? The same bed?

Ridiculous. Allison was willing to maintain this charade, but not to the extent of sharing a bed with a man she'd only met yesterday. Even if she *was* drawn to him by a dizzy attraction she couldn't begin to explain.

If Nick didn't request separate rooms, Allison hoped for his sake their room had a big, comfortable chair. Because otherwise Nick was going to spend the night on the cold, hard floor.

The car stopped again, this time across the street from an outdoor market that obviously catered to tourists. Nick handed Allison a wad of pesos. "Where'd you get these?" she asked in surprise.

"At the bank. Would you mind hopping out and buying something over there?"

She stared at him. "Could you be a little more specific? What exactly do you want me to buy?"

"It doesn't matter—just some tourist junk. Pottery, a big sombrero, sandals . . . get several things."

"You're certainly easy to please," she grumbled, getting out of the car. Nick had picked a pretty strange time to stop for souvenirs.

"And don't try to bargain them down," he called after her. "We're in a hurry."

"Then why are we wasting time here?" Allison muttered through her teeth as she pushed her way through the crowd of shoppers. At the first stand she came to, she plunked down a stack of pesos and picked out a donkey piñata, a fringed serape and an orange ceramic pot.

After lugging her treasures back to the car, Allison shoved the remaining pesos at Nick. "Here's your change. What's next? Are we going to take in a bullfight as long as we're in the neighborhood?"

"Maybe next time," he said absently, steering the car out into the traffic.

In the back seat, Danny was eagerly examining the piñata. "When can we break this open, Dad?"

"Hmm?" With Nick engrossed in driving at the moment, Allison turned to Danny.

"The piñata's empty. We have to buy our own candy and toys to put inside it."

"Oh." Danny's face fell. Then with a shrug, he looked out the window, apparently forgetting about the papier-mâché creature.

His reaction told Allison more than she wanted to know about the kind of life Danny had led for the past two years. Most kids would have raised a ruckus about the piñata, begging their parents to stop and buy candy to fill it.

But Danny's matter-of-fact acceptance of the disappointing situation demonstrated an emotional maturity far beyond his seven years. She couldn't help wishing Danny behaved a little more like a kid and a little less like an adult. Living on the run had forced him to grow up too quickly, robbing him of precious childhood innocence. And once lost, that innocence was gone forever.

Allison wondered if Nick realized the full impact of his decision to hide Danny from his mother. She knew exactly what Nick would say: that Sheila's abusive behavior left him no choice. But was Nick aware of the detrimental effects their secretive, rootless life-style was having on his son?

Studying Nick's tense expression, Allison was sure he must be. She'd seen that haunted look in his eyes—the look of a man torn by conflict. Nick must have doubts about the wisdom of his choice. He must know that dragging Danny all over the country—and out of the country—had to be traumatic. Constantly uprooted just when he'd gotten used to a new home and a new school, when he'd managed to make some friends—Danny had to be confused and frightened by the lack of permanence in their lives. How must it feel to a seven-year-old to live constantly with the knowledge that some strange man is searching for you, chasing after you no matter where you go?

Allison sighed. Was there a better alternative for Nick and Danny? Obviously Nick didn't think so. At any cost, he was determined to keep his son from the threat of physical harm. Was Nick's ex-wife really as violent as Nick claimed?

Or had Nick merely fabricated the whole story to justify stealing Danny away from his mother...?

That's why she was there in the first place, Allison thought. To find those answers. Maybe to convince Nick that taking Danny back to Boston would be in the boy's best interest.

She sighed again. Even after such a short acquaintance, Allison knew that trying to change Nick Caldwell's made-up mind would be an uphill battle. The man was as stubborn as an ox once he was convinced he was right. How far did Allison dare interfere?

Absently she patted her purse, where Raymond Kellogg's phone number was tucked away.

She forced the thorny problem from her mind for the time being. She was committed to spending a few days with the Caldwells, so any action she decided to take was still a ways off. She might as well enjoy the scenery since she was along for the ride.

As Nick navigated the tangle of Tijuana streets, Allison became hopelessly lost. She didn't have the best sense of direction in the world, but she was almost positive they were heading north.

But that didn't make sense! That was the direction they'd come from....

Then she spotted the line of cars, the low buildings, the signs.

"Nick Caldwell," she exclaimed. "Would you mind telling me why we're about to cross back over the border?"

Chapter Five

Danny slumbered in the back seat, one arm draped over the piñata. When she was satisfied he was fast asleep and wouldn't be awakened by a raised voice or two, Allison turned sideways in her seat.

"I want some answers, Nick. Now."

They'd just been waved through the border crossing. After being stuck behind a long line of cars and inhaling exhaust fumes for half an hour, it was a relief to be cruising down the freeway again.

What Allison couldn't figure out was why they were reversing their route along the same freeway they'd traveled only a couple of hours ago.

"Did you forget something in L.A.?" she prodded. "Whatever it is, it can't be worth driving all the way back."

"I didn't forget anything."

"Change your mind about hiding out in Mexico? What's the matter—didn't you like the food?"

The corner of Nick's mouth curved up slightly. "I never intended to stay in Mexico."

"Then what's this all about?" Allison nearly shouted, lowering her voice at the last second as she remembered Danny. "Nick, you can't keep me in the dark like this. If you're afraid I'll sneak off to the nearest pay phone the minute your back is turned and reveal your grand scheme to Kellogg, fine. You don't have to tell me everything." She raked her fingers through her tangle of long auburn hair. "But you can at least tell me where we're going to spend the night. And why did we drive to Mexico and go through all that rigmarole if we were just going to turn around and—oh!"

Nick watched comprehension dawn on Allison's face. Her eyebrows, furrowed with exasperation, arched in surprise. Her pursed lips parted. He couldn't help smiling at her astonished expression.

"You want Kellogg to *think* we're in Mexico," she said slowly. "You're trying to throw him off the track."

Nick nodded. "That's why I bought the auto insurance and changed some money to pesos. Kellogg's good. If he follows us to the border, he'll undoubtedly snoop around until he finds the people who sold me insurance and exchanged my money. Maybe if he thinks we're in Mexico, he'll give up the chase."

"You don't really believe that."

Nick glanced at Allison. A shadow crossed his brow. "No," he said. "I don't believe that for a moment."

They sat in silence. Then Allison asked, "Why did we buy all that junk back in Tijuana?"

"I didn't want the border guard to notice anything odd about us, because then he might remember us later.

I figured with a carload full of souvenirs, we'd look like any other American family visiting Mexico for the day.''

"And if we didn't look like tourists, he might wonder what we were doing in Mexico.''

"Right.'' Nick guided the car off the freeway and into the parking lot of a large shopping center.

"What now?'' Allison asked.

"One more thing to cover our trail. Do you have a screwdriver?''

"Sure. In my toolbox back home.''

"That won't help us much. How about a metal nail file?''

"How is a manicure going to cover our trail?''

Nick shook his fist at Allison in a mock threat. "Never mind. Do you have a nail file or not?''

"I think so....'' Allison rummaged through her shoulder bag. Really, one of these days she was going to have to organize this purse....

She found the nail file beneath a theater program from a play she'd attended last fall. "Here it is!''

Nick scrutinized the nail file. "Hmm. I guess this'll have to do.''

Before Allison could inquire "Do what?'' Nick was out of the car and kneeling in back of a station wagon parked next to them. Allison craned her neck. When she saw what Nick was doing, she gasped in horror and leaped out of the car.

Crouching next to him on the pavement, she whispered, "Are you crazy? Are you trying to get us arrested?''

"Are you aware you're standing on my foot?'' he replied. With two flicks of his wrist, Nick unscrewed one of the bolts of the station wagon's rear license plate.

"You can't steal these license plates! It's against the law!"

Nick spared her a wry glance, never pausing in his attack on the remaining bolt. "Allison, I've defied a court order, abandoned my career and everything I own, and lived like a fugitive for two years. All for my son. Do you think I'm going to let a little thing like petty larceny stand in the way of Danny's safety?"

The bolt came loose with a harsh squeak. Allison raised her head above the car, nervously scanning the parking lot. Nick had chosen a spot far enough from the stores so there weren't lots of people passing by, but with enough cars parked around them to provide cover.

"Someone's coming this way!" she whispered urgently.

Nick froze, and they both held their breaths until the elderly woman with the shopping cart had passed them by. Then Nick scooted to the front of the station wagon and started unscrewing the other license plate.

Allison scuttled after him. "Nick, I don't feel right about this. The owner is going to have to pay for new license plates."

"What am I supposed to do? I'd tuck some money under the windshield wiper, but I have a feeling it wouldn't be there by the time the owner got back."

"But he'll have to drive around without license plates...."

"No, he won't. Because I'm going to put *your* plates on his car. Hopefully he won't notice the switch for a few days."

"Then how will I get *my* plates back?" Allison exclaimed.

"We'll worry about that later. You can say some prankster must have switched them or something."

"Well...I don't know." Allison swung her gaze around the parking lot. She hadn't bargained on this new twist to their relationship. She'd wistfully imagined herself and Nick as Romeo and Juliet—not Bonnie and Clyde. Yesterday she'd been Nick's getaway driver; today she was his lookout. What next—his gun moll?

"There," he muttered, finally yanking the license plate free. Moving to Allison's car, he started working on her plates. Allison watched in dismay, feeling as if events were slipping out of her control.

Who was she kidding, anyway? Since throwing in her lot with the Caldwells, Allison hadn't controlled anything—least of all her feelings for Nick. It was a bit disconcerting to discover she was falling for a modern-day desperado—one who rustled cars instead of cattle.

Suddenly she said, "Wouldn't it be better to swipe out-of-state license plates?"

Nick glanced up at her with surprised admiration. "That's not a bad idea," he said. "Kellogg and his contacts in the highway patrol will be on the lookout for California plates." Shrugging, he moved back to the station wagon and began to attach Allison's plates. "On the other hand, California plates are less conspicuous here. The important thing is that we get rid of *your* plates, since your license number is the one they'll be watching for."

"I still can't believe Kellogg has the resources to trace my car."

Nick frowned. "Believe me, he couldn't have trailed Danny and me to L.A. without a lot of cooperation from law enforcement agencies. Those guys do each other favors all the time." Just then the overworked nail file broke in half. "Damn!" Nick jammed his thumb to his mouth.

"What's the matter?" Allison asked anxiously.

Inspecting his thumb, Nick said, "I cut myself when the tip of the file broke off."

"Let me see it."

"It's nothing." Nick jerked his thumb back and finished attaching the plates to the station wagon.

"Nick, you're really bleeding!" Allison pointed to several red drops spattered on the pavement.

"It's not as bad as it looks."

"How do you know? You haven't even looked at it." She snatched his hand.

"Allison, we don't have time for—"

She paled. "Nick, this is a deep cut. You can't just ignore it."

"I can until these plates are changed and we're safely out of here."

"Oh, for heaven's sake, I'll put on the damned license plates! Give me your handkerchief."

Meekly, Nick complied. Allison clamped her lips together in disgust. Why did all men insist on acting like big babies when they got a hangnail, and like macho hemen when they were really hurt? *Shucks, Miss Kitty, this here bullet wound in my chest ain't nothin'....*

Allison wrapped the handkerchief tightly around Nick's thumb. "There. Keep pressure on that until it stops bleeding." Picking up one of the license plates Nick had swiped from the station wagon, she screwed the bolts as tightly as she could with her fingers. The nail file was now useless. She scrambled to the other end of her car and attached the second plate.

Dusting her hands together, she said, "That'll have to do. I can't get these bolts any tighter without a screwdriver."

"They'll be fine." Nick opened the door and slid halfway into the driver's seat. "Come on, let's get out of here."

"Hold your horses. We're not going anywhere before we fix up that thumb of yours."

Nick waved his hand impatiently. "I told you, it's just a little cut. Come on, get in."

Allison propped her hands on her hips. "What if it gets infected? Would you rather take time to find a doctor? Maybe spend a few days in the hospital? A lot of good you'll do Danny if you come down with gangrene or something."

Nick grimaced. "All right, you win."

"Good. I'll run into that drugstore over there and get some bandages and antiseptic."

As Allison scanned the store's shelves for the supplies, she couldn't help feeling mildly smug that she'd finally scored a victory over Nick. She'd convinced him that his way of doing things wasn't always the best way. Maybe now he would share more of his plans with her.

But she wouldn't count on it.

Back in the car, Allison gingerly peeled the handkerchief from Nick's thumb. She couldn't stifle a sharp inhalation at the sight of the ugly wound. "It's still bleeding, Nick. That's not a good sign."

"Cuts are supposed to bleed. That way the germs get washed away."

She raised a skeptical eyebrow. "I suppose you learned that in your high school biology class."

"Nah. I learned it from watching TV."

Allison giggled, then her face grew somber. "Maybe we should find a hospital and go to the emergency room. I think this cut needs a stitch or two."

"I've had worse cuts before. It'll heal just fine. I promise!" Nick said, crossing his heart when Allison looked at him doubtfully.

She opened the bottle of antiseptic and liberally doused a cotton ball. "I'd tell you that this is going to hurt me a lot more than it hurts you, but unfortunately that isn't true. This is going to sting like hell, Nick."

"I know. Just get it over with."

Taking a deep breath, Allison began to cleanse the cut as best she could. Nick flinched once, but made no sound. She wound a gauze bandage tightly around his thumb. Had the bleeding slowed? Or was that merely wishful thinking?

Allison knew she was being ridiculous. Nick was a grown man, and it wasn't like he'd broken his arm or something. But even this minor injury concerned her. Visions of infections and gangrene and blood poisoning danced through her head. She wasn't used to having someone to worry about. The sensation was strange, but not—she had to admit—entirely unpleasant.

Once she'd finished the task of bandaging Nick's thumb, Allison found herself at a loss. His hand was cradled between hers, and he seemed to have no intention of removing it anytime in the near future.

His skin was dark brown against the stark white bandage. Allison studied the sprinkling of fine black hairs, the solid ridge of knuckles. With a will of their own, her fingers lightly stroked his, feeling their strength, their callused pads. She turned his hand over and continued her exploration of his palm, tracing the pattern of creases and lines.

Nick held his hand motionless, and when Allison glanced up, he was gazing at her with acute concentration, as if he, too, were bewitched by a magic spell. His eyes glowed like sapphires; the bold angles of his face were arranged in a combination of wonder and desire.

Suddenly looking at Nick wasn't enough. Allison raised her hand and touched his square chin, his lips, his furrowed brow, skimming over his rugged features with fascination.

A shudder ran through Nick's body. Then he lifted his good hand and slid it alongside Allison's face, tangling his fingers in her hair, stroking her earlobe sensually with his thumb.

Slowly...irresistibly...like two magnets being drawn together, they bent their heads toward each other. As Nick's face loomed inches from hers, Allison closed her eyes. The first contact of his lips on hers was indescribably sweet. As he moved his mouth languidly on hers, Allison savored the taste and smell of him—a heady, masculine blend that made her dizzy.

Nick shifted his body closer to hers, trying to bridge the gap between their seats. His movement made Allison aware of their close quarters—the way the car enclosed them in a steel-and-glass cocoon, shutting out the outside world. Once again a feeling of peace and security drifted over her—as if her subconscious mind had already decided to trust him.

"Mmm..." A contented growl rose from Nick's throat, evoking a responding sigh from Allison. She could happily stay like this forever, Nick's hand caressing her face, his lips roaming over hers....

His kiss was tender, undemanding, as if they had all the time in the world and no need to rush things.

Unfortunately, that wasn't true. Nearby a car door slammed, and Allison's eyes flew open as she and Nick jerked apart. What if the station wagon's owner had returned?

"Whew!" Nick wiped a hand across his brow, watching a young mother load her children into a car several places away.

"Nick, let's go." Allison's pulse was racing. This scare, following the thrill of Nick's kiss, was almost too much for her. Her heart couldn't take this much excitement.

Nick reached for the ignition, then turned back to Allison. He touched her cheek again. "Thank you," he said softly, as she found herself drowning once more in the depths of his gaze.

"For what?"

"For caring. For this." He lifted his bandaged thumb. "Just for being here."

Allison averted her eyes, unable to face the naked emotion visible in his strong features. Nick was grateful to her now, but she couldn't guarantee that she would continue to be a help and not a hindrance to him. She cringed at the thought of how rapidly Nick's feelings for her would change if she decided—for Danny's sake—to report their whereabouts to Kellogg.

Nick ran his uninjured thumb slowly along her jawline, then pressed it lightly against her lips. The smoldering gaze he gave her when she finally looked up sent a flood of heated desire coursing through her body. If only they had more time...if only circumstances were different.

Reluctantly Nick removed his hand from her face. She could still feel the imprint of his flesh lingering where he had touched her. She shivered.

It took a moment for her to notice that Nick was having trouble starting the car.

"You can't drive with that injured thumb," she exclaimed. "Let me drive." She started to get out of the car to trade places with him.

"Stay there," he commanded. "I'm perfectly capable of driving."

"You can't even get the car started. And how are you going to work the stick shift?"

"I can manage." Nick grimaced in frustration, then muttered, "If you'll help me out."

"You are positively, absolutely, without a shadow of a doubt the most stubborn, pigheaded man I have ever—"

"Save the compliments for later. Right now I need you to turn the key for me."

With a groan of exasperation, Allison surrendered. Leaning over, she switched on the ignition. As she rebuckled her seat belt, she said, "I suppose you want me to shift gears for you, too?"

Nick experimented with the stick shift, wincing slightly as he gripped the knob. "I think I can handle shifting. And once we're back on the freeway, I won't need to change gears."

With that, he backed the car out and headed for the freeway. Soon they were driving back through San Diego. As they headed north, Allison tried to dismiss the ridiculous worry that somehow Kellogg, trailing them south down the same freeway, would spot her car as they passed each other at a relative speed of more than a hundred miles per hour.

Really, she was getting as paranoid as Nick!

Yet despite all of Nick's previous precautions, the detective had somehow managed to track the Caldwells to Los Angeles. Allison knew the man was only human; he didn't possess a crystal ball or have some supernatural power that enabled him to find Nick and Danny no matter where they tried to hide. The man was simply good at his job.

But Allison couldn't help glancing nervously over her shoulder from time to time, half expecting to see a brown sedan tailing them like a shark sniffing after a helpless swimmer.

If she was this nervous after only half a day on the run, what must Nick be feeling after two years of living like a criminal, constantly on the alert, knowing that at any moment Danny could be snatched away and whisked back to Boston . . . ?

Or had Nick simply grown used to it? Maybe his clever precautions were second nature by now. Perhaps time and practice had sharpened his survival skills while simultaneously dulling the knife-like edge of fear.

But Nick was a grown man, with an adult's understanding of the world around him. What worried Allison was how this uncertain, fearful life was affecting Danny. Surely the specter of a real-life pursuer must be even more terrifying than any bogeyman who ever lurked under a child's bed at night.

Danny's childhood fears were real. They couldn't be soothed away by a comforting hug or banished by a night-light. Other kids worried about monsters in the closet, but knew their dads could chase the monsters away.

But Danny's monster was chasing his dad as well.

Allison sensed that Nick had done everything in his power to make his son feel secure. But every few months, the monster found them again. Once again Danny was uprooted, his precarious sense of stability destroyed. He was a sensitive child, and there was no way Nick could completely hide his own anxiety from his son.

Was Nick subjecting Danny to a life even more psychologically damaging than Sheila's abuse?

That's what she had to decide over the next several days, Allison thought as she watched the familiar Los Angeles sights fly past the car window.

Danny had awakened an hour ago and was sitting quietly in the back seat, clutching an old baseball.

"I bet you and your dad play catch with that ball a lot," Allison said brightly, trying to draw Danny out of his shell.

His blue eyes widened in horror. "This is my Ted Williams autographed baseball!" he exclaimed indignantly.

Nick chuckled, then immediately assumed a somber expression when Allison glared at him.

"Is that a special kind of baseball?" she inquired.

Danny stared at her as if she'd asked him what planet they were on. "Ted Williams autographed this baseball," he repeated.

"And who's Ted Williams?"

Danny's jaw dropped, but no words came out. Nick shot his son a sympathetic glance over his shoulder. "Girls," he said, shrugging. "What do you expect?"

"Hey, don't teach him that kind of sexist attitude," Allison said. "Baseball doesn't happen to be one of my interests, that's all. Can I help it if I never heard of Tim Williams?"

"*Ted*. Ted Williams," Nick said.

"Right. Ted. That's what I meant." Throwing Danny a feeble smile, Allison temporarily gave up her attempt to establish a meaningful rapport with Nick's son.

But at least she could try to recover some of her dignity. "I'm not completely ignorant about sports," she said to Nick.

"No?"

"No. As a matter of fact, I was the sports reporter for my high school newspaper."

"I take it your school didn't go much for baseball."

Allison threw him a wry glance. "As a matter of fact, we had a very good baseball team."

"But Ted Williams didn't play on it, and that's why you never heard of him."

"Very funny." Allison could see her attempt to impress Nick with her sports expertise was failing miserably. "Actually, my biggest scoop was my locker-room interview with the varsity football team."

Nick arched his eyebrows. "They let a *girl* reporter into the locker room?"

He was playing right into her hands. "Not exactly. That was part of the scoop."

"Then how did you . . . ?"

Now she had him hooked. "I stuffed my hair under a cap, borrowed some of my brother's clothes and used an eyebrow pencil to draw on a mustache. Then after the game, I just pushed into the locker room with everyone else."

"I bet you looked cute in a mustache." Nick's eyes wandered appreciatively over Allison's lush curves. "But I find it difficult to believe you were able to fool them into thinking you were a boy."

"Well . . . I wasn't as . . . developed back then. And I didn't fool them for very long."

Nick grinned. "What happened?"

"Two of the players got into a scuffle, and in the commotion, my cap got knocked off."

"And all that beautiful long hair was a dead giveaway."

Allison nodded. "That was the end of my budding career as a sports journalist, I'm afraid. I also got suspended from school for three days."

"Any regrets?"

"Not a one." She sighed happily. "When my story appeared, it became the most popular issue of the paper in school history. Besides that, I got to ogle all those sweating male bodies. That alone was worth the price." She shook her head in wonder. "I'll never forget the sight of all those big shoulders, big biceps, big—"

At that moment, she noticed Danny leaning his head forward with wide-eyed interest.

"Oh, never mind," she mumbled, slouching down into the seat.

Nick's shoulders shook with silent laughter, as Danny sank back, disappointed.

Somehow, the story about her enterprising reporting hadn't impressed Nick and Danny much after all. Well, why should she care if they both considered her a sports ignoramus? She'd never been bothered by other people's opinions of her before.

But this time, Allison *did* care what they thought of her. She wanted Nick and Danny to like her; she wanted to be one of the gang.

And she wasn't entirely pleased with this realization. *She* was supposed to be assessing *Nick's* character. Why did it matter so much what he thought of her? After all, in a few days she would be saying goodbye to him and would never see him again—

"Last chance to back out," Nick said quietly, interrupting her thoughts.

Allison whipped her head around to look at him. "What do you mean?"

"If you're having second thoughts about coming with us, now's the time to say so. You could drop us at the bus station and be home in half an hour."

"Not a chance, pal! After what I've been through today? Sneaking across the border, stealing license plates, bandaging wounds...no way am I quitting now. I've got too much invested in this crazy escapade already."

Nick smiled. "I was hoping you'd say that."

Allison eyed him suspiciously. "I should think you'd be happy to get rid of me."

"Oh, I don't know. You're kind of handy to have around sometimes."

"Handy, huh?"

"Well, sure. Like when you fixed up my thumb."

"Is that all?" she asked casually.

"Is what all?"

"Is that the only reason you want me along? Because I'm *handy*?"

Nick reached for her with his injured hand. "No," he replied, his voice warm and low. "That's not the only reason I want you along." He squeezed her hand and threw her a meaningful smile that sent an excited tingling through her body.

This was insane, Allison thought—the way she and Nick kept dancing around the subject of their mutual attraction. They were like two children dancing around a bonfire, darting forward to poke a stick at the embers and send a blaze of sparks skyward.

The problem about playing with fire was...sometimes you got burned.

Allison considered that disturbing fact as they left Los Angeles behind, swinging west from the freeway to hook up with the highway that hugged the coastline. North they sped, through Santa Barbara, Santa Maria and San

Luis Obispo, where they stopped at a coffee shop for a quick dinner.

Nick was silent while they ate, his eyes darting frequently to the parking lot. Danny seemed to pick up his father's preoccupied mood, and even Allison's best jokes failed to elicit a smile from him.

As darkness fell, they were back on the coast highway, skirting the cliffs above the crashing waves of the Pacific Ocean. Danny soon fell asleep again.

Allison had to bite her tongue to prevent herself from asking Nick where he planned to stop for the night. This stretch of the coast was sparsely populated, and their choice of lodging was likely to be rather limited.

Just to display her utter lack of interest, she yawned.

"Tired?"

She looked at Nick in surprise. "The mummy speaks! I didn't think I was going to hear another word from you."

The lines of his face creased into a grimace. "Sorry I haven't been much of a conversationalist this evening." He turned the steering wheel sharply. "Besides, I've got to concentrate on navigating these curves."

The road had narrowed, and for the past hour had been climbing and swooping like a roller coaster along an endless chain of hairpin curves. In the darkness it was especially hard to drive.

"Don't let me distract you," Allison said hastily.

Silence descended again, and Allison found it increasingly difficult to keep her eyelids propped open. On one hand, she longed for sleep, since the tortuous, never-ending curves were making her decidedly queasy.

On the other hand, she intended to keep an eye on Nick no matter what. Allison wasn't going to let him out of her sight until she finally decided what to do. For the next several days, she had to be constantly on alert, her eyes and ears open for any indication that Nick Caldwell wasn't what he claimed to be.

Allison's head jerked up. Damn! She must have dozed off for a few seconds.

"Have a nice nap?"

She jumped at the sound of Nick's voice. "I wasn't sleeping."

"Do you commonly snore while you're awake, then?"

"I don't snore," she said indignantly, brushing a lock of hair from her face.

"Must be something wrong with the car, then. For the past half an hour there's been a constant buzzing noise coming from the passenger side."

Half an hour! Good grief, was it possible she'd slept so long? Ignoring Nick's unchivalrous comments about her snoring, Allison asked, "Where are we?"

"Big Sur."

"Big Sur?" she exclaimed, noticing they'd left the coast highway and were traveling along a narrow dirt road beneath a dense canopy of trees. "What is this, some trip down memory lane back to your wild hippie days during the sixties?"

Nick made a sour face. "Please. I was fourteen years old when the sixties ended."

"Then what are we doing here?"

"Spending the night. That is, if this lodge has a vacancy."

Just then the trees thinned a little and they drove into a clearing past a sign that read Redwood Cabins. A pale yellow light illuminated the word "Office" on a small building.

"I don't see any cabins," Allison said.

"They're probably up in the woods behind the office." Nick switched off the Volvo's engine. The silence was deafening.

"How did you know about this place, anyway?" Allison instinctively lowered her voice to a whisper.

"I saw a billboard along the highway while you were asleep. Excuse me, I mean while you were practicing your buzz-saw imitation."

Allison thumped Nick on the upper arm. "Ow!"

"Shh. You'll wake up the raccoons," she said sweetly.

Nick glanced in the back seat. "Not to mention Danny." He opened the car door. "I'll get us a room. Be right back, so don't wander off."

Allison watched Nick's shadowy figure slip inside the office. Wander off? Not likely—not in the middle of pitch-black woods that were no doubt filled with bears and wolves and other creatures that go bump in the night. For all she knew, Bigfoot was lurking nearby.

Nick's words echoed in her ears. "I'll get us a room," he'd said. *A* room. Singular, not plural. Meaning one room, not two.

Allison propped her chin in her hand and waited for Nick's return. She couldn't tell if the butterflies in her stomach were from anxiety...or anticipation. But whatever the cause, the night ahead promised to be very interesting, indeed.

Nick returned and tossed a room key into her lap. "We're in luck," he said. "They had a vacancy."

He pulled the car into a parking area behind the office. "Can you manage the luggage while I carry Danny?"

Allison followed Nick up a sloping trail that led to a small log cabin beneath the trees. Their meager luggage wasn't that heavy, and the trail wasn't that steep...but she was breathing rapidly by the time they reached the cabin. Her heart pounding loudly in her ears was the only sound in the still night.

As Nick stepped aside, Allison jabbed the key at the lock, missing her target several times before the key finally slipped in. Pushing the door open, she allowed Nick and his sleeping son to precede her into the cabin.

With shaking hands, Allison stuffed the key back into her pocket. Then she sighed, squared her shoulders and followed the Caldwells inside.

Chapter Six

In her dream they were still driving along those dark, towering cliffs, only this time someone was chasing them. Peering fearfully over her shoulder, Allison couldn't see another car, only Danny's terrified white face, but she knew someone was after them, was gaining on them, and would soon catch them or drive them over the side of the cliff into the bottomless ocean below.

Nick's face was a rigid mask as he steered the car left...right...left again, forcing the overworked Volvo to cling precariously to the road's endless curves. All around them was blackness. The only sound was the maddening screech of tires as the car barreled around the curves, swinging wide each time, nearly plunging over the cliff. If they met another car coming the other way, it meant certain death for all of them.

Then Allison felt herself rising, as if the car had already crashed into the ocean, and she was fighting her way to the surface. Yet the awful screech of tires still filled her ears as she struggled for breath, flailing her arms and legs wildly, searching for Nick and Danny—

Her eyes flew open as she surfaced from the dream like a swimmer exploding from the water. For a moment the only sound was her own rapid breathing, but then she realized that the crazy sound of screeching tires still persisted.

Propping herself up on her elbows, Allison searched for the source of the racket that had penetrated her dream. Daylight filtered into the bedroom through a calico-curtained window. Strange. It sounded like the noise was coming from right outside that window.

Casting aside the bedclothes, Allison slipped out of bed and tiptoed to the window. She peeked cautiously out, then flung the curtain aside.

A squirrel, chattering indignantly at a crow in a nearby tree, took one look at Allison, dropped the nut between his tiny paws and fled. She watched him scamper across the carpet of brown pine needles and scurry up the tree to join his avian adversary. Who said life in the country was quiet? she wondered.

She turned away from the window, pausing at the sight of the room's other inhabitants.

After all of Allison's anxiety, the sleeping arrangements hadn't turned out to be so extraordinary after all. Their one-bedroom cabin contained two double beds, so Allison had claimed one and Nick and Danny had shared the other.

Danny looked as if he hadn't budged one inch from the position Nick had gently laid him in last night. Nick, on the other hand, looked as if he had done his share of thrashing around during the night. The bedclothes were a wild tangle, one sheet slashing diagonally across his chest, baring a tantalizing view of his hard, well-developed pectoral muscles. A wiry covering of black hair rippled as he breathed deeply in his sleep.

One arm was flung above his head, as if Nick had tried to ward off some danger during one of his dreams. Allison hoped his dreams had been more peaceful than her own—but she doubted they were.

The room was a bit chilly, and as Allison tugged the sheet up over Nick's chest, her hand brushed against him. She shivered, though not from the cold. The urge to skim her palm across that broad chest, to tease the coarse curls with her fingertips, was nearly irresistible.

Sighing, Allison resisted. She could just picture Nick's reaction upon waking up to find her caressing his hard, tanned flesh. Hmm. Actually, his reaction might be rather exciting.

But not with Danny in the room, she thought, stepping back hastily.

In sleep, Allison could see the resemblance between them for the first time. Nick's face had softened, losing that tense, guarded look she was used to. His lips were slightly parted, and a lock of black hair strayed across his forehead.

Allison's eyes darted to Danny, then back to Nick. Okay, so Nick really was Danny's father. That much of his story, at least, was true. But what was his real reason for taking Danny away from his mother?

She desperately wanted to believe Nick, partly because she didn't want to believe she could fall for a man who would tell such a horrendous lie.

And Allison was honest enough to admit—to herself, at least—that she *was* falling for Nick. Her feelings for him had already progressed beyond intense physical attraction. She wanted to know everything about him, and not simply so she could decide what to do about Danny.

Yet Allison knew virtually nothing about Nick. Only his name and that he came from Boston. That much she'd learned from Kellogg, so it must be true.

Today, she vowed, she would break through Nick's resistance and find some answers.

She only hoped they were answers she could live with.

Allison dressed quickly in the bathroom, moving as quietly as possible so as not to waken Nick and Danny. She hadn't had much chance to notice their surroundings last night; it had been dark and she'd been exhausted.

The cabin was furnished plainly yet cozily. The walls were paneled in pine, and a framed seascape hung above the stone fireplace in the living room. Braided rag rugs lay on the hardwood floors. Adjoining the living room was a small but perfectly adequate kitchen, the sight of which started Allison thinking about breakfast.

Since her roommates were still asleep, she might as well see about rustling up some food, she decided. She grabbed a sweater, let herself out the door and followed the path down the slight hill to the lodge office.

Inhaling deeply, Allison filled her lungs with the scent of cedar and wood smoke. The faint tang of salt wafted in from the ocean, which was probably half a mile away, she figured. Birds chirped in the trees, and small animals scurried unseen through the underbrush. Redwoods and shorter pines loomed overhead.

Smoke unfurled from the chimney of the office cabin. A plump, middle-aged woman with curly gray hair looked up from the counter as the door banged shut behind Allison. "Good morning."

"Good morning," Allison replied, smiling. "I'd like to whip up some breakfast for my, uh…family, but I'm afraid we didn't bring any groceries with us. Is there a little market or something here at the lodge?"

The woman shook her head regretfully. "No, dear, I'm afraid not." She set down her pencil. "That was something my husband, Edgar—God rest his soul—and I always talked about adding someday, but we never got around to it. And now that Edgar's gone, I'm afraid I just don't have the gumption left to start a big project like that."

The woman sighed. "Seems it's all I can do these days just to keep this place breaking even. Oh, but you don't want to hear all this." She dismissed her troubles with a wave of her hand. "There's a general store about three miles up the highway. Go back to the lodge entrance, turn north, and it'll be on the right. You can't miss it— there's a big red sign out front."

"Isn't there anything closer? Within walking distance? It's such a lovely morning, I thought I'd like to get some exercise."

"No, dear, I'm sorry. The general store is the nearest market."

"Well, thank you. You've been very helpful." The woman beamed as Allison backed out of the office.

So, she would have to take the car. No big deal…except, she remembered suddenly, Nick still had the key. She sneaked into the bedroom, half expecting to find them awake by now, but they were still sound asleep. Allison found Nick's pants slung over a chair and fished delicately into his pockets. Her fingers found the key almost immediately, but they touched something else as well. Nick's wallet.

She drew it out slowly, hardly daring to breathe. Nick owed her some answers, and maybe some of them were here. Goodness knows, a thorough exploration of Allison's purse would yield the story of her life. Would Nick's wallet yield some of his secrets as well?

Casually, she flipped the worn leather wallet open. Driver's license. Name... Nicholas Anthony Caldwell. Well, she'd known that already. Birth date... that made him thirty-four years old. Hair... eye color... weight— Allison slapped the wallet shut. What the hell did she think she was doing? There had to be a better way to discover more about Nick than by violating his privacy.

She slid his wallet back into his pocket, half expecting an angry hand to clamp down on her shoulder while her back was turned. What had she expected to find in his wallet, anyway? A folded-up wanted poster offering a reward for his capture?

Not likely. One thing Allison *did* know about Nick: he was too careful to carry something incriminating on his person. If he were injured in an accident, for example, and they searched his pockets at the hospital, anything linking him to his life in Boston might very well result in a phone call that would lead Sheila straight to Danny.

Allison escaped undetected from the bedroom, and in minutes was driving up the coast in search of breakfast. She found the general store with no problem, but standing in front of the shelves realized she had no idea how much food to buy. Should she stock up for a few days? Or was Nick planning to leave immediately?

She decided to buy eggs and milk and some nonperishable items they could pack in the car if Nick insisted on hitting the road right away.

Arms full of groceries, Allison hiked up the trail to the cabin, feeling rather domestic and humming softly under her breath. Pushing the door open, she braked to a stop at the sight that greeted her.

Nick, his shirt unbuttoned, his feet still bare, was throwing things into his suitcase as fast as possible, while Danny stood to one side, watching his father nervously, clutching his backpack. "Have you got everything, Shortstop? We've got to get out of—"

The words died on Nick's lips when he saw Allison. The look on his face when their eyes locked together was something she would never forget. Nick froze, and in his narrowed blue eyes she watched a succession of emotions tumble over each other—surprise, fear, relief, anger...and something that amazingly resembled affection. That wary, hunted look was back on his face, his lips tightly pressed together, his jaw set at a determined angle.

Slowly, he rose from his stooped position. "You're here," he said in a measured, even tone.

With a thud, Allison dumped the grocery sacks on the coffee table. "Yes," she replied. "But I guess if I'd come back a few minutes later, you two wouldn't have been."

"Allison—"

"You thought I'd run out on you. You thought I'd sneaked off to call Kellogg."

A muscle flickered in Nick's jaw. "What was I supposed to think? You were gone, the car was gone—"

"You could have trusted me, Nick! You could have given me the benefit of the doubt and figured there was a perfectly innocent reason why I'd taken the car."

"I don't know you well enough to trust you," he said quietly. In that moment, Allison felt as if they were complete strangers. What had happened to that easy camaraderie they'd developed? What about the kisses they'd shared, and those smoldering, meaningful glances Nick had given her?

How insignificant those things must really be, if Nick's suspicions could sweep them aside so easily.

"Why didn't you leave a note?" he asked.

"I didn't realize I was required to," she replied icily. Deep down inside, Allison supposed she couldn't really blame Nick for jumping to the wrong conclusion. But her feelings were hurt. The realization that Nick still didn't trust her after what they'd been through was like a slap in the face.

"Danny, why don't you go play in the bedroom for a little while?" Nick said.

"Aren't we gonna leave?" Danny's voice was small and scared.

Nick knelt beside him and took the backpack from his fragile shoulder. "No, we're not leaving. For a while, anyway." He rubbed his son's head. "It's okay, Danny. Go play in the other room for a few minutes."

The fearful look Danny gave Allison as he left the living room nearly broke her heart. Obviously Nick had conveyed his own doubts about her to his son. Would she ever make friends with Danny now?

"I'll make breakfast," she said, gathering the groceries in her arms. "That is, if it's all right with you. Or should I write you a note about it?"

"Let me help you," Nick said, moving toward her.

"I can manage, thanks." She carried the sacks into the kitchen and set them on the counter. "What would you like for breakfast?"

"Allison—"

"French toast?"

"Will you please lis—"

"Pancakes?"

"Allison—"

"Maybe an omelet? Of course, we did have eggs for breakfast yesterday, so if you're worried about cholesterol—"

"Allison, will you please listen to me for one minute and stop talking about breakfast?" Nick shouted.

Allison stared at him. "There's no need to raise your voice," she said quietly.

Nick pounded his fist on the counter. He rolled his eyes toward the ceiling, closed them and took a deep breath. Never, in his entire life, had he encountered such a maddening female, such an aggravating, frustrating...gorgeous...desirable female. In a moment he regained his self-control.

"If my not trusting you offended you, I'm sorry," he said. "But put yourself in my position, Allison. I can't afford to trust anyone, because if I make a mistake, Danny would suffer for it."

"So you say."

Nick felt his temper inching upward again. "I guess that makes us even. I don't trust you, and you don't believe me."

Allison turned from the cupboard, clutching a box of crackers to her chest. Her eyes shone at him with dismay. "Oh, Nick, why does it have to be like this? I thought we were getting on so well, and all of a sudden we're at each other's throats."

Nick's irritation drained away. He took the box from her, set it on the counter and drew her to him. She came—not reluctantly, but cautiously—into his arms, resting her cheek against his chest.

He stroked her hair, running his fingers through the long auburn tresses. "I don't want things to be this way, either, Allison. But I don't think either of us can afford to trust the other yet. We need more time.''

"We don't have a lot of time, Nick." Her voice was muffled. Then she raised her head and looked up at him. "I can't go running away with you forever."

"Why not?" The words escaped Nick's lips before they even had a chance to register on his brain.

Allison's eyes widened; her eyebrows knit together. "What do you mean?"

What *did* he mean? Nick wasn't even sure himself. "I mean, there's really no specific date you have to get back to L.A., is there?"

Allison's intent expression softened with what Nick could have sworn was disappointment. "I won't lose my job if I'm not back on a certain date, no," she admitted. "That's one of the benefits of being your own boss. But I have a responsibility to Marilyn, and to our customers. I can't simply take off for a week or a month...or longer...whenever I feel like it."

"Mmm, no...I suppose not." Nick couldn't take his eyes from Allison's lips. Fascinating, the way they moved when she spoke, the slight quiver as she breathed. They were pink and luscious and full...and suddenly he could no longer resist the urge to taste them once more.

Lowering his face to hers, Nick watched her startled expression melt into anticipation, and when their lips touched she responded with an eagerness that delighted him.

Her mouth was warm and welcoming, her tongue joining his in a sensual union. Nick felt her lush breasts press against him as she arched her back, molding her body into his as her arms tightened about his waist.

He felt a quickening in his loins, and slid his arms more possessively around her, kneading her back with his fingers, sliding one hand down to cup her bottom and draw her even more snugly against him.

Allison writhed slightly against his hardness, and a faint moan welled up from her throat. *Good,* Nick thought, *she wants me as much as I want her.* He kissed her with even greater fervor, savoring the softness of her lips, plunging his tongue deeper into the sweet moistness of her mouth.

Spanning Allison's waist with his hands, Nick swung her up into a sitting position on the counter, their mouths never breaking contact. Their faces were on the same level now, and when Nick opened his eyes, Allison's lowered lashes fluttered directly across from him. Her eyelids were creamy ivory, and a tiny vein pulsed delicately at her temple.

"You're so lovely," he murmured, tearing his lips from hers to feast on the delicious curve of her throat.

Allison slid her hands up Nick's back and over his shoulders, tangling her fingers in his hair, massaging his neck. Her head fell back, allowing Nick easier access to her sensitive flesh.

Nick felt as if he could never get enough of her, could never explore Allison long enough or far enough to satisfy the insatiable desire building in his abdomen. She was so soft, so sweet, so willing. . . .

He parted her knees and insinuated himself between her thighs. Seeking her mouth again, Nick pulled her closer until their bodies were joined in intimate contact, separated only by several layers of clothing. Yet for all the heat that surged between them, they might as well have been completely nude.

Allison wrapped her legs around Nick's hips, creating a delicious pressure that he thought would make him explode. He slid his hands across her back, squeezing and stroking, while he bestowed kisses on her eyelids, her temples, the dimple in her cheek.

"Ah, Nick..." Allison whispered his name, her breath a warm caress in his ear.

He buried his face in her hair, inhaling the wonderful scent of pine, unable to resist returning to her mouth a moment later to sample the flavor of her lips.

Sliding his hand to her waist, Nick sought the sleek satin of Allison's skin beneath the thin pullover sweater she wore. He slipped his fingers beneath her clothing, nudging the sweater aside as he explored her softness, tracing her ribs, brushing against her lacy bra.

Despite this annoying obstacle, Nick cupped Allison's breast in his hand, kneading the luscious flesh, teasing the hardened nipple. His sensual caresses elicited faint purrs of pleasure. At this point, Nick had no intention of stopping without definite discouragement, but—to his satisfaction—Allison seemed to be enjoying this as much as he was.

Unclasping her bra, Nick pushed her sweater aside to gaze with pleasure upon her round, creamy breasts. Licking his lips, he bent his head to one rosy peak. Capturing the pebble-hard tip in his mouth, he flicked his tongue across it until Allison groaned.

"Nick, please ... oh, please ..."

Was she begging him to stop? Or urging him to continue?

Her body was responding to him in a way that left no doubt in Nick's mind. Allison was as consumed with desire as he was.

An overwhelming passion swept over him, blotting out all awareness except for the one thought that he must possess this woman, satisfy her, share with her the incredible ecstasy their lovemaking would ignite.

In a swift, confident motion, Nick gathered Allison into his arms, hugging her against his chest as he carried her from the kitchen. She wrapped her arms tightly around his neck. He could feel the excited pounding of her heart, and wondered if he would be able to make it all the way to the bedroom before laying her down and tearing the clothes from her sexy body.

The sight of Danny's backpack on the living room floor was like a bucket of ice water dashed in his face.

Nick halted instantly. "Oh, my God," he said in a low, tortured voice. "What the hell are we doing?"

Allison scanned Nick's face, then followed the direction of his eyes. In a second, she'd leaped from his arms to the floor, hurriedly pulling her sweater down over her bare breasts.

They stood frozen for a moment, a good three feet apart, panting rapidly. Finally Allison pushed a lock of hair from her eyes and gave Nick a wavery smile. "Oops," she said weakly.

"Allison, I'm so sorry, I don't know how I could have forgotten—"

She cut him off with a wave of her hand. "No apologies necessary. We both got a bit carried away, that's all. It happens." *But it's never happened to me before,* she thought. *Not like this.*

Nick shook his head, looking bewildered and angry at the same time. "I don't understand how I could have simply... forgotten about Danny."

"Don't be so hard on yourself. What, um, what we were doing has a way of being ... rather distracting."

"You don't understand." Nick jammed his hands in his pockets and began pacing the floor. "For two years, Danny has been foremost in my mind. Every moment. He's had to be my primary focus at all times, because one lapse on my part—'' he grimaced ''—one moment of forgetfulness, and I could lose him forever.''

Nick's eyes were accusing as he studied Allison from across the room. Was he accusing her? Or himself?

Allison shrugged, exasperated. With Nick...and herself—because his partially bare chest, visible beneath his unbuttoned shirt, continued to stir tantalizing images in her brain. "It's over," she said. "No harm done. There's no point in beating yourself up about it. Let's forget it, shall we?"

"No," he said stonily. "We can't forget. We have to remember, to prevent its recurrence. Allison—" Nick wiped his hand across his brow. "We can never let this happen again."

The silence was deafening.

"Don't worry," she replied tartly. "It won't." Then she turned her back on Nick and headed for the kitchen.

Lips sewn tightly together, Allison made French toast and contemplated her situation. Obviously, living in close quarters with Nick wasn't going to work out. She cracked a couple of eggs, dumped the contents into a shallow dish and beat them with a fork.

This overwhelming physical attraction they had for each other wasn't going away. It was getting stronger. Even worse, it was passing beyond the physical realm and entering a dangerous region where emotions were involved. She attacked a loaf of bread with a butcher knife and carved half a dozen thick slices.

Now Nick was adding new ground rules to the ones he'd laid down in the beginning. No more stolen kisses, no more secret embraces. Allison slapped two slices of egg-soaked bread into the frying pan. They sizzled angrily.

Fine. If that's the way Nick wanted it, that's the way he would have it. Allison would be cool as a cucumber. Aloof. Distant. Butter wouldn't melt in her mouth. She flipped the French toast, banging the spatula against the pan.

But if Nick could change the rules, so could she. She was tired of his secretiveness. She'd played fair with him; now it was time for him to come clean.

She wanted some answers, and she wanted them today. She didn't have time to keep pussyfooting around the issue. As she'd pointed out to Nick, she had responsibilities back home. She didn't have time to trail around the country after him, waiting for him to drop an occasional tidbit of information about his past.

Today. Sometime today she would corner Nick and demand some answers. And if he clammed up, well, what choice did she have but to call that detective? Let others more qualified than she make the decisions about Danny's future.

Allison was worried about the child. She'd seen for herself some of the harmful effects all this running away was having on the poor kid. Nick had better come up with some pretty convincing facts to convince her that the life Danny faced back in Boston was any worse than this.

And he'd better produce them quick. Today. Allison would give Nick one more chance to persuade her that his way was the best way for Danny.

She flipped the French toast onto a plate, then bowed her head. God, how she hoped Nick could convince her! How she wanted to believe him....

Don't blow it, Nick, she prayed silently. *Tell me the truth. Tell me everything. Don't force me to pick up that phone and make a call I don't want to make.*

Stubborn . . . pigheaded . . . always so sure of himself . . .

Allison slammed the cupboard door shut.

"Breakfast's ready!" she yelled.

Chapter Seven

Nick lay back on the sand, propped up on his elbows, his eyes closed. The warm sun felt good on his face. He was more relaxed than he'd been for two days—ever since he'd come out to his truck and seen that detective parked across the street.

He knew this peaceful interlude wouldn't last, and he intended to take advantage of it—to recharge his batteries, so to speak. Then he would be ready once again to make the critical decisions that would affect his and Danny's future. Nick needed this period of rest so that his wits would be sharpened, his reflexes lightning-quick when it came time to fight for Danny again.

Opening one eye, he studied Allison. She sat several feet away, arms circling her bent knees, toes buried in the sand. She was staring out over the ocean with a troubled expression on her face.

A surge of guilt washed over Nick. He knew he was responsible for the lines that creased her forehead, the downward twist of her lovely mouth. It had been his idea to drag her along with them, and Nick didn't have to be a mind reader to tell that Allison regretted coming.

He could hardly blame her. She'd been an amazingly good sport so far, putting up with his silence, his elaborate precautions. Most women wouldn't have stuck it out this far. Sheila, for example. Nick couldn't picture his ex-wife throwing a few things in a bag and taking off for an unknown destination on the spur of the moment. Sheila was the kind of woman who never went anywhere without her curling iron.

Nick peered at Allison again. The brisk sea breeze lifted the long strands of her reddish-brown hair from her shoulders, baring her beautiful neck. Nick shifted uncomfortably, as his body reacted to the memory of their earlier encounter in the kitchen. He shook his head, still unable to believe that anyone or anything could so bewitch him that he could forget his son—if only for a moment.

Nick had to be on guard in two directions now—from Kellogg and from Allison. Yet this knowledge in his mind directly conflicted with messages from his heart and body. Allison had already come to mean more to Nick than a sexy potential bedmate. He cared about her in a deeper way, and it tore him up inside to recall the hurt look in her eyes this morning when he'd told her that any further physical involvement was off-limits.

Nick sighed. Somehow he suspected he was going to have trouble following his own advice.

Allison turned her head at the sound. "I was beginning to think you'd fallen asleep," she said.

"After that huge, delicious breakfast you cooked for us, you could hardly blame me."

"Mmm. I did notice that you were more than willing to finish what Danny and I couldn't eat."

Was she calling a truce to the war of silence that had prevailed between them since this morning? Nick wished he could see the look in her eyes, but her dark sunglasses disguised whatever she was really feeling.

"Where's Danny?" Nick asked, suddenly sitting up straight.

Allison pointed. "He's right on the other side of that rock, building a sand castle. I've been keeping an eye on him."

"I guess he's pretty safe down there, as long as he doesn't go too far out into the water."

Nick's gaze wandered across the scene in front of them. After breakfast he'd suggested walking across the highway to the beach. Danny had been so excited at the prospect that Nick had had to grab his arm quickly to prevent him from dashing into traffic. Once they were safely across the road, the boy had charged on ahead, racing to the water's edge and flinging himself into the surf with cries of delight.

Allison and Nick had followed more sedately, more silently, kicking off their shoes and plodding through the sand dunes. The rugged shoreline of Big Sur was far different from the smooth, sandy beaches of Southern California. Here the short, rocky stretches of beach were bisected by cliffs and curved into small coves. Sea grasses and stubbly green shrubs covered the cliffs and dunes.

It was on one of these dunes, some distance above the water's edge, that Nick and Allison had plopped themselves down into the sand.

"Too bad we didn't bring bathing suits," Nick said.

Allison shivered. "It's too cold to go in the water. I refuse even to dip my toe into the ocean until at least July."

Which was one nice thing about being here early in the season, Nick reflected. There weren't a lot of other people around—people who might remember them if a detective showed up asking questions. The only other beach-goers in sight were another family about fifty yards up the shore.

Another family. Well, *a* family. Why did Nick keep slipping into the illusion that he and Danny and Allison were a family, too? Because it was so damn easy. Because ever since his last family had disintegrated—Kevin's death, Sheila's alcoholism—Nick had dreamed of someday finding again the happiness and security that came with a family—a family that enveloped its members in peace and love.

But how could Nick build a family for Danny and himself as long as he had to keep shutting other people out, turning away from them before they got to know him too well, before they discovered his secrets—

"You know, there are a lot of things you haven't told me about yourself." Allison's words startled him, both by their suddenness and by their reflection of what he'd been thinking.

Nick dusted sand from his hands and watched Danny splash about in the shallow water near the shore. "What would you like to know?" he replied casually.

"Well . . . what you did back in Boston. For a living, I mean."

"How do you know I didn't simply live off my wife's money?"

Allison made a moue of disgust. "I know you well enough not to believe *that.*"

Nick picked up a twig and rolled it between his fingers. "Actually, I was an architect."

"An architect?" Allison's jaw dropped.

"Why does that surprise you?"

"I don't know...." She shrugged. "I guess it's hard to imagine an architect skipping town, going on the run, living like a fugitive. Architects always seem so...so law-abiding. I'd pictured you as more of a renegade."

"What, like a gunrunner or something? A smuggler?" Nick grinned.

Allison smiled back. "Something like that."

"Sorry to disappoint you."

"Did you work for a big firm?"

"Not a big firm, but my own."

She arched her eyebrows. "You must have been pretty good."

"I was." Nick tossed the twig away.

"Successful?"

"Mm-hm."

"Making a lot of money?"

He nodded.

Allison was silent for a moment. "You really gave up a lot, didn't you?" she said softly.

Nick fixed her with a level gaze. "It meant nothing to me," he said. "Not compared to what I gave it up for."

She swallowed and looked away. After a few minutes, she said, "How have you made your living since then?"

"The same way I started out when I was younger. As a construction worker, handyman, that sort of thing. The kind of work where they pay cash and don't ask a lot of questions."

"Like I'm doing now."

SILHOUETTE GIVES YOU SIX REASONS TO CELEBRATE!

MAIL THE
BALLOON
TODAY!

INCLUDING:

1.
4 FREE
BOOKS

2.
A LOVELY 20k GOLD
ELECTROPLATED CHAIN

3.
A SURPRISE
BONUS

AND MORE!

TAKE A LOOK...

Yes, become a Silhouette subscriber and the celebration goes on forever.

To begin with we'll send you:

4 new Silhouette Special Edition® novels — FREE

a lovely 20k gold electroplated chain—FREE

an exciting mystery bonus—FREE

And that's not all! Special extras— Three more reasons to celebrate.

4. FREE Home Delivery! That's right! We'll send you 4 FREE books, and you'll be under no obligation to purchase any in the future. You may keep the books and return the accompanying statement marked cancel.

If we don't hear from you, about a month later we'll send you six additional novels to read and enjoy. If you decide to keep them, you'll pay the low members only discount price of just $2.74* each — that's 21 cents less than the cover price — AND there's **no** extra charge for delivery! There are **no** hidden extras! **You** may cancel at any time! But as long as you wish to continue, every month we'll send you six more books, which you can purchase or return at our cost, cancelling your subscription.

5. Free Monthly Newsletter! It's the indispensable insiders' look at our most popular writers and their upcoming novels. Now you can have a behind-the-scenes look at the fascinating world of Silhouette! It's an added bonus you'll look forward to every month!

6. More Surprise Gifts! Because our home subscribers are our most valued readers, we'll be sending you additional free gifts from time to time — as a token of our appreciation.

FREE! 20k GOLD ELECTROPLATED CHAIN!

You'll love this 20k gold electroplated chain! The necklace is finely crafted with 160 double-soldered links, and is electroplate finished in genuine 20k gold. It's nearly 1/8" wide, fully 20" long — and has the look and feel of the real thing. "Glamorous" is the perfect word for it, and it can be yours FREE in this amazing Silhouette celebration!

SILHOUETTE SPECIAL EDITION®

FREE OFFER CARD

4 FREE BOOKS

20k GOLD ELECTROPLATED CHAIN—FREE

FREE MYSTERY BONUS

PLACE YOUR BALLOON STICKER HERE!

FREE HOME DELIVERY

FREE FACT-FILLED NEWSLETTER

MORE SURPRISE GIFTS THROUGHOUT THE YEAR—FREE

YES! Please send me my four Silhouette Special Edition ® novels **FREE**, along with my 20k Electroplated Gold Chain and my free mystery gift, as explained on the opposite page. I understand that accepting these books and gifts places me under no obligation ever to buy any books. I may cancel at any time for any reason, and the free books and gifts will be mine to keep!   235 CIS RIYJ (U-S-SE-02/90)

NAME
_____
(PLEASE PRINT)

ADDRESS _____ APT _____

CITY _____ STATE _____

ZIP _____

Remember! To receive your free books, chain and a surprise mystery bonus, return the postpaid card below. But don't delay.

DETACH AND MAIL CARD TODAY

If offer card has been removed, write to: Silhouette Reader Service, 901 Fuhrmann Blvd., P.O. Box 1867, Buffalo, NY 14269-1867

FILL OUT THIS POSTPAID CARD AND MAIL TODAY!

BUSINESS REPLY CARD

FIRST CLASS   PERMIT NO. 717   BUFFALO, N.Y.

Postage will be paid by addressee

SILHOUETTE BOOKS®

901 Fuhrmann Blvd.,
P.O. Box 1867
Buffalo, N.Y. 14240-9952

NO POSTAGE
NECESSARY
IF MAILED
IN THE
UNITED STATES

Nick scooped up a handful of sand and let it dribble through his fingers. "I guess you're entitled," he said.

She turned back to him. "Then I have a few more questions to ask."

Nick took a deep breath. He didn't like people prying into his past. But then, Allison wasn't just another busybody. Her life had become entangled with his, through no fault of her own. He himself was responsible for her involvement. He supposed he owed her some answers.

"Shoot," he said.

Allison twisted herself to face him, crossing her legs Indian-style. "Okay. You told me that your ex-wife abused Danny, and that Danny was living with you after the two of you separated."

"That's right."

"What I don't understand is why she decided to turn around and sue for Danny's custody after the divorce proceedings started. It seems to me that up until that point she wasn't really interested in keeping him."

Nick sighed. "You can't imagine how many times I've asked myself that same question. But knowing Sheila, I think I can make a pretty good guess."

Allison waited.

"As I mentioned before, Sheila came from a prominent Boston family. Very wealthy, very old guard, very status conscious. The first Hammonds came over on the Mayflower—or so their descendants claim. Anyway, I think it was that family background, that obsession with upholding a proper image in front of society, that made Sheila put up a fight."

"You mean she was worried about how it would look if the court awarded you custody?"

Nick nodded. "Since the mother usually retains custody of the children after a divorce, Sheila was worried people would suspect her of something terrible if Danny stayed with me. She couldn't bear to tarnish the family name by letting people assume the courts had pronounced her an unfit mother."

"But wasn't she risking that very thing by starting a custody battle? Surely she knew that her drinking and her abusiveness would come out in court?"

Nick shrugged. "I guess she figured it was an acceptable risk. And she was right. Sheila was playing with a stacked deck, and sure enough, she won."

Allison tore off her sunglasses. "What kind of justice system do we have in this country, anyway? I just can't believe a judge would side with an abusive mother just because her family is powerful and has political connections...damn it, Nick, it's just not fair!"

In Allison's eyes, Nick saw a fresh image of his own indignation—the sense of outrageous injustice he'd felt when the judge handed down the verdict, pronouncing the words that had sent Nick's heart plummeting to his feet and made him almost physically ill.

He remembered the emotion he saw in Allison's face, although he no longer felt it himself. Two years had blurred the sharp edges of his rage, dimming his vivid sense of frustration. These days his emotions were more basic and instinctive: survival, protecting Danny, keeping a roof over their heads and food on the table. Nick no longer had the luxury of worrying about abstract concepts like justice.

Allison shook her head slowly. "You never had a chance, did you?" she asked.

"*Danny* never had a chance," Nick replied grimly. "So I had to give him one."

"Taking him away from Boston must have been a difficult decision."

"No. On the contrary, it was quite easy in a way. I had no choice. There was no way I could put my son in danger." Nick paused, remembering that fateful day, that fateful moment. He'd never told another living soul about it. But now he wanted to tell Allison.

Once Nick began speaking, the words spilled out as if a dam had burst. "It was a Tuesday," he said. "The day after a long Memorial Day weekend. It was the date the judge had set for me to turn Danny over to Sheila." Nick clenched his fists. "I'd taken Danny on a fishing trip over the holiday, to take both our minds off what was coming. It didn't work, of course. At least, not for me. All I could think of while we were sitting in that rowboat out in the middle of the lake was that in three days...in two days...in one day I'd have to surrender my son to a person who was unfit to raise him, who'd verbally tormented him and physically abused him."

Nick's forehead was sheened with sweat. "We were packing Danny's suitcase that Tuesday morning. I had to have him at Sheila's by noon. Danny sat cowering in the corner. He hadn't spoken a word since we'd gotten back from our fishing trip. I'd explained as best I could why he had to go and live with Mommy, and that we'd still see each other and I'd still be able to take him to baseball games at Fenway Park. But he was only a little kid. How could I make him understand why he couldn't live with me anymore, when I didn't understand it myself?"

Nick wiped the back of his hand across his forehead. "Danny just sat there, watching me put his clothes in a suitcase, following my every move with these enormous, bewildered, terrified eyes. That was the hardest thing I ever had to do—keep calm in front of Danny and pretend that everything was going to be all right. Because I knew it wouldn't be. Sheila didn't want him for the right reasons—she only wanted him to protect the family honor. She was still drinking like a fish. The least little irritation would send her into a rage. And when she lost her temper, she lost control of her actions and took her rage out on Danny.

"The clock kept inching forward, moving closer and closer to noon. I could see Danny watching it. I kept throwing things in his suitcase like some kind of robot. That's what I felt like—a zombie. I didn't want to break down in front of Danny, so I tried my damnedest to keep my emotions bottled up until after it was all over. I tried not to think, not to feel, until after Danny was gone." Nick's hands trembled slightly. "I snapped the suitcase shut, finally, and the sound echoed in the room like a gunshot. Danny and I stared at each other for a minute. Then his little face crumpled, and he launched himself out of that chair and into my arms. He hung on to me for dear life—he was practically strangling me. Then I heard him say, his voice muffled against my shoulder and choked with tears, 'Daddy, I'm scared of Mommy!'"

With a quick, embarrassed gesture, Nick brushed his eyes. Clearing his throat, he looked directly at Allison. "That was when I knew I could no more turn my son over to Sheila than I could throw him into a den of lions. I tossed some of my things into Danny's suitcase, we took the subway out to the airport, and we hopped on the first plane out of state. I suppose the ticket agent remembered us, and that's how Kellogg picked up our trail."

Allison's face had gone white. Tears stained her cheeks. Her mouth quivered as she whispered, "Oh, Nick..." She flung her arms around his neck, pulling him close.

He buried his face in her neck, clenching his jaw until it ached, squeezing his eyes tightly shut. Ridiculous, this urge to cry. He hadn't cried since his parents died. Clinging to Allison like a drowning man clutching a lifesaver, he never wanted to let her go.

She stroked his hair, patted his back. "It'll be okay," she soothed. "Everything will be all right...."

Nick's body heaved in one great shudder, then a series of harsh sounds reached his ears. To his amazement, he realized they were his own sobs. Slowly, relief spread over him like a healing balm. He'd covered up his emotional wounds for so long, they'd never had a chance to heal. By relating the unhappy past to Allison, Nick had finally exposed his pain to light and air. Maybe now his psychological bruises would begin to fade.

Nick hadn't realized how desperately he'd needed to share his nightmare with someone. But Allison had been there for him. He could never thank her enough for that. He tightened his arms around her, then drew back and pressed his damp cheek against hers.

Allison's heart was full enough to burst—with compassion for Nick, with sorrow for what he and Danny had suffered, with happiness that Nick had finally opened up to her. How could she help believing his story now? Doubts still nagged her about the wisdom of Nick's present course of action, but at least she no longer had to worry about any hidden motives.

The only problem was, from now on it would be harder than ever to restrain her increasingly tender feelings for Nick.

But she could deal with that later. Right now, all she knew was that Nick needed her. His newly revealed vulnerable side made her want to protect him, reassure him, comfort him.

She kissed his temple, patted his dark, wavy hair. "Don't worry," she murmured, "I'm here...." Her lips brushed his forehead, his eyelids, his cheek. She kissed his mouth lightly, almost playfully.

Then some quality in their embrace shifted, subtly altered. They found themselves gazing into each other's eyes in stunned, frozen silence. An instant later Nick seized Allison's mouth with his, blotting out the sky and the sea and the sun, everything but the intoxicating, exquisite pressure of his lips on hers.

Nick parted her lips impatiently with his tongue, and Allison met him with an equally ardent response. Their hot breaths intermingled as the depth of their kiss deepened. It was as if they were each frantically seeking some basic need that only the other could provide—a need as elemental and primitive as water, food, air....

Allison's head hit the sand as Nick swung her down to lie beneath him. He tangled his fingers in her hair, cradling her face between his hands while he plundered her mouth with his tongue.

Allison savored Nick's weight on top of her. Running her hands over his broad, hard back, she traced every ridge, every muscle, as if this would somehow stake her claim on him.

Sounds reached her ears from very far away...the cry of gulls reeling overhead, the crash of breakers against the shore. Drowning out these distant distractions were the moans of pleasure that rose from her own throat, and Nick's labored breathing as he moved his lips to her neck.

Allison arched her back into the hardness of his body, digging her nails into his back. Flames of passion licked across her skin, threatening to consume her entire body. Only Nick had the power to douse those flames, to satisfy the raging inferno inside her.

Then those distant sounds of the sea registered on her brain. Allison opened her eyes and saw puffy white clouds floating overhead and knew that this was impossible. Danny could stumble upon them at any moment, not to mention any other beach-goer who happened to walk by.

Automatically she stiffened. Nick apparently understood her signal, for his hands loosened their fevered grip, his kisses slowed. Finally he raised his face above Allison's and bent his head so their foreheads touched. In his eyes, so close to hers, she read the same resignation, frustration and defeat that she was feeling right now. Why couldn't they have met under different circumstances... in a different time and place where they could concentrate only on each other for a while and let the rest of the world fend for itself?

Nick planted a kiss on the tip of her nose. With a heavy sigh, he levered himself off her and helped her sit up. Dusting the sand off herself as best she could, Allison watched Nick closely. Would he use this incident as an excuse to shut her out again?

The breeze whipped his hair back from his face as he cocked his head to one side, looking down at the water. Then the anxious expression faded as he spotted Danny. Jamming his fingers into the sand, he shot her a sideways glance. "Sorry about that," he mumbled.

She shrugged. "It was as much my fault as yours."

"What? Oh, er, no—I didn't mean that." Without looking at her, he reached for her hand and took it in his.

"I meant I'm sorry about earlier, when I, uh, kind of broke down. I don't know what came over me."

Allison brushed a patch of sand from his well-muscled forearm. "You've had to be strong all this time, for Danny's sake. You've been repressing your own feelings so he wouldn't see them. It's no wonder something finally snapped."

Nick's mouth curled up ruefully. "I guess I'm kind of rusty at this crying business."

"Don't be silly." She squeezed his hand. "I'm glad you finally were able to tell me about those things."

"Allison, thank you. I can never repay you for what you've done—just by being here. By listening. I only wish there were some way I could show you—"

"Shh." She laid her finger across his lips. "You don't owe me anything. I'm happy you felt you could open up with me, Nick."

He pressed her fingers against his lips. "You're the first person I've known in a long time whom I *wanted* to open up with. You're a very special person, Allison Reed. I only wish I were going to have the opportunity of proving to you how much I mean that."

She lowered her gaze after his last statement. He slid his hand to her leg, bare below her rolled-up jeans. He stroked her calf. "As for what happened just now between us..." He let his words trail off.

Allison mustered a faint smile, aware of the worried furrows across his forehead. "We don't seem to be able to keep our hands off each other, do we? Despite our best intentions." She drew an aimless pattern in the sand with her finger. "I'm no good at keeping New Year's resolutions, either."

"Allison." Nick tilted her chin up with his finger, forcing her to meet his eyes. "I can't let you distract me.

Too much is at stake. One slip on my part, one instant of carelessness . . . and I could lose Danny forever. After what I've done, no judge would allow me near him until he turns eighteen. And by that time, who knows how much damage Sheila will have done? Maybe she'll have poisoned his mind against me, so that he'll never want to see me again.''

"Nick, don't you see? That's all the more reason for you to take Danny back to Boston now, before it's too late."

Ignoring the dark expression on his face, Allison plunged ahead. "If you bring Danny back of your own accord, the judge will certainly go easier on you. You can explain why you took him, and maybe the judge—"

Nick cut her off with an angry slash of his hand. "That's out of the question. I won't even consider it."

"You damn well better consider it," Allison said, beginning to lose her temper. "You could be doing that boy more harm than good by continuing this insane life you're leading."

The muscles in his face tightened as Nick clenched his teeth. Releasing Allison's hand, he pulled his knees up and circled them with his arms. He stared out to sea without saying a word. She could sense the anger radiating from his tense body.

"Nick," she said gently. She touched his arm. "Nick, I only care about what's best for Danny. For both you and Danny." His eyelids flickered. Allison shook him gently. "Hey, believe it or not, we're on the same side. We have different ideas about the best solution to the problem, that's all."

A moment later Nick placed his hand over hers. "Sorry," he said gruffly. "I know you mean well. But *I* have to be the one to decide what's best for my son."

Allison opened her mouth to argue with him, then decided to leave it alone for the time being. They'd made a real breakthrough today, when he'd told her the whole story of his decision to take Danny from Boston. If Allison gave this newfound trust a little more time to grow, maybe she could persuade Nick to at least consider another alternative.

"Okay," she said, smiling at him. "You're the boss." She squeezed his arm. "But remember, I'm here if you ever want to talk about it."

Nick's eyes radiated a tender caring that surprised her. How volatile this man was! A moment ago he'd blocked her out with his anger. Now he was looking at her with an open vulnerability that touched her heart.

"Thanks," he said softly. "You don't know how much that means to me." Suddenly he bundled her into his arms and tucked her head under his chin. "You're pretty nice to have around," he said. "Even if you *are* a terrible distraction."

Allison looked up at him. "Are we friends again?"

Nick arched an eyebrow as if seriously considering her question. "Sure, why not?" he replied. "We're friends. Buddies."

"Pals."

"Chums."

"Comrades."

"Amigos,"

"Okay, okay, I get the picture." Allison rolled her eyes.

Nick's even, white teeth flashed as he gave Allison a grin that was like the sun coming out from behind a cloud. Then he lowered his mouth to hers and gave her a playful kiss that was quick and sweet and, well . . . downright friendly.

Her eyes sparkled as she gazed up at him. Then a nearby movement caught their attention simultaneously.

Danny stood there, white and frail-looking in only his shorts. His fine, blond hair was plastered to his head; glistening runnels of water dripped from his thin little body. Patches of sand clung to his legs.

But what startled Allison more than Danny's sudden appearance was the expression on his face—a mixture of shock and confusion and disgust. His mouth worked soundlessly; his eyes were huge, dark circles filling his pale face. He dropped the long streamer of brown kelp he'd dragged up from the beach. Then he turned and fled.

Allison collapsed against the sand as Nick scrambled to his feet. "Danny!" he shouted. "Danny, come back!"

Nick's head swiveled between Allison and the rapidly retreating figure of his son. He raked his fingers through his hair. As he helped Allison to her feet, she saw that his face was drained of all color.

"Oh, my God," he said raggedly. "He must have seen us together. Allison, I—I—" With a final tortured glance in her direction, he took off after Danny.

Allison watched Nick bound over the dunes, his feet kicking up tufts of sand as he chased after his son. She could see Danny running along the water's edge, his legs pumping frantically as he tried desperately to escape the unexpected horror he'd witnessed.

When she saw the distance between them narrow and realized that Nick was about to catch up, she turned

away, pressing her palms to her cheeks. Slowly, she
trudged through the sand back toward the lodge. Her
heart had sunk to the vicinity of her stomach.

She would never win Danny's friendship now. The
look on his face had told her that much—that look of
total rejection . . . of resentment . . . of hatred.

Her heart went out to the boy. It must have been a
terrible shock, stumbling upon her and Nick that way,
locked in each other's arms, kissing. . . .

How ironic that what Danny had seen was meant as
an act of friendship, a sealing of their bargain to be
friends . . . and nothing more.

But she couldn't expect a seven-year-old to understand that. All he knew was that the stranger who had so
abruptly entered their lives less than two days ago had
somehow gotten her hooks into his father.

No wonder Danny had reacted the way he did. He'd
been used to having Nick all to himself for so long, the
thought of having to share his dad with someone else
must have been terrifying.

Crossing the highway, Allison knew this unfortunate
incident had destroyed any slight chance she and Nick
might have had for a meaningful relationship. Obviously Nick's first loyalty was to his son—and that was
as it should be. The last thing Allison wanted was to
come between them.

But her heart gave a painful throb at the thought of
what might have been. . . and at the memory of what she
and Nick had already shared. The caress of his
hands . . . the feel of his strong arms around her . . . the
delightful excitement of his kiss still lingered.

Well, that's all she would have from now on. Memories. Nothing more. No anticipation, no expectation that

the aching, unfamiliar desires Nick aroused in her would ever be fulfilled.

It had to be that way... for Danny's sake.

As she walked up the trail beneath the tall pines, Allison's view of their cabin was blurred by a veil of tears.

Chapter Eight

Allison slammed her book shut. "I'm going out," she announced.

The only response from the room's other two occupants was an absentminded grunt from Nick. He didn't even bother to look up from his newspaper as Allison slipped out of the cabin.

Outside, she felt like a newly released prisoner on his first day of freedom. The atmosphere inside the cabin had been so oppressive, so fraught with unspoken words and undercurrents of resentment, Allison had thought she would scream if she had to remain there one more minute.

Breathing deeply, she drank in the fresh air and the woodsy scent and the salty ocean tang. What an idiot she'd been, staying cooped up in the cabin for so long, when the rugged, majestic beauty of Big Sur lay right outside her door.

She wandered past a few of the lodge's other cabins, then found a sign marking the start of a hiking trail. With one final backward glance, Allison squared her shoulders and started walking.

She enjoyed the sensation of her heart pumping steadily in her chest, the tingling touch of a cool breeze against her face. Birds twittered in the rustling pines.

As her head cleared, Allison was able to assess her present situation more objectively. One thing was certain: she had no intention of falling victim again to the depressing malaise that had settled over the cabin since yesterday.

Allison had spent an anxious hour or so pacing the floor while she waited for Nick and Danny to return from the beach. How had Nick explained the embrace Danny had stumbled upon? What was taking them so long to come back? Was Danny refusing to set foot in the same cabin with the woman who threatened to take his father away from him?

Chewing her nails, Allison had cursed herself and Nick a thousand times. They should have been more careful. They weren't teenagers, for God's sake! Why couldn't they have kept their hands off each other until there was no chance of Danny accidentally seeing them?

When the cabin door finally opened, Allison's pulse hammered frantically.

Nick ushered Danny into the cabin. Danny's eyes were glued to the floor, and without a word, he marched into the bedroom and shut the door behind him.

"Well?" Allison asked. The word seemed to stick in her throat.

Nick shrugged. "I told him it didn't mean anything, that you'd been a big help to us and I was just trying to thank you."

"Do you think he believed you?"

"Not for a second." Nick dropped into a nearby chair. "He's not blind, Allison. He saw us kissing. He saw the way we were looking at each other. He knows there was more to it than that."

"What are we going to do?"

Nick regarded her thoughtfully for a moment. "Stay away from each other." His voice sounded wooden; his expression was numb.

Allison nodded. What more was there to say?

Turning away from Nick, she sought refuge in the kitchen. And that was where she'd spent most of the past day and a half, cooking meals, setting the table, washing dishes. She understood all too well why Nick didn't offer to pitch in. Look what had happened the last time they were alone in the kitchen together.

When the three of them sat down to eat, no one spoke a word. No one looked at anyone else. The food tasted like sawdust to Allison, and she ended up throwing half of it away. Nick and Danny didn't seem to have much appetite, either.

The rest of the time, Danny sat cross-legged on the floor in front of the television set, watching the screen with a glazed expression. The few times Allison had spoken to him, he'd ignored her. The only reaction she'd stirred was unintentional. She'd been straightening up the living room, and picked up Danny's baseball from a corner of the couch, intending to put it with the rest of his things.

Danny had seen her. "Gimme that!" he cried angrily.

"Danny!" Nick warned. It was the first time Allison had ever heard Nick use a harsh tone with his son.

Pushing out his lower lip, Danny snatched the ball when Allison handed it to him. He returned to watching the TV, sulking silently.

Nick spread his hands and shrugged at Allison. He looked tired . . . tired and unhappy. Then he hid his face behind the newspaper again.

Aside from reading the paper, Nick had passed the hours poring over a road map of California he'd gotten from the glove compartment of the car. Allison had no idea what he was planning, and she didn't dare ask. There was something forbidding about the determined, square set of his jaw, the furrow of his dark eyebrows.

She'd finally walked down to the lodge office and borrowed a thick paperback novel from the gray-haired woman who owned the place. Burying her nose in the dog-eared pages, she'd vowed to escape from her problems for a while. But she couldn't summon much interest for the melodramatic trials and tribulations of the brave immigrant family and their descendants. She had too many trials and tribulations of her own to care about anyone else's right now.

Reaching the highest point of the hiking trail, Allison dropped onto a log to rest before heading back down. The view was spectacular, and she couldn't stave off a twinge of regret that Nick wasn't here to share it with her.

The sun was sinking slowly into the sea, painting the western sky with bold splashes of pink and orange and gold. The shoreline was hidden by a ridge of tall trees, but as Allison gazed over the sea to the horizon, she saw clearly what she had to do.

She had to go back home.

Her presence was only making matters worse. Danny hated her; Nick was barely speaking to her. She herself was nothing but a wedge between father and son. What was the point of staying with the Caldwells any longer?

Allison had gotten to know Nick pretty well in the past few days. All *too* well, as a matter of fact. It was obvious that he loved his son, and that Danny wanted to be with his father. Nick was making a mistake by not going back to Boston to face the music, but maybe he was right—that was *his* decision and no one else's. Certainly Allison didn't have the right to step in and make that decision for him.

One thing she *had* decided: she would never turn Nick over to that detective. If Nick took Danny back to Boston, it had to be of his own free will. Otherwise, the courts would go hard on him.

Besides, if Allison called Kellogg, Nick would never forgive her. And that was a thought she simply couldn't bear.

But it was time for Allison to call it quits. She'd satisfied herself that Danny was in no danger with Nick; in fact, she could hardly imagine anyplace he would be safer. Her conscience would be clear when she let the Caldwells slip out of her life.

But her heart would be close to breaking.

It was amazing how much Nick had come to mean to her in just a few days. Not that she was in love with him or anything…but Nick Caldwell was somebody special. She'd never been so instantly attracted to a man before. And after getting to know Nick better, she hadn't been disillusioned; her feelings for him had only grown stronger.

Well, none of that mattered now. Time to go back to Los Angeles, lick her wounds, cry on Marilyn's shoulder and wait for time to heal the ache that already throbbed in her heart.

She and Nick had no future. It was unfortunate they hadn't met under other circumstances, but nothing could alter the past. Time to behave like a responsible adult, cut her losses and try to pick up the pieces of her life.

No matter how much it hurt.

Shadows crisscrossed the ground as Allison descended the hard dirt trail. The sun was now a glowing orange semicircle hanging on the edge of the horizon. By the time she reached the cabin, the woods were shrouded in gloom. She was about five yards away when a movement in front of the cabin startled her, making her draw up short. Her hand flew to her heart.

It was Nick.

"Sorry if I scared you," he said. He was leaning back against a wood railing, his long legs crossed in front of him.

Allison came and stood beside him. "I didn't see you at first."

"It *is* kind of dark out here." He rubbed his chin. "Where did you go?"

"For a walk. Up there." She waved her hand. "I found a hiking trail."

Nick coughed. "I got kind of worried. You were gone so long."

She glanced at him in surprise. Shadows fell across his face, obscuring his expression. But he certainly *sounded* genuinely concerned....

"I had a lot of thinking to do," she said.

"Oh? What about?"

"What do you think?"

Nick was silent a moment. "Things are kind of a mess, aren't they?" he said finally.

"You can say that again."

"Allison, I'm sorry for—well, for everything, but I—"

She stopped him with her raised palm. "Nick, before you say anything more, I have something to tell you. Something I decided a little while ago."

Her words sent a knife of apprehension slicing through his chest. Whatever she'd decided, he had a feeling he wasn't going to like it. "What is it?" he asked casually.

"I've decided to go home. Tomorrow."

Nick's heart dropped like a rock. But he knew better than to try to change Allison's mind with a head-on attack. "May I ask why?"

"It's obvious, isn't it? Things aren't working out. This whole situation has gotten out of hand. For heaven's sake, no one's even speaking to anyone else!"

Nick turned to her, placing his hands on her shoulders. "Allison, I'm sorry. I didn't mean to give you the silent treatment—but it's difficult, when Danny's there...."

She nodded. "I understand. But it's more than that, Nick. It's the way Danny resents me, and the way I've come between the two of you."

"You haven't come between us. Nothing could do that."

Allison shrugged Nick's hands off her shoulders. "Okay, maybe not. But you have to admit that you guys aren't exactly best buddies right now."

"Danny will get over it."

"Where *is* Danny, anyway?"

"Getting ready for bed. Allison—" Nick searched desperately for the words that could make her change her mind. He hadn't realized before how important she'd become to him—until he was faced with losing her for-ever.

And the worst of it was, he had no one but himself to blame. It was his fault that Danny had discovered them together. But it was so damn hard not to touch her when she was near him, so hard to resist the urge to take her in his arms and kiss her soft, pliant lips and caress her luscious curves. Nick wanted her so much...but that was no excuse for letting his hormones rage out of control. He'd lost sight of what was most important to him: Danny's well-being.

And now not only was he losing Allison, his son might be in jeopardy as well.

Nick swallowed. "Have you decided what you're going to do about—I mean, are you planning to..."

Allison smiled a faint, bitter smile. "I'm not going to phone Kellogg, if that's what you're worried about, Nick. I still think living on the run like this is more harmful to Danny than taking him back to Boston would be. But you're his father. It has to be your decision."

Relief flooded Nick, making his knees weak. He leaned back against the wood railing.

"Well, now that I've set your mind at ease, I'll go pack my things." She turned away, but Nick grabbed her arm.

"Allison, wait."

She turned back, and in the darkness, Nick thought her face contained a glimmer of hope.

"I want to apologize for the way I've been treating you since yesterday."

Her hopeful expression died away. What had she been waiting to hear him say?

"That's all right," she said. "I understand what a predicament you're in—trying to reassure Danny."

"He's not used to having someone else around. He hasn't had to share me with anyone for a long time, and I think he's just plain jealous."

"It's okay, Nick." Allison placed her hand alongside his face. "Of course he's jealous. And scared. It's only natural. But don't you see? That's another reason I have to leave."

"Allison—" Nick turned his head and pressed his lips against her palm. "I don't want you to leave." There! He'd said it.

In the dim moonlight, Nick detected a suspicious glitter in Allison's eyes. Her voice was low and even when she finally spoke. "It's best if I go, Nick. Then I won't be a distraction to you, or an object of resentment for Danny."

"You're more than just a distraction to me, you know."

"I know." She swallowed. "All the more reason for me to leave right away, before things go any further between us."

She was right, of course. How could he argue with her logic? But logic seemed a feeble force compared with the depth of his feelings for her. Lately he'd indulged himself with impossible daydreams that the three of them could someday be a family. How he longed for a normal life—a life full of love and warmth to share with the people he cared most about!

But when Allison left, she would be taking those wonderful dreams with her.

Nick had to let her go—but maybe not just yet.

"You've been an enormous help to Danny and me," he said. "Can I ask one final favor before you leave?"

"I suppose so, although I want to hear what it is before I make any promises."

"Without your car, Danny and I will have to catch a bus or a train or a plane someplace. Big Sur isn't exactly a transportation hub. Can you drive us to Monterey tomorrow before heading back to L.A.?"

Allison tilted her head to one side, considering. "Okay. I wouldn't want to strand you here."

Nick heaved a sigh of relief. "Thanks. I really appreciate it."

Allison clasped her hands together. "I don't suppose you'd be willing to tell me what your plans are after that?"

Nick gazed at her, noting the shine of her hair in the moonlight, remembering what her hair felt like against his face, tangled in his fingers. He memorized her lush, full lips, her pert nose, her long-lashed green eyes.

"I think it's better if I don't tell you," he said softly.

Allison bowed her head. She started back toward the cabin, then whirled suddenly and flung herself into Nick's embrace. She wrapped her arms around his neck and pressed her face against his.

Nick hugged her tightly, feeling her heart thudding against him, savoring for the last time the fresh scent of her floral shampoo, the satiny touch of her skin. He squeezed his eyes shut. He wanted to say something that would comfort her, and make things right between them.

But even if he'd been able to find the right words, he couldn't have spoken them through the lump in his throat.

He ached for Allison, and longed to kiss her one more time. But for once, he intended to control his desire. His impulses had already cost him Allison. He didn't intend to make their parting any more difficult by starting something he knew he couldn't finish.

After a moment, they drew apart. She fled inside the cabin without meeting his eyes, without saying a word.

He watched her go, knowing she thought he still didn't trust her, and that was why he wouldn't reveal his plans to her.

But the truth was, Nick hadn't the foggiest idea where he and Danny would go after Allison Reed exited from their lives forever.

Allison's mood matched the weather—raw and gloomy. As she drove north toward Monterey, the ocean was a sheet of gunmetal off to her left. Gnarled cypress trees drooped over the cliffs, wringing their branches and swaying mournfully back and forth in the wind. Gray clouds hovered overhead with oppressive nearness, and sporadic bursts of rain spattered the windshield. Gusts of wind made it difficult to steer.

Next to her, Nick's face was dark and grim as a thundercloud. The only person in the car who was in a good mood was sitting contentedly in the back seat, humming quietly to himself and watching the scenery pass by.

Nick must have told Danny that Allison would be leaving today. She was glad to see the boy in good spirits again, but the knowledge that her imminent departure was the cause didn't do much for her ego.

Sighing, she rubbed her forehead. If only this were all over, and the moment of separation nothing but an unhappy memory....

Yet part of her wished the short drive from Big Sur to Monterey were longer...much longer. Even if it meant prolonging the agony.

"Could you please stop at the coffee shop up ahead?" Nick asked suddenly. "I want to ask directions to the—er, bus station."

Or to the train station or to the airport, Allison thought, swinging the car left into the parking lot. It hurt that Nick still felt he had to be secretive with her.

The only spot left in the parking lot was next to a beat-up black van surrounded by a group of rather rough looking teenagers. They lounged in the open rear door of the van, drinking beer out of cans and smoking what Allison hoped were cigarettes. Their raucous laughter filled the silence when she turned off the engine.

Nick eyed them with disgust as he opened the door. "I won't be long," he said. "I, uh, suggest you lock the door after me."

"Nick, wait a second—" Allison glanced in the back seat. She wasn't too keen on the idea of being left alone with Danny. But Nick was gone.

As she leaned over to lock the door, a long-haired kid wearing an army surplus jacket and a skimpy three-day growth of beard leered at her. "Hey, baby, wanna party?"

Allison set her mouth in a straight line and sat back in her seat, ignoring him. The rest of the gang broke up into loud hoots and hysterical laughter before they forgot about her and went back to plotting mayhem or comparing tattoos or whatever they were doing.

Allison's annoyance turned to concern in a few minutes, however, after she'd overhead their foul language and a few of their crude jokes. Checking in the rearview mirror, she saw that Danny was as fascinated as she'd feared.

"Hey, look out in the ocean! See the sea lions on those rocks out there?"

Her attempt to distract Danny succeeded. Instantly he forgot about eavesdropping on hoodlums and pressed his nose against the window, straining for a glimpse of the sea lions. "Where?"

Allison pointed. "On those rocks. See them?"

Danny squinted. "I think so." Then he opened his door and was halfway out of the car before Allison could react.

"Hey, Danny, wait, don't go—oh, well, I guess it's okay," she mumbled. She had a pretty good suspicion that Danny wouldn't obey her anyway. She stepped outside the car and watched him run toward the ocean.

He stopped in front of a low metal guardrail a short distance from the parking lot, where the ground dropped away in a sharp slope. "Don't go past that rail!" Allison called. She folded her arms across the top of the open car door, keeping an eagle eye on Danny. At least his attention was focused on the sea lions instead of those delinquents in the van.

Allison shivered as an icy gust of wind whipped her hair about her head. A sudden surge of raindrops pelted her face. It was really too cold for Danny to be outside without a jacket.

"Danny!" she called. "Danny, come back to the car!"

At first she thought he hadn't heard her over the howl of the wind and the crash of breakers below. She opened her mouth to call him again. Then Danny turned and looked straight at her. Even at a distance Allison could see his defiant glance and the way he stuck out his lower lip.

She slammed the car door and stepped toward him.

In a flash he had disappeared, his head sinking out of sight behind the guardrail.

Allison's annoyance turned to fear. "Danny!" she shouted. "Danny, come back!" She dashed to the guardrail and peered over the edge. About ten feet below her, Danny was climbing down the rocky slope like a mountain goat.

"Oh, my God!" Allison gasped. Another fifty feet below Danny the waves boiled and spumed over bare rocks that clustered along the shore like jagged teeth.

She dug her nails into her palms, swiveling her head from left to right, uncertain what to do. Then she stepped over the guardrail and prepared to follow Danny.

At that moment she spotted Nick leaving the coffee shop. She scrambled over the rail. "Nick!" she screamed. "Nick, hurry! Come quick! It's Danny!" She jumped up and down and waved her arms over her head.

Nick sprinted across the parking lot. His face turned white when he looked over the cliff's edge. Without a moment's hesitation, he started climbing down the slope.

"Nick, be careful!"

He moved cautiously yet rapidly down the rocky escarpment, searching for handholds, testing each footrest to make sure it would hold his weight.

"Danny!" Allison heard Nick's hoarse cry. "Stay where you are! Don't move!"

The wind carried Danny's faint, quavering reply to Allison's ears. "Daddy, I'm stuck! I'm gonna fall!"

"Don't move, Danny. I'll be right there!"

"Daddy, I'm scared!"

Tears mingled with the rain on Allison's cheeks. Dear God, please let them both be all right....

Maybe she should go get help, she thought. But she couldn't leave Nick and Danny alone. What if they needed her? Besides, by the time a rescue party arrived, the storm might already have torn Danny from his precarious perch and dashed him onto the boulders below.

She would wait until Nick reached him. Then if he couldn't make it back up the slope with Danny, she would run for help.

The moments seemed endless as Nick crept closer to Danny. Allison could see Danny's pale, terrified face peering up at his father. How fragile he looked, clinging to the steep slope while the ferocious breakers clamored for him....

Then Nick lost his foothold and skidded down the embankment in a shower of rocks and debris. Allison screamed.

Somehow he managed to regain a hold on the slope. He paused, and Allison could see his entire body shudder with the effort to catch his breath.

By now he was only a few feet above Danny. Thank God Nick's fall hadn't started an avalanche, which would surely have swept the boy to certain death.

At last Nick reached his son. Allison couldn't make out the words, but Nick's reassuring tone drifted up to her. As Nick carefully turned his back, Danny put his arms around his father's neck and hung on for dear life.

Then Nick started slowly, painfully up the slope, carrying Danny piggyback while he used both hands to pull them upward. Allison held her breath, expecting at any moment to see Nick lose his balance and topple over backwards.

Inch by inch...foot by foot...yard by yard, Nick crept up the treacherous slope carrying his precious cargo. Allison couldn't take her eyes off them. Wind and rain lashed her skin, but she was oblivious to the icy chill on her face and bare arms. The steady roar of the crashing breakers filled her ears, competing with the deafening thud of her heart.

After what seemed an eternity, they reached the top of the cliff. Allison grabbed Danny and swung him to safe ground, as Nick clambered over the edge. The three of them collapsed in a panting heap.

Then Nick pulled Danny into his arms and hugged him tightly. Over Danny's damp head he gave Allison a weary look. He winked.

Allison didn't know whether to laugh or cry, so she did a little of both. Then she wrapped her arms around both Caldwells and squeezed her eyes shut. Her head rested against Nick's. His body was soaked with sweat and rain, and wracked by deep, heaving breaths. Danny shook with sobs.

Several minutes passed before their shaking, sodden huddle broke up. Nick held Danny at arm's length. "You okay, Shortstop?"

Danny nodded wordlessly.

"How are you doing, Allison?"

She mustered a tremulous smile. "I've had better days, I must admit. But I'm fine." She reached for Nick's hand, then recoiled when he flinched at her touch.

Looking down, she saw that Nick's hands were a bloody mess. His desperate climb had reopened the cut on his thumb and torn open a few others as well. Grit and gravel were embedded in his palms.

Allison sucked in her breath. "Oh, Nick, your hands!"

He yanked them back and examined them. "Funny. I didn't feel a thing." He frowned. "Damn. I've already gotten blood on your shirt."

"It doesn't matter." Allison took his hands again. "Come on. Let's get back to the car and patch these up."

"Okay." Nick rose stiffly to his feet. "But no doctors."

"I know, I know," Allison replied. "Where have I heard this before?"

Danny clung to his father's legs. Nick started to pick him up when Allison pushed him aside. "Don't be silly. You can't carry him with those hands." She knelt and picked Danny up swiftly, leaving no time for protests. But the boy offered no resistance, and hung limply in Allison's arms as they made their way back to the car.

She laid Danny on the back seat, and after a quick inspection determined that—physically, at least—he was in good shape. He was shivering like crazy, however, so she laid his jacket over him. "You'll warm up soon," she promised.

After sending Nick into the coffee-shop restroom to wash his hands, Allison rummaged in the glove compartment for the first-aid supplies she'd bought a hundred years ago for Nick's thumb. When he slid into the car a few minutes later, she gingerly examined his hands.

"Hmm. These cuts aren't as bad as they looked at first," she muttered, dousing them with antiseptic.

"Ow! What are you, some kind of sadist?" Nick grinned painfully at her.

"Why, yes! And now I have you completely in my power." Allison cackled wickedly as she wrapped gauze around his hands.

When she finished taping the first hand, Nick raised it to her face. "Thanks," he said softly.

"For what? Letting Danny climb down a cliff and nearly get both of you killed?" She tore a piece of tape with a violent gesture.

"Sweetheart..."

The unexpected endearment brought tears to Allison's eyes. Blinking, she clenched her jaw and focused on bandaging Nick's hand.

He tilted her chin up so she had to look in his eyes. "Allison, it wasn't your fault."

"How do you know? You weren't here."

"No. But I know what little boys are like. I know sometimes they disobey. And I can't believe you gave Danny permission to go past that guardrail."

"No..."

"Well, then." Nick stroked her cheek with his fingers. "I'll deal with Danny later," he whispered. "Right now I want to make sure you're not blaming yourself for what happened."

Allison drew a long, quavering breath. Then tears spilled down her cheeks. "Oh, Nick..." She leaned forward, resting her head on his shoulder. "You could have been killed," she choked out.

Nick patted her back with his bandaged hand, murmuring soothing words in her ear. "Shh, everything's okay now. Danny and I are safe."

Allison wished she could stay close to Nick like this for a long, long time. But Danny was in the back seat. She didn't want to stir up any more resentment than she had already.

Clearing her throat, she wiped the tears from her face and finished bandaging Nick's other hand. She sensed him studying her, the blunt angles of his face arranged in watchful concentration, his blue eyes narrowed beneath the bold, dark streak of his brow.

"There, all finished." Allison gazed back at Nick. His tangled, wet hair was plastered in black clumps to his head; Allison noticed a patch of raw skin near his jaw, where rocks or gravel had grazed his face.

Never had he looked so handsome . . . or so desirable. Nearly losing him in a tragic accident had made her realize how much she cared for him. A startling thought rocked her.

Was it possible . . . could it be . . . that she was falling in love with Nick Caldwell?

The idea so confused Allison that she immediately sought a distraction—something to occupy her attention while her subconscious mind wrestled with this disturbing possibility.

She turned around to check on Danny. His shivering had subsided, and he lay across the seat with his eyes closed, clutching his jacket to him.

Nick turned to follow her gaze. "Hmm."

His puzzled tone captured Allison's attention. "What's the matter?"

Nick frowned. "Did you put my suitcase in the trunk?"

"No . . . you wanted it in the car, remember? So you and Danny could hop out quickly when I dropped you at the bus station or wherever. You put it in the back . . . seat."

Allison's jaw dropped.

Nick's suitcase was gone.

"Give me the key to the trunk," he said sharply.

As Allison got out of the car with him, she said, "I told you, it's not in the trunk. Could you have left it back at the—"

Nick slammed the empty trunk shut in disgust. "No. I distinctly remember putting it into the back seat. Remember? I joked with Danny about buckling the other seat belt around it.''

"But then where—" Allison's hand rose to her mouth. Her eyes widened. "Those kids!" she breathed. "Those teenagers in the van."

She and Nick wheeled simultaneously toward the next parking space.

The black van was gone.

In its place was a tan station wagon with a child's car seat in the back.

Nick slammed his fist on the trunk of Allison's car and growled a chain of curses through his clenched teeth.

Allison shook her head in amazed annoyance. "They stole it," she said. "Those rotten kids actually stole your suitcase out of my car while we were—"

She banged her own fist against the car. "Those sneaky little rats! Those thieving, foulmouthed, beer-swilling—" She started toward the coffee shop. "I'm calling the police."

"No, wait." Nick grabbed her wrist. "No police, Allison. The last thing we want is a crowd of cops asking us a bunch of questions."

"But Nick, we can't let those punks get away with it!"

"Yes, we can." Nick raked his fingers through his tangled hair. His face had turned pale, his eyes darting back and forth. "We can't risk any contact with the police. There's nothing we can do, Allison. The suitcase is gone for good."

She sensed that Nick was trying to convince himself more than her. "I guess you're right. Calling the police would create more problems than it would solve." She patted Nick's shoulder. "Besides, it's only a bunch of clothes. You can always buy more."

"You don't understand.". Now the despairing expression on Nick's face began to alarm her.

"Nick, honestly. I'll help you pick out a whole new wardrobe, I promise."

He shook his head and swallowed with a dry, clicking sound. Turning away, he banged the heel of his hand against his forehead. "I can't believe this," he groaned.

"Nick, what's the matter with you? Why are you so upset over this?" Allison stepped in front of him, shaking him by the shoulders.

Nick's eyes were hollow tunnels, rimmed with anxiety and shot through with near-panic. "Allison—" He gripped her shoulders. "Allison, that suitcase wasn't just full of clothes." He swallowed. "There was over three thousand dollars cash in that suitcase."

Allison gasped in horror.

"It's all the money I have in the world, Allison. All the money Danny and I have to live on." Nick's voice cracked with anguish. "It's the money I need to stay ahead of Kellogg. And now it's gone."

Chapter Nine

Allison poked the red snapper with her fork. Across the table, Nick picked at his order of linguine with clam sauce. Danny was the only one with an appetite. He gobbled his fried shrimp, dipping them into the little container of tartar sauce, then mopping up ketchup with his french fries.

Well, lunch had *seemed* like a good idea at the time.

Allison's treat, of course. After the disastrous theft of Nick's suitcase and all his savings, he hadn't exactly been in the mood to splurge on a nice seafood lunch.

But Allison had managed to persuade him by pointing out that they hadn't eaten breakfast, and surely getting some food in their stomachs would help them think more clearly. Besides, where else did Nick plan to go? With only the money in his wallet left, his options were rather limited. They could figure out their next step while eating lunch.

So here they were in a quaint, cozy restaurant on Monterey's Cannery Row, seated at a table right next to the window overlooking Monterey Bay. The ceiling and walls were decorated with fishing gear and photographs from various movies based on the novels of John Steinbeck.

The place was cute as hell, really. And Allison was sure the food was delicious. But it was hard to appreciate, with the specter of doom occupying the extra place at the table.

Nick refilled his glass from the carafe of white wine. Tilting his head back, he drained half of it in one gulp. As he set the glass back on the table, his eyes locked with Allison's.

"I guess that won't help much, will it?" he muttered.

She swallowed a bite of fish. "No. But I can't say I blame you, all things considered."

Nick pushed the carafe toward her. "You finish the rest. I need to keep a clear head."

"And I suppose it doesn't matter if *I* get plastered?"

"I didn't mean that. Sorry." He propped his head between his hands for a moment, then looked up at her. "Actually, I'd appreciate any suggestions you have."

Allison swirled her wine around her glass. "Take Danny to the aquarium."

"Yeah, Dad!"

Nick stared at Allison. "I suppose after that I should buy a set of golf clubs in case I feel like playing eighteen holes out at Pebble Beach."

"I'm serious."

"You're nuts."

"Dad, can we go to the aquarium? Huh? Please?"

Nick scowled at Danny. "After the stunt you pulled this morning, kiddo, the only place I should take you is out to the woodshed."

Danny's eager expression wavered, as if he didn't quite understand the allusion, but suspected he was in trouble.

"Nick, the aquarium is right down the street. It's one of the best aquariums in the world. It would be educational and interesting and fun—for all of us. And it's someplace to go while we try to figure out what to do next."

"I'm hardly in a financial position to pay for an afternoon of entertainment, remember?"

"*I'll* pay for it," Allison pleaded.

Nick's frown deepened. "I can't let you spend your money on us. I shouldn't even have let you pay for this lunch."

"Nick, we need something to cheer us up. What's your alternative? Sitting in my car all afternoon and watching coastal erosion?"

"It's a waste of money and time. How do you expect us to enjoy ourselves, knowing that we're only postponing the problem?"

"Trust me." Allison patted Nick's hand. "Everything will be all right. Waiter, could we have the check, please?"

A few minutes later she was standing in the ticket line at the aquarium.

"Here you go!" Allison pressed two tickets into Nick's hand as a crowd of tourists pushed them toward the entrance.

"Where's yours?" he asked, puzzled.

"I'm not going with you."

"What?"

"I have an errand to run."

"Allison, what the hell—"

"I'll meet you out front in a couple of hours. Have fun!" She waved as the mob of people swept Nick and Danny into the aquarium. Her last glimpse was of Nick's irritated scowl.

Oh, well. He would forgive her later, once he learned her reason for tricking him. Allison walked back to her car, whistling.

Two hours later, she collapsed, breathless, on a bus bench across the street from the aquarium. She scanned the exiting sightseers for any sign of Nick and Danny. Good. She'd made it back in time.

These few minutes by herself gave her a chance to reflect on what she'd just done, and on what she was about to do. A twinge of doubt nagged her. Was she doing the right thing? If only there were someone she could discuss the matter with, someone who could advise her.

But Allison was all alone on this one. She thought about her family back in Minnesota—Mom and Dad, her brother and sister and their families. Practical people. Her father and brother were both accountants, and you didn't get much more sensible than that.

Allison loved them all dearly, and knew they loved her. But that didn't mean they understood her. She'd always been the different one. Dreamy...carefree... impulsive...what had her father called her once? A free spirit.

Allison knew exactly what the people she loved and respected would say if they knew about her current predicament.

They would say she was crazy.

That she was foolish not to have called the police after Nick hijacked her van.

That she was reckless to have invited him into her house that night.

That she was nuts for joining Nick and Danny in their flight.

And for what she was about to do, they would probably have her committed to a lunatic asylum.

Allison sighed. She could picture her whole family right now, shaking their heads, wagging their fingers at her, warning her not to do it.

But Allison had to follow her heart. That was what she'd done all her life, and she hadn't done too badly, had she? Sure, she'd wound up in a few sticky situations, and there were several past episodes in her love life that still made her cringe.

But Allison believed in listening to her instincts. And her instincts told her that this was the right thing to do.

She jumped to her feet and waved as Nick and Danny appeared. Danny was chatting happily with Nick, bouncing along with an enthusiastic smile on his face.

"Hi! How was the aquarium?" Allison asked when they reached her.

Danny's smile faded. He stuck his hands in his pockets and looked down at the ground.

Allison felt as if she'd been kicked in the stomach.

"We had a great time, didn't we, Shortstop?" Nick frowned and nudged Danny. "Tell Allison what we saw."

Danny mumbled something incomprehensible.

"Danny," Nick said in a stern voice, "we didn't hear you."

Danny scuffed his toe on the sidewalk. "Fish," he said sullenly. "And some sea otters."

"Tell her about the tide pool."

"I got to pick up a sea urchin," he said to the ground.

Nick threw Allison an apologetic glance. "It's okay," she said. "Come on, let's go back to the car. I have a surprise for you."

"You're full of surprises today," Nick said, falling in step beside her. "What was the big idea? All that talk about the aquarium and then you don't even come with us."

"I had other things to do," she replied airily.

"Oh? Such as?"

"You'll have to wait and see." Allison's good humor was returning with her anticipation of Nick's reaction.

When they got back to the car, Danny scrambled into the back seat. "What are all those shopping bags?" Nick asked, peering inside the car.

"Surprise! Or part of it, anyway. I went shopping and bought you some new clothes. I hope they fit. If not, we can exchange them. And here!" She dug an envelope out of her purse and handed it to Nick.

His dazed expression turned hard when he looked into the envelope. "What's this?" he asked in a level voice.

Allison's smile flickered. "It's money!" she exclaimed. Looking nervously around, she lowered her voice. "You know, money. Federal Reserve notes. Greenbacks. For you and Danny."

"And where did it come from?" Nick's voice maintained its neutral tone, but Allison detected something disturbing in it.

"It's mine. Or rather, it *was* mine. Now it's yours. Yours and Danny's. It's not quite as much as you had stolen, but it's all the money I had in my savings account. Everything else is tied up in my business."

"I can't accept this." Nick stuffed the envelope back into her hand and walked away.

Allison stared, then ran after him. "Nick, please! What's the matter? Why can't you take it?"

"I don't accept charity," he replied. His chin jutted out slightly. "Not from you. Not from anyone."

"Who said anything about charity? Consider it a loan. You can pay me back."

"Forget it."

"Nick..." Damn! She should have foreseen this reaction and handled the situation more delicately. Of course a man like Nick was too proud to take handouts! What an idiot she was, practically clapping her hands with glee as she handed Nick the cash, acting like Lady Bountiful, pretending she was Santa Claus, expecting Nick to fall to his knees with boundless gratitude.

Well, maybe it wasn't totally unreasonable to expect Nick to be the teensiest bit grateful. But his cold refusal, his stubbornness, his *anger*...had definitely caught Allison off guard.

Her own anger flared in response. "You're not exactly in a position to turn up your nose at this," she said. "What are you going to feed Danny with? Pride?"

Nick's eyes gleamed with fire as his face grew dark with rage. "That was a low blow, Allison. A cheap shot."

Instantly she regretted her words. "Nick, I'm sorry. I didn't mean it."

"Yes, you did." He jammed his fingers through his hair and glared at her. "Don't ever question my ability to take care of my son, Allison. Danny and I got along fine before you came along, and we'll get along fine after you're gone."

"Good. Well then, I'll just be on my way. Can I drop you somewhere before I leave? Or are you planning to hoof it from now on?"

Without waiting for a reply, she started back to the car. Nick grabbed her arm.

"Allison," he said, gritting his teeth, "you didn't have all that money in your purse this whole trip, did you?"

"No, of course not. Do you think I'd be stupid enough to carry my life's savings around with me? Unlike *some* people I know," she muttered.

Nick let her remark pass. "Then how did you get that money?"

She shrugged. "I used my credit card to get a cash advance. I found a local branch of my bank, and I— Nick? Nick, what's the matter?"

Nick had closed his eyes. His brows were dark slashes against his sudden paleness.

"Nick, what's wrong?"

He opened his eyes, and she saw that his anger had drained away, to be replaced by tired worry. "Allison," he said slowly, "don't you realize what you've done? Our friendly neighborhood detective undoubtedly has spies keeping an eye on your accounts. This transaction will show up on the computer, along with the location of the bank."

Allison's eyes widened in horror. "You mean . . . ?"

"By withdrawing that money, you might as well have drawn Kellogg a map, with an arrow pointing right to us."

Nausea roiled in her stomach. "Nick, you don't really think Kellogg can find out—oh, my God!" Allison turned away, cupping her hand over her mouth. How could she have been such a fool?

Her eyes burned with tears. She'd been so pleased with her own generosity—her first big chance to help Nick and Danny—and all she'd done was bring disaster crashing down around their heads!

Sobs shook her body as panic darted along her nerve endings. She doubled over, afraid she was going to be physically ill as well as sick at heart.

Then Nick was close behind her, hugging her shoulders, trying to comfort her. "Allison? Allison, don't cry. Come on, don't worry. Things aren't as bad as all that. Sweetheart, please don't cry."

Tears blinded her as she straightened up. "Oh, Nick, I'm so sorry! My God, what have I done? If only I'd thought—I'd never have—I didn't mean to—" She dropped her head onto Nick's shoulder as he wrapped his arms around her, patting her back, stroking her hair.

"Shh, it's all right, honey. We'll figure out what to do. Everything will be okay."

"How can you say that?" Allison wailed into his chest.

He hugged her tightly. "We've been in tough spots before. This isn't the end of the world."

Her sobs subsided into ragged hiccups. "If only I hadn't tried to give you that money. What a dumb idea! Oh, Nick, I didn't mean to offend you ... I only wanted to help...." Her voice rose to a choked squeak as she started crying again.

Nick hushed her softly, cradling her face against his hard, reassuring chest. He kissed the top of her head, squeezed her shoulders. Patiently, he let Allison's weeping play itself out.

Finally she drew back, brushing her eyes with her knuckles. "I must look a mess," she mumbled.

Nick chuckled. "Now I *know* you're feeling better." Allison's eyes were puffy, her tearstained cheeks red and blotchy.

Nick thought she'd never looked more beautiful.

Because Allison's beauty involved more than her sexy green eyes and kissable mouth and satiny auburn hair. Allison's true beauty radiated from her heart.

Holding her in his arms, soothing her tears and trying to comfort her, Nick had had a chance to reflect on Allison's gesture. He understood now that her motives were decent and honest. She'd offered him the money not to trap him or humiliate him, but because she truly wanted to help.

And Allison's reaction when she realized she'd unwittingly placed them in danger told Nick even more about her.

It told him that Allison had already made up her mind not to report their whereabouts to the detective. It told him that she'd decided Danny belonged with his father.

And it told Nick that maybe—just *maybe*—his wistful, impossible dream about creating a new family wasn't so impossible after all.

He planted a kiss on Allison's forehead. "Come on," he said with a wink and a smile. "Let's get out of here."

Nick found a not-too-expensive hotel near downtown San Francisco, agreeing to accept a small loan from Allison—just to tide him over until he could earn the money to pay her back.

After they toted their remaining luggage and the shopping bags and the takeout hamburgers up to their adjoining rooms, Allison stuck her head through the connecting door. "I'm going to take a shower before dinner. Go ahead and eat without me."

"We'll wait," Nick said, sending a warning glance Danny's way. "Danny and I need to have a talk first, anyway."

"Hmm. Okay. I'll be through in about fifteen minutes." She shut the door gently behind her.

Nick took a partially unwrapped cheeseburger from Danny's hands. "Come over here and sit on the bed next to me," he said. "You and I need to get some things straight."

Danny shuffled to the bed and sat down, swinging his legs over the side. Nick eased himself down next to his son. His muscles were already incredibly stiff and sore after the ordeal of climbing the cliff. By tomorrow Nick would be lucky if he could even get out of bed.

The brim of Danny's baseball cap was lowered, hiding his eyes. Nick flipped the cap off. "There, that's better."

Stifling a groan, he turned his aching body toward Danny.

"What you did this morning was really dumb, kiddo. Crawling over the edge of that cliff was dangerous. You could have been hurt or killed. And *I* could have been hurt or killed trying to rescue you. Not to mention Allison. She was ready to risk her life by going after you, even though the reason you were in trouble in the first place was because you disobeyed her."

Fidgeting, Danny mumbled, "I thought you said she was leaving today."

"And that's another thing. Look at me." Nick grasped his son's shoulders. "I don't like the way you've been treating Allison. She's been very nice to us, and how do you thank her? By acting rude. By ignoring her. I want this behavior to stop, Danny, and I want it to stop right now. Understand?"

Danny nodded once, his lower lip protruding.

"Okay." Nick released him. "You can go eat your cheeseburger now."

But Danny stayed where he was, kicking his heel against the bed frame.

"Danny? Aren't you hungry?"

Thud, thud, thud went the bed frame.

"Hey, Shortstop..." Muscles screaming in protest, Nick knelt on the floor in front of Danny.

Danny looked at him in anguish, his mouth pinched shut as if to keep from crying.

"Danny, what is it?"

"Are you gonna leave me behind?" he blurted out.

Nick nearly toppled backward in surprise. "Leave you behind? Of course not! Why would I leave you behind?"

"'Cause you like *her* better than you like me!" With that, Danny's face crumpled and tears spilled down his cheeks.

Nick pulled his son into his arms. "Danny, Danny," he whispered, his throat aching as it constricted. "You're the most important person in the world to me, Danny. I'd never leave you behind—never! I love you, Shortstop. I love you so much...." With that he hugged his son tightly, unable to speak for a moment.

Finally he lifted Danny back onto the bed. Ruffling his son's blond hair, Nick said, "I want you to put that crazy idea right out of your head, Shortstop. I'm never going to leave you behind, and no one's ever going to take you away from me. We're a team, partner. You and me. Forever."

Danny rubbed his eyes with his fists. "What about *her*?" he asked tearfully.

Sighing, Nick put his arm around Danny. "Allison is a very special person," he said carefully. "And she likes you a lot. She really wants to be your friend, if you'd only give her a chance."

"Is she going to live with us from now on?"

Nick shifted uncomfortably. "Well . . . to tell you the truth, I'm not sure how long Allison will be staying with us."

Danny considered this for a minute. "I guess it's okay if she stays for a while," he said. He slid off the bed. "Dad?"

"Yes?"

"Does she know that you and me are a team?"

Nick smothered a grin. "Yes, Danny. She knows."

"Good." With a satisfied nod, Danny proceeded to attack his cheeseburger.

Later, while Danny was glued to the television watching a San Francisco Giants game, Nick knocked on the connecting door of Allison's room, where she'd retreated shortly after dinner.

"Come in!"

Nick closed the door behind him. Allison was sprawled diagonally across the bed doing a crossword puzzle. She lay on her stomach, legs crossed in the air behind her. She was tapping a pen thoughtfully on the folded newspaper.

"Don't tell me you're one of those people who do crossword puzzles in ink," Nick joked, settling himself in the chair next to the bed.

Allison looked up from the puzzle. "Don't tell me you came in here just to criticize my choice of writing implements."

Nick grinned. "No. As a matter of fact, I came for two reasons—to offer an apology and to ask a favor."

Allison tossed the newspaper aside. "No apologies are necessary. As for the favor, you know I'll do whatever I can to help."

"Yes, I know." Nick rubbed his chin ruefully. "Which leads me to my apology. Allison, I'm terribly sorry I acted the way I did when you offered me that money. You caught me by surprise, and I—well, I hope you can forgive me."

She brushed his apology aside. "Forget it. I should have handled it differently, instead of making such a production out of it."

Nick leaned forward and rested his arms on his knees. "You see, there were times in the past when people tried to pressure me into accepting money. I've always been determined to make it on my own, without financial help from anybody, and the whole issue of taking money is kind of a touchy subject with me."

"Hmph." Allison swung herself into a cross-legged sitting position. "I wish people had tried to give *me* money. Then I wouldn't have had to wear my feet out waiting tables while I was trying to become an actress."

Nick blinked. "You wanted to be an actress?"

Allison blushed. "Corny, isn't it? I came out to California after I graduated from college. I was like thousands of other star-struck kids, getting off the bus in Hollywood with nothing but a hundred dollars in my pocket and a head full of dreams."

Nick studied her. "You're certainly pretty enough to be a movie star. What happened?"

"Thanks. But pretty girls are a dime a dozen in Hollywood. I wound up like most of the rest of them, waiting tables while waiting for my big break. Only it never came."

"How did you get into catering?"

"My partner, Marilyn, was one of the regular customers at the coffee shop where I worked. She had this dream of starting her own business, but she was afraid to try it alone. I had some money saved up, and one day I realized I was sick of getting pawed by male customers and stiffed out of tips. I quit my job, and Marilyn and I went into business together. The rest—as they say—is culinary history."

"Any regrets about giving up your acting career?"

Allison winced. "There wasn't a lot to give up. And working with Marilyn to build up our own business has been very satisfying. So—no, I don't have any regrets."

Nick nodded eagerly. "I know exactly how you feel. I worked my way through college, then went to work for somebody else before starting my own architectural firm. Building that company from the ground up was the most rewarding thing I've ever done in my life." He fell silent, remembering how much his business had meant to him... knowing that he'd lost it forever. His clients would have gone elsewhere by now, his equipment and supplies would have been sold, his office space rented to someone else.

Allison cleared her throat. "So," she said brightly, "who were all these people trying to give you their money?"

Nick shook his head free of the bittersweet memories. "Actually, it was one person. My father-in-law. He didn't think I was capable of supporting his daughter in the style to which she was accustomed. When Sheila and I got married, her father offered me a job with Hammond Industries. I declined, and then he offered to set me up in my own architectural firm, which I also declined. After I kept turning down his money and job offers, he finally realized he'd have to take the indirect approach. So he proceeded to lavish gifts on Sheila. Clothing, furs, jewelry, vacations..."

Nick scratched his head. "Needless to say, this was kind of a sore spot in our marriage. And after Kevin and Danny were born, Sheila's father stepped up the pressure again. But I was determined to prove to him and everyone else that I was perfectly capable of supporting my own family. Eventually, my firm grew quite successful. Although my income never approached Hammond standards, of course."

He should have foreseen that money would be a problem between him and Sheila, but in those early days, Nick had been too dazzled to worry about such things. He remembered the first day he'd met her, when she'd come to the construction site of her father's latest office building. Nick had been a college student, working his way through school by construction work and any other odd jobs he could find.

How well he recalled that moment . . . the sun burning his bronzed skin, sweat pouring down his face and naked chest as he set down his shovel. He winced as he tried to straighten the kinks out of his back.

When he opened his eyes, he was staring at a vision. That's how Sheila seemed to him, standing on the edge of the square earthen crater, her gauzy white dress rippling in the whispering breeze. She'd looked so cool . . . so elegant . . . so lovely.

Nick didn't discover whose daughter she was until their third date. By that time he was already bewitched. To a poor kid from a working-class background, Sheila seemed like a beautiful exotic bird. Nick had been flattered by her attention.

Naturally, Lawrence Hammond tried to put a stop to their relationship. But Sheila was his only child. After his wife's death years before, Hammond had lavished his attention and wealth on his daughter. Sheila was spoiled and headstrong and thought the idea of falling in love with a common laborer was just too, too romantic.

In the end, Hammond hadn't the heart to deny Sheila anything she really wanted. So he'd let her have Nick. And he'd never stopped pressuring Nick to accept his money and the other rewards of the Hammond power, status and influence.

Despite this constant source of disagreement, Nick and Sheila's marriage might have endured if it hadn't been for Kevin's death. The drinking, the abuse, the emotional isolation that followed could have destroyed even the strongest marriage.

But one precious thing survived from those disastrous years. And Nick intended to keep him.

"What's the favor?"

"Huh?"

Allison snapped her fingers in front of Nick's nose. "And when you wake up, you will remember nothing of your hypnotic trance."

"You didn't make me run around the room and squawk like a chicken, did you?"

Allison laughed. "No, but next time you might not be so lucky."

"I'll remember that."

"Good. Now, what's the favor?"

"What favor?"

Allison groaned. "The favor you came in here to ask me!"

"Oh, right." Nick folded his bandaged hands and studied his fingers. "I was wondering if you'd consider staying on for a couple more days. I want to start looking for some temporary work tomorrow, and it would be a big help if I could leave Danny with you during the day."

Allison arched her eyebrows. "What kind of work are you going to find, with your hands all beat up like that?"

"I'll find something, don't worry."

"Hmm." She chewed her lower lip. "I suppose I could stay a while longer," she said slowly. "But I don't think Danny will be too thrilled to have me as his babysitter."

"That won't be a problem," Nick said. "Danny and I had a talk."

Allison frowned doubtfully. "Well, if you say so."

"Then you'll stay?" Nick couldn't keep the eagerness out of his voice.

"Sure, why not? In for a penny, in for a pound. Besides, I can't leave until you repay the money you borrowed, right?"

Relief and happiness mingled with Nick's gratitude. He hadn't realized how worried he'd been that Allison would want to leave the next day. He clasped her hand in his. "How can I ever thank you?" he said quietly.

Allison's skin was satiny smooth, her eyes deep pools of gold-flecked green. Fascinated, Nick watched her soft lips curl slightly into an uncertain smile.

Warning alarms erupted in his brain, but it was no use. How could he resist the lure of those full, sensual lips...?

Nick bent his head toward hers, closing the gap between them slowly, inch by agonizing inch. Her shallow breaths fanned his mouth seconds before his lips touched hers. He saw her eyes flutter shut as he kissed her languidly, sliding his hand to the nape of her neck, tilting her chin up so he could kiss her more thoroughly, more deeply.

Her hair was still slightly damp from her shower. The tresses clung to Nick's fingers as he combed his hand through her hair. The scent of flowers rose to his nostrils.

He parted Allison's lips, running his tongue behind her teeth, exploring the moist, warm furrow behind her upper lip. She purred like a kitten, the sound stirring an even greater desire within him.

How he cherished this woman! She'd brought gaiety and laughter into his life at a time when he needed it most. She'd stood by him even when she didn't agree with him. In Allison, Nick had finally found someone with whom to share his thoughts and fears and dreams.

As he moved his body to sit on the bed beside her, Nick realized he wanted to share even more with Allison. Much, much more.

He pressed his lips to her temple, her eyelids. "I want you so much," he muttered gruffly. He eased her back against the mattress, sliding one of his legs across her. Her heart was beating rapidly, exciting him. He moved his hand to cover her breast. Even through her sweater and the gauze taped around his hand, he could feel her nipple grow hard against his palm.

"I want to make love with you, Allison," he whispered. "So much...so very, very much..."

He sought her lips again, but she turned her head to one side. "Nick," she breathed, "Nick, we have to stop this before it's too late."

He raised his head, touched her cheek with his fingers. "It's already too late," he murmured. "Too late to be just friends. Too late to forget what it feels like to hold you, to touch you."

"Nick." She tangled her fingers in his hair, gazing deep into his eyes. "I feel the same way you do. I want you, too, Nick, but—" She pressed her hand against his chest as he lowered his face toward hers. "But we have to face reality. We may never see each other again after—after we say goodbye in a few days." She drew a deep breath. "I can't be satisfied with only a few days, Nick. If things go any further between us, I don't think I could bear to say goodbye."

"Then don't."

Allison shook her head sadly. "You're only saying that in the heat of the moment. You know that any serious relationship between us is impossible—as long as you keep living on the run."

Nick pushed himself up and sat on the edge of the bed. Head in his hands, he said, "I have no choice. You know that."

Allison placed her hand on his shoulder. "I know you *think* you have no choice. And that's really all that counts, isn't it?"

When Nick looked at her, he saw in her eyes and her expression a reflection of his own torment. He turned away. "I'd better go check on Danny," he mumbled.

Chapter Ten

During the night the connecting door between their rooms opened, and a shaft of light fell across Allison's face.

Normally it wouldn't have awakened her, but her sleep had been haunted by nightmares of Nick and Danny being torn from the cliff by the storm, plunging onto the rocks below and disappearing beneath the raging sea.

So when Nick tiptoed into her room, Allison was instantly awake, her heart hammering in her chest. Had he come to share her bed, despite their earlier agreement that making love would be making a mistake?

And what would her reaction be when Nick slipped beneath the sheets beside her? Allison didn't know if she had the strength to turn him away, feeling toward Nick the way she did.

"Allison?" he whispered. Then, more loudly, "Allison, are you awake?"

A funny way to begin a seduction, she thought—calling from across the room. She sat up, pulling the covers up to her neck.

Nick was silhouetted against the light from the other room. "I'm sorry to wake you, but do you have any Tylenol? I think Danny has a fever."

She whipped off the covers. Her bare feet padded against the carpet as she walked over to her purse. "I think I have some." She rummaged around, vowing once again to throw some of this junk out as soon as she got a chance to sort through it.

"Here," she said finally, handing Nick a small bottle. "Take the whole thing."

"Thanks."

"Is Danny really sick?"

She couldn't see Nick's face clearly in the dark, but the worry in his voice was unmistakable. "I don't know. His forehead is hot. He was shaking so hard with the chills, he woke me up."

"Do you want me to take a look at him? No, that's silly. You know more about sick kids than I do."

"He probably caught a cold from being out in that storm. I'm sure he'll be better in the morning." Nick patted Allison's shoulder reassuringly before leaving the room.

But Danny was no better the next morning. His head was congested, his body achy and sore. Despite the Tylenol, his fever persisted.

Nick and Allison stood back from the bed, conferring out of Danny's earshot.

"I hate to leave him when he's like this," Nick said, frowning. "But I'm anxious to get out there and find work. If I don't leave soon, the construction contractors will have hired all the day laborers they need for to-day.''

Allison laid her hand on his arm. "I can watch him, Nick. He's probably just got a bad cold. I've had plenty of those myself, so I know how to take care of him.''

"You're sure you don't mind?''

"No, of course not. Why don't you run out and find a drugstore before you go to work? Bring back some decongestants and cough syrup and stuff. Oh, and you'd better buy some children's Tylenol.''

"Are you sure you'll be okay with him all day?''

"Quit worrying," Allison said, pushing Nick toward the door. "I'll order up some chicken soup from room service. We'll be fine.''

Nick didn't look totally convinced, and he brought back enough medical supplies to open their own pharmacy. "Tell Danny I said goodbye, will you?'' he whispered, gazing down at the sleeping figure of his son. Danny's breathing was shallow and ragged. His face was flushed.

"I will," Allison said. She was a bit apprehensive about Danny's reaction when he awoke to find his father gone and himself in custody of the Wicked Witch of the West, but she wasn't about to let Nick see her anxiety.

"I'll see you tonight," he said softly, kissing her quickly before slipping out the door.

Allison turned away with a dreamy smile on her lips. She could get used to these cozy domestic moments with Nick. Then her smile faded. The last thing she wanted was to get used to this. Because leaving would be that much harder when the time came.

Sighing, she picked up a spy thriller novel Nick had thoughtfully brought back from the drugstore. She pulled up a chair next to Danny's bed and sat there watching him with a worried frown.

He slept until nearly noon, when a spasm of racking coughs shook him awake.

"Where's my dad?" he asked weakly when the coughing had subsided.

"He went to work," Allison said, placing her hand on his forehead, uncertain what she was supposed to feel. Danny seemed warm, but how did she know what was normal and what wasn't? She didn't exactly have a lot of expertise in this field.

"Your dad will be back in time for supper," Allison promised Danny. "You were asleep when he left, so he said to tell you goodbye."

Danny jerked his head away from Allison's touch, turning toward the wall. She pressed her lips together and got up to check whether Nick had bought a thermometer at the drugstore. When she came back, Danny was lying against the wall, his back to her, shaking.

Alarmed, Allison rolled him over to see what was wrong. To her dismay, she saw he was crying.

"Oh, Danny, come on, don't cry! Your dad will be back soon. I know you don't feel well. Would you like something to eat? Some soup or toast or something? Sweetie, please don't cry!"

Her attempts to comfort Danny were in vain. His thin, feeble sobs alternated with fits of coughing, and he pulled away from Allison when she tried to put her arm around him.

She'd never felt so helpless in her life. In a minute she would be crying right along with him.

Pushing her hair out of her face, Allison gritted her teeth. *Get a grip on yourself,* she thought. *You can't let Nick and Danny down.*

She got the bottle of cough syrup and poured a dose into the plastic cap. "Danny, listen to me." She sat next to him. "I know you're upset, but you've got to calm down and take this medicine. It'll make you feel better, I promise."

Danny's weak crying persisted.

"Come on, Danny. Swallow this cough syrup, and then we'll find something to watch on TV. Maybe there's a baseball game on." Desperation rose in her chest. "Danny, that's enough. Quit acting like a baby and swallow this."

His arm flailed out, knocking the cough syrup all over the sheets and Allison. Red, sticky cough syrup. The kind that stained.

She fought back her irritation. Danny was sick and scared; he wasn't really responsible for his behavior. Nick should never have left Danny alone with her.

Then her own words came back to haunt her. *We'll be fine, Nick, don't worry. I know how to take care of him.*

She had no one but herself to blame for this mess.

As darkness began to fall over San Francisco, Allison's self-pity had long since given way to fear and despair. Danny's condition had grown steadily worse all day. His coughs erupted from deep in his chest, and he was flushed and hot with fever. Yet he refused to take any medicine or food from Allison. When he wasn't sleeping, his pitiful sobs lashed her like a whip.

She paced the hotel room, wringing her hands and checking her watch every two minutes. Where, oh where on earth could Nick be?

When the key clicked in the lock, relief bubbled up inside her. She'd let Nick and Danny down, but at least Nick was here now. Danny would take his medicine and eat something and start to get better.

Nick's face was etched with lines of exhaustion when he came through the door.

"Oh, Nick, you don't know how glad I am to see you!"

He smiled absently. "How's Danny?"

"Not doing so well. Nick, I tried, but I couldn't get him to take any medicine or eat anything. He's been crying all day, and I think his fever's gone up and he's coughing something awful."

In two seconds Nick was sitting on the bed next to Danny, who'd fallen into a restless doze a few minutes ago. Nick ripped the bandages off his right hand. His face paled when he felt Danny's forehead. "Allison, he's burning up."

"Maybe you can get him to take some Tylenol," she said hopefully.

"Get some cold wet washcloths from the bathroom." Nick shook two orange Tylenol tablets into his hand. "Danny . . . Shortstop . . . time to wake up."

"Maybe you should let him sleep."

Nick shook his head. "We've got to get his fever down as quickly as possible. Danny, come on, kiddo, wake up."

When Allison returned with the washcloths, Danny was propped up on the pillows, washing down the Tylenol with a glass of water Allison had brought him earlier. As she laid the cool cloths across his forehead, she was shocked by the dull, glazed look in his eyes. But he wasn't fighting her anymore, now that Nick was here.

"How about eating some soup, Danny? Can you do that for me?" Nick's voice was gentle, but Allison could see the worry in his face.

"I'm not very hungry, Daddy," Danny croaked.

"I know you're not, but getting some food in your stomach will make you feel better. Okay?"

Danny nodded as a coughing spell seized him. Nick held his son's hand until it passed.

Allison had her hand on the phone receiver, ready to dial room service, when Nick asked over his shoulder, "Have you eaten anything yourself?"

She hesitated. "Actually, no. I forgot all about eating."

"Better order some sandwiches for us, then. And soup for Danny."

Allison ordered enough food to feed an army, believing somehow that food equaled health, and if they could just surround Danny with enough food, he would get well. When room service arrived, she paid the man quickly so their order wouldn't be added to the bill for the room, which Nick was sure to insist on paying.

Nick eyed the overloaded serving cart with surprise, but made no comment. Danny swallowed a few spoonfuls of soup before dozing off again.

"Has he ever been this sick before?" Allison asked while she and Nick ate their sandwiches.

If she'd been hoping for reassurance that Danny had bounced back from worse illnesses, she didn't get it.

"No," Nick said quietly, worried furrows creasing his forehead.

"Maybe we should call a doctor."

"No."

"Nick, the hotel probably has a doctor on call. He could come right over, and—"

"No doctor, Allison. He'd just be one more way for Kellogg to track us down."

"But Danny's so sick!"

"He'll get better," Nick said firmly. "I know he will. He'll be better after a good night's sleep."

Nick sounded as if he were trying to convince himself more than Allison. When she finally went to bed shortly after midnight, Nick was still sitting in a chair beside Danny's bed, watching the labored rise and fall of his son's chest.

Exhausted, Allison slept through the night without waking up once. When at last she opened her eyes, bright sunshine was streaming through a crack in the curtains. Everything was so still—no coughing, no sneezing, no sobs.

Still wearing her nightgown, she scuffled into the other room, yawning. Nick was still in the chair, but he was slumped across the bed. Danny's slow, tortured breathing broke the silence. Edging closer, she saw that Nick was asleep. Dark circles rimmed his eyes. Sleep had done nothing to soften the harsh lines of anxiety engraved on his face.

Glancing at Danny, Allison nearly gasped. His complexion was an ugly, sallow color; his closed eyes were sunk back into his skull, giving him a deathly look. His mouth hung open, and every breath was torture, as if an enormous weight compressed his thin chest, preventing him from breathing.

Allison touched Nick's shoulder. Instantly he lifted his head. "Nick, I'm calling a doctor right this minute."

He rubbed his hand across his face. "Allison, I told you—"

"And I'm telling *you*, keeping Danny from seeing a doctor is child abuse. It's worse than anything Sheila ever did to him."

Her sharp point struck home. Nick recoiled as if stung by a hornet. He shifted his gaze to Danny, and all the color drained from his face.

"My God," Nick breathed. "He looks terrible." He gripped Allison's wrist. "Please, call a doctor—quick."

It seemed forever before a knock sounded on the door. Allison flew to open it.

"Hello, I'm Dr. Waverly. I got a message that—"

"Come in, please come in, Doctor." Allison grabbed the woman's hand and practically dragged her into the room.

Dr. Waverly was a stout, no-nonsense woman with snow-white hair that made it difficult to guess her age. As she put her stethoscope back into her medical bag after examining Danny, she glowered at Nick and Allison over the tops of her bifocals.

"You certainly took your time about calling me, didn't you?"

Nick flushed. "We thought it was just a cold, that he'd get better. He—he *is* going to get better, isn't he?"

"No thanks to his parents." She shook her head in disgust. "Why do people insist on waiting so long before calling a doctor?"

Nick and Allison exchanged guilty glances.

"He'll have to be hospitalized, of course."

"Doctor, are you sure that's necessary?" Nick asked. "He'll be scared in the hospital, and my—my wife and I can stay with him around the clock. Isn't there any way we can take care of him here?"

"Young man, your son is on the verge of pneumonia."

"But that—that's not quite as serious as *having* pneumonia, is it?"

Dr. Waverly stuck her hands in the pockets of her white coat and considered what Nick had said.

"No," she said finally, "it's not as bad as *having* pneumonia. But he'll have to be watched every minute, even during the night."

"We can do that," Allison said eagerly. "I promise, we'll take good care of him."

"I suppose the child *would* be happier with his parents than in the hospital...."

Nick and Allison held their breaths, waiting for the doctor's verdict. Finally her grim expression relaxed. "All right," she agreed. "He can stay here for the time being. But if he takes a turn for the worse, you're to call me immediately. *Immediately*, do you understand?"

They nodded as Dr. Waverly pulled a prescription pad from her medical bag. She scribbled something and said, "Have this filled at the drugstore right away, and follow the directions *exactly*."

"Don't worry, we will," Nick said.

Dr. Waverly tore off the prescription and handed it to him. "I'll be back tomorrow morning to check on the boy, and if he's no better, then into the hospital he goes."

"Doctor, how can we ever thank you?" Allison asked.

"By taking care of that little boy and seeing that he gets better. Give him plenty of fluids, try to see that he eats something and make sure he gets the antibiotics I prescribed." She glanced at the collection of pills and potions Nick had purchased yesterday. "Keep giving him Tylenol and cough syrup, but the rest of that stuff is useless. And keep him covered with cool, damp cloths until his fever goes down."

The doctor started toward the door, then paused and put her hand on Nick's shoulder. "And get some sleep yourself, Mr. Caldwell. You look awful."

Nick mustered a tired grin. "Thanks, Doctor. For everything."

"I'll be back tomorrow morning." She gave Danny a sympathetic glance before leaving.

Her solid, reassuring footsteps had barely died away when Allison headed for the drugstore to have the prescription filled.

By the time she returned, Nick was slumped across the bed again. "Come on," she said, dragging him into the other room. "You need to get some real sleep."

"Don't wanna leave Danny," he mumbled.

"You can't do Danny any good if you're dead on your feet," she said, tucking Nick into her bed. "I can watch him for a while. You get some rest."

Nick's reply was muffled as he buried his face in the pillow and dozed off.

Back in the next room, Allison squared her shoulders and prepared to do battle with Danny. He had to take the first dose of medication right away. Gently she shook him awake. By now the poor kid was too sick and weak to fight with her, and he swallowed the medicine without an argument. She even got him to take some more Tylenol. Before she had time to screw the cap back on the bottle, Danny was asleep again.

While the Caldwells slept, Allison picked up the room, throwing away the remains of last night's sandwiches and scooping up a blizzard of crumpled tissues. She moistened the cold cloths for Danny and laid them across his forehead and chest again.

Several hours passed before Nick emerged from the other room, his eyes barely open, the lower half of his face shadowed with whiskers. "How is he?" he asked in a gravelly voice.

Allison glanced up from her book. "About the same, I think."

Nick stood over Danny, a concerned frown on his face. "He hasn't shown any sign of improvement yet?"

"It takes a while for the medication to have any effect," Allison reminded him. "It's still too soon to tell anything."

"Isn't he sleeping an awful lot?"

"Probably the best thing in the world for him right now." Allison rose to her feet. "How about some lunch? I spotted a delicatessen on the way to the drugstore. I bet they have terrific chicken soup, too."

"It'd be easier to call room service."

"Too expensive."

"That's true." A dark cloud flitted across Nick's face for a moment. Allison knew he was worried about money, but he had an even greater concern right now.

When she got back with the food, Danny was propped against the pillows, looking a little better, she thought. He ate some soup while watching TV, and Nick persuaded him to nibble a couple of crackers. After a spell of hacking coughs, Nick spooned some more cough syrup into him.

"After you're feeling better, we can take in a baseball game at Candlestick Park. Would you like that?"

Danny's throat was swollen and red, preventing him from speaking. But he looked up at his father with sunken, adoring eyes and nodded. Nick hugged him.

"Would you like a coloring book and some crayons? I could run out and get them for you," Allison offered.

Danny shook his head, then pointed at the corner of the room.

"Your backpack? You want something out of your backpack?" she asked.

"Your baseball, right?" Nick said, smiling when Danny's head bobbed weakly up and down. "Allison, could you please bring him his baseball?"

"Sure," she said, anxious for any chance to earn her way into Danny's good graces.

He clutched the baseball to his chest and leaned back, closing his eyes. After he fell asleep, Nick said softly, "I think he's breathing easier, don't you?"

Allison hesitated. Danny sounded no better to her, but Nick looked so hopeful, so desperate. "I'm sure he'll be better by morning," she replied. "Now, come on—let me change the bandages on your hands."

"I think they've healed enough so I don't need the bandages anymore." Nick unwrapped the remaining gauze.

Allison inspected his hands. "They look pretty good," she admitted. "Well, why don't you go lie down in the other room, then? I'll sit with Danny."

"Thanks, but I think I'll stay here for a while."

She tried again. "Remember the doctor's orders, Nick. She told you to get some rest."

"I'm going to stay with Danny."

Allison shrugged helplessly. As she turned to go back to her room, Nick reached up and took hold of her hand. "Allison," he said, "thanks." His tired eyes gazed at her with gratitude and affection. When he looked at her that way, Allison could forgive him anything.

"That's okay," she murmured. Impulsively, she bent forward and kissed him on the cheek. The stubble on his unshaven face scratched her skin, making her lips tingle. A unique—and delightful—sensation, she decided.

Nick squeezed her hand. In his face Allison saw that strange, resigned longing again. It was the same look a thirsty desert traveler might have when spotting an oasis far in the distance, then realizing it was a mirage.

Back in her room Allison tried to lose herself in the spy novel, but her thoughts kept returning to the man and boy in the other room, and how important they had become to her.

The hours passed slowly. Nick refused to leave Danny's bedside, despite Allison's protests. Danny swallowed some more soup, but by evening, Allison could still detect no improvement in his condition. She said nothing to Nick, knowing he was aware that Danny didn't seem to be getting any better. Nick's worry showed itself in the rigid way he sat forward in the chair, staring at Danny, clutching the arms of the chair so that his knuckles turned white.

Late that evening Danny awoke and couldn't go back to sleep. Coughing fits racked his small body—deep, hoarse sounds that frightened Allison. He thrashed beneath the bedclothes, flinging his arms from side to side, moaning softly.

Even Nick's attempts to soothe him were in vain. Watching his son suffer, Nick's mouth was clamped into a tight line. The planes and angles of his face were sharpened in tense concentration. Nick's eyes burned with a fever of their own, but whenever he spoke to Danny, his voice came out calm and reassuring.

Allison sat helplessly by, her nerves stretched taut as piano wire. When a car backfired in the street below, she gasped as if she'd been shot. Nick threw her a sympathetic glance before returning his attention to Danny.

Allison chewed her thumbnail. What if she and Nick had waited too long before calling the doctor? What if their reluctance to put Danny in the hospital was a mistake? What if—God forbid—Danny died?

Her stomach churned with queasy fear. Losing Danny would destroy Nick—of that Allison was certain. Her eyes filled with tears as she watched Danny's torment. Every harsh cough was like a stab through her own heart. Poor little kid...why, oh, why wasn't there something they could do to help him?

Late evening turned to early morning, and still the nightmare continued. Nick's face was a stony mask, but Allison saw the despair in his eyes, heard the quaver that crept into his voice when he spoke softly to Danny.

As a faint glow appeared in the eastern sky, Danny fell quiet at last. But the sudden peace was almost worse than the agitated hours just past.

Allison had dozed off, her head lolling against her shoulder, when Nick's urgent voice awoke her.

"Allison, come here—quick! I think there's something wrong with him!"

In a flash she was next to Nick, leaning over Danny.

"Feel his forehead," Nick said.

Allison placed her hand on Danny's forehead, then felt the rest of him. "Nick, he's so cold! And he's soaking wet!" She had to struggle to keep the horror out of her voice. Panic wouldn't solve anything.

Nick bounded to the phone. "Where's the doctor's number?"

Allison grabbed the scrap of paper she'd written Dr. Waverly's number on. "Nick, she said she'd be back this morning. Maybe we should wait until she stops by."

Nick dialed the phone, his fingers jabbing awkwardly at the numbers. "No way. I'm through taking chances where Danny's concerned. The only reason he's so sick is because I was stubborn and wouldn't call the doctor and wouldn't let her put him in the hospital, and ... oh, God, Allison, what am I going to do if something happens to him?''

She put a shaky hand on his shoulder. "Danny will be fine, Nick. I'm sure of it." But she wasn't sure at all.

Dr. Waverly arrived amazingly soon, considering Nick had roused her from a sound sleep. She bustled into the room and headed straight for the bed. Nick followed right behind her. "He's so still, Doctor, and his skin is cold. He's soaked with sweat."

Dr. Waverly ran her hands over Danny, took his pulse and pressed the stethoscope against his chest. When she stood up, she nodded curtly. "Just as I suspected, from what you described over the phone."

"What is it? What's wrong with him?" Nick's voice was hoarse with fear.

"Nothing to worry about, Mr. Caldwell," the doctor replied, putting her stethoscope away. "Quite the opposite, in fact. Danny's fever has broken, that's all."

"That's good right?" Allison asked quickly. "It means he's getting better, doesn't it?"

Dr. Waverly nodded. "The worst is over. I expect it'll be a week or so before he's back to his usual self, but he'll be all right."

Allison collapsed against Nick.

"Thank God," he muttered. She felt a tremor run through his body.

Dr. Waverly rummaged through her medical bag. "Here," she said, handing Nick a small packet. "The best thing for Danny is rest. Next time he wakes up, have him eat something, and give him one of these. It'll knock him out for a while, so he can get some sleep. Otherwise his cough may keep him awake."

"You're sure he'll be all right? He doesn't need to go to the hospital?"

Dr. Waverly shook her head. "He'll be fine here. Just keep on doing whatever you've been doing. And see that he keeps taking the antibiotics for ten days, even if he seems perfectly well."

She opened the door, then looked back at Nick and Allison. "Danny's a lucky boy to have such caring parents," she said gruffly. "I can see you two were awake all night with him. Get some sleep, both of you. I have quite enough patients already."

The door closed behind her. With a weary grin, Nick pulled Allison into his arms. Resting his chin on the top of her head, he whispered, "Danny's going to be all right, Allison. My boy's going to be fine."

Allison clung tightly to Nick as relief flowed through her limbs. Now that the crisis was past, she felt light-headed and buoyant, as if she could rise to the ceiling like a helium balloon. Then without warning, she yawned—an enormous, jaw-cracking yawn.

Nick held her at arm's length. "Poor Allison," he said. "You didn't know what you were getting into when you signed on with us, did you?"

She managed a tired half smile. "I'd have come anyway," she replied. "Does that mean I need to have my head examined?"

Nick kissed her forehead. "No. But I do think you need some sleep."

"So do you," she retorted. "So what do we do? Flip a coin?"

"Nope." Nick turned her around and gave her a gentle push toward the other room. "We do it my way."

"Why do we always have to do things *your* way?" she grumbled sleepily.

"'Cause I'm bigger than you. Now scoot!''

"Tyrant," she muttered, closing the connecting door between the rooms. She'd show Nick she didn't need any sleep. First she'd take a shower and wash her hair, then she'd pop out for some breakfast, then she'd straighten up their rooms....

She got as far as a shower and washing her hair. Toweling her hair dry, she yawned at her reflection in the mirror. Well, maybe a quick nap wouldn't hurt, just to pep up her energy level a bit. She slipped into her bathrobe and lay down on the bed.

A short nap. Forty winks or so. Then she'd be revitalized and ready to take on the world. She'd close her eyes for maybe ten minutes, then . . .

Allison awoke with a start. When her eyes flew open, she found herself gazing at the ceiling, disoriented. Where was she? What time was it?

Then she remembered the doctor's visit . . . Danny's fever had broken . . . he was going to be all right. A lazy smile curved her lips. Arching her back, she stretched like a cat. Her right arm encountered something bulky next to her.

Allison flipped hastily onto her side. Not ten inches from her lay Nick. Snoring.

Chapter Eleven

Allison had never seen Nick look as peaceful as he did sleeping next to her. She lay very still, not wanting to disturb him and lose this opportunity to study him while his guard was down.

He must have showered and shaved earlier. The strong planes and angles of his face were smooth, and the clean scent of soap emanated from his body. Dark lashes fringed his sturdy, resolute cheekbones, and from his slightly parted lips, his breath warmed Allison's hand.

Her fingers fairly tingled with the desire to trace those lips and the faint, sexy cleft in his chin. A lock of jet-black hair curled across his forehead.

Even in sleep, Nick's body radiated a confident masculinity. Allison sensed that his muscles, though now relaxed, could tense and be ready for action in an instant. His eyes would fly open at the slightest sound and dart from side to side, wary and alert.

Had he always slept like this? Allison wondered. Like some wild animal in the forest, where falling too deeply asleep could mean the difference between life and death. Or had his senses been honed by two years on the run, so that even in sleep, he was tuned in to his surroundings, so that the slightest sound penetrated his slumber...?

Allison inched ever-so-carefully closer to Nick. She wished she dared lift his arm and curve it snugly around her, or sling one of her legs across his. But people only did that when they were used to sleeping with each other. And she had a feeling she and Nick would never have the chance to become that familiar.

Her gaze drifted to his hand, which lay palm upward between them. His thick calluses seemed to have done a good job protecting his hands; the recent cuts had healed to faint red lines. She imagined Nick's hands sliding down her body, and shivered.

What time was it, anyway? With the curtains drawn, it was hard to guess the time of day, and her watch lay on the bedside table, on the other side of Nick. He must have given Danny that pill to make him sleep, or surely he wouldn't have left Danny alone in the other room.

Lying perfectly still next to Nick, Allison had a chance to consider all she'd learned about Nick and his son since Danny had gotten sick. Whatever doubts had lingered in her mind had been swept away in the face of Nick's devotion and concern.

She'd never met Nick's ex-wife Sheila, of course, but Allison couldn't picture that rich, spoiled woman keeping an all-night vigil next to her son's sickbed. Might ruin her beauty sleep or something.

Maybe that wasn't fair. After all, Allison had only Nick's description of Sheila to go by. And Nick could hardly be expected to present a perfectly objective version of his ex-wife's character.

Nonetheless, Allison believed with all her heart that Nick wanted what was best for Danny. If circumstances were different, if Danny could have a better life with his mother, Allison knew with complete certainty that Nick would give up his son.

Look at all the sacrifices Nick had already made for Danny—giving up a wealthy life-style, a successful architectural business, and any chance of leading a normal life. Wouldn't it actually be easier for Nick to let Danny go back to his mother?

But Nick would never take the easy way out where Danny's welfare was concerned. That was one of the reasons Allison loved him.

The realization dawned like a sunrise, spreading light and warmth throughout Allison's body. She loved Nick. Of course she loved Nick. Had there ever been a time when she *hadn't* loved him?

It was as if she'd loved him all her life—as if there'd been this empty space in her heart just waiting for him to come along and fill. And then one day he'd jumped into her catering van and threatened to shoot her with a set of keys.

Was it any wonder she'd fallen in love with him?

But knowing she was in love with Nick created more problems than it solved. How could they build a life together with a detective hot on their heels? Allison didn't care about having a house with a white picket fence, but she did care about *some* things. Like staying in one place long enough to make friends, to put Danny in school, for Nick to find a steady job.

Even Allison, with all her spontaneity and impulsiveness, needed some stability in her life. And she had responsibilities she couldn't simply dump like unwanted baggage. Her catering business, for one thing. She and Marilyn were partners, and Allison couldn't just disappear without a word.

And what about her family in Minnesota? Allison couldn't bear the idea of cutting off all contact with the people she loved, never letting them know where she was, never knowing how they were doing.

It was impossible, of course. As long as Nick believed he had to hide Danny from Sheila, he and Allison had no future. And Allison wasn't about to try to change Nick's mind. She'd given it her best shot, and been rewarded with anger and stony silences.

Of course, maybe Allison's dilemma didn't exist. Maybe Nick didn't love her anyway, would never love her, and wouldn't dream of asking her to stay with him and Danny.

Well, that was certainly a cheery thought.

Allison shifted her position slightly, and her hand came to rest a mere inch from Nick's face. Tentatively, she touched the back of one finger to the bold ridge of his jaw.

Nick's eyes drifted open. "Hi," he said sleepily. His lips twitched with the beginnings of a smile.

"Hi yourself, sleepyhead," Allison replied softly.

"What time is it?" With a groan, he twisted around and groped for her watch. Bringing it in front of his face, he blinked twice, either to clear his vision or because he couldn't believe how late it was.

"Well?" she asked.

Nick dangled the watch in front of her eyes. "Oh, my gosh, I've been asleep for nearly five hours," she exclaimed.

"And you call *me* sleepyhead," Nick retorted, laying the watch back on the table. "I've only been snoozing for a couple of hours."

Allison propped her head on her arm. "Did you give Danny his pill?"

Nick nodded. "He finally woke up, so I got him to eat some crackers and drink some juice. Then I gave him the sleeping pill and the antibiotics and some more Tylenol. He should sleep quite a while."

"Does he seem any better?"

"Oh, yes." Nick gave her a relieved grin. "He was much more alert, and some of the color's come back to his face. He was even hungry."

Allison fell back against the pillow. "Nick, I can't tell you how relieved I am."

"You don't have to. I know exactly how you feel." Clearing his throat, Nick raised himself up on one arm. "Allison, Danny and I can never repay you for the way you've helped us. No, let me finish," he said, brushing her protests aside.

He clasped her fingers in his big hand. "Most people would have bailed out on us long ago. Hell, most people wouldn't have come with us in the first place."

"You didn't exactly give me much choice," she said wryly.

"You could have turned us over to Kellogg. You could have let us go and just forgotten about us. But you didn't." Nick pressed the tips of her fingers to his lips. "You're one in a million, Allison. I'll never forget you."

His last words were like a bucket of ice water sloshed in her face. This sounded suspiciously like a goodbye scene. Bravely, Allison smiled. Her glance faltered and she fastened her gaze on the row of buttons on Nick's shirt. "I'm glad I could help," she said, her mouth feeling as if it were stuffed with cotton.

The row of buttons moved. "You've done much more than help," Nick said, bending his body over hers. He lowered his face, filling Allison's vision, filling her heart as his lips touched hers with an indescribably tender pressure.

She wrapped her arms around his neck, drawing him closer, as if she were clinging for dear life to the secure fortress of his strong, wide shoulders. His mouth touched and drew back, touched and drew back, deliberately preventing them from tasting fully of each other.

Allison locked her wrists behind his neck and buried her fingers in Nick's coarse, wavy hair. Instinctively she raised her body against his, as if afraid Nick were planning to get up and walk out of her life at any moment.

He appeared to be in no hurry to leave, however. His kiss deepened, his tongue sliding languidly between her lips as if he were savoring a particularly rare delicacy. Allison met his tongue with hers, their gentle duel stirring a smoldering fire deep inside her.

His taste was sweeter than honey, and more addictive than any drug. Desire surged through Allison's bloodstream, spilling to the tips of her toes and the ends of her fingers. Every cell in her body cried out for Nick's touch.

He slipped his hand beneath the folds of her robe, and she recalled with a start that she was wearing nothing underneath. Now she was glad she'd fallen asleep before getting dressed.

Nick cupped her bare breast in his hand. The rough calluses were a strangely arousing contrast to her soft, vulnerable flesh. Gently he kneaded her breast, while his breath fell hot against her face.

"Nick," she murmured, "Oh, Nick...darling..."

He gave a satisfied sound as her nipple hardened against his hand. He spiraled his finger around the rosy bud, and Allison felt something wild and primitive uncoil inside her. She arched against him, her lips moving against his with a kind of desperation.

She wanted Nick with a frenzied passion that was totally new and unfamiliar. They had so little time left together, and at any moment they could be interrupted by a cry from Danny or by the hotel maid knocking on the door. So little time, so much of each other to explore.

"Easy," Nick crooned. "I want to make this last a long...long time." His lips tickled her ear, while he slid his hand down the curve of her waist, pushing her robe aside. He raised himself up to look at her with a lazy, admiring smile. "You're so beautiful, Allison. Just lovely..." He trailed his fingers across her satiny smooth body, searing a path of pleasure into her skin.

He tugged her robe from her arms and cast it to the floor. Then he rose to his knees and unbuttoned his shirt, his eyes sending a sizzle of sparks to hers, his mouth curved slightly upward.

Allison lifted her hands and undid the last several buttons. Then, shyly, she unzipped Nick's jeans. As she touched him, she was vividly aware of the caged passion she was about to set free. The thought excited her, made her shiver with wanton expectation.

Nick stood and slid off his jeans. A patch of sunlight illuminated him, giving his skin a bronze glow. As he stood before her, proud and erect, Allison raked his body with a frank, lustful glance.

The physical perfection of his body amazed her. Years of hard work had carved his thick muscles and sinews into sleek, efficient lines. Black hair covered his broad chest, tapering to a fine sprinkling at his belly. His narrow hips and long, lean legs were those of an athlete.

Allison drew in her breath sharply as Nick moved over her with the natural grace of a leopard. His eyes were hooded with desire, his limbs radiating heat and power and passion.

At the first delicious contact of his naked body against hers, Allison gasped with pleasure. She ran her hands across his back and around his waist, exploring every square inch of him.

Nick buried his face in her neck, kissing, sucking, licking her skin until Allison was on fire. She molded her body against his, aching for the exquisite fulfillment only Nick could give her.

"So impatient," he murmured. "What's your hurry, sweetheart?"

"Nick, I—I need you."

A contented growl rose from his throat. He pressed his hands to her breasts, stroking, teasing, arousing. He fluttered his fingers across the swollen tips, sending Allison nearly over the edge with ecstasy.

Then he dragged his hand lower, questing, seeking out the white-hot, urgent core of her being. She writhed against him, clamping her teeth together to keep from crying out.

He cast a fiery glance at her face, then raised himself above her and entered her with slow...agonizing... barely restrained passion.

Their union sent Allison soaring to dizzy heights of longing and rapture. As Nick stroked back and forth, he urged her higher and higher. He seized her mouth with his, then broke off to gasp tortured words in her ear. Allison wrapped her legs around him, matching her movements to his. She was filled to the brim, with Nick's body and with her overwhelming love for him.

She scanned his dark eyes, so close to hers, for any sign that he returned her feelings. But his expression, strained with pleasure, gave away no secrets.

It didn't matter. She gave herself to him freely, with no strings attached. Her love for him was motive enough. She wanted to give him pleasure, to raise Nick to the same thrilling heights of ecstasy their lovemaking had brought her.

Her hands ranged across his solid, heaving body, fingers exploring, palms caressing. This might be her last chance to acquaint herself with the delightful mysteries of Nick's body. She wanted to remember every detail forever.

"Allison," he panted, "sweetheart, it's so good to be with you like this." His lips moved against her flushed cheek. "I've wanted to make love to you for so long...."

He lowered his mouth to her breast and captured her pebble-hard nipple. His tongue drew lazy circles, then fluttered rapidly against the straining peak.

She gasped at his touch.

His lips were a blazing brand against her creamy white skin. Deep inside her abdomen, some force was unleashed, building in strength until no power on earth could stop it.

"Nick!" she cried, arching her back, accelerating their joined motion. "Ah, Nick!"

"Yes, sweetheart," he breathed, drawing back to watch her face.

Seconds after Allison careened over the edge, she felt and saw Nick join her, his face contorted with an intense rapture that matched her own. Together they spiraled downward, pulses slowing, arms wrapped around each other as they collapsed, sated, on some wonderful, newly discovered shore.

Nick fingered a long strand of Allison's hair, which spread across the pillow like reddish-brown silk. Her skin was still burnished with a rosy glow; her eyes, shining like emeralds, followed his every move.

"That was wonderful," he murmured, splaying his hand across her flat belly, noting with delight the way she trembled at his touch.

Allison entwined her fingers with his. "Mmm, yes...wonderful." She drew her knees up and cuddled against Nick. "Your arm's not falling asleep, is it?"

"Hmm? Oh, no...it's fine." He liked the weight of her pressed against his arm, the snug way she fit into the curve of his embrace. Their bodies could have been molded just for each other, he thought.

How ironic, then, that this might be the first, the last, the *only* time he and Allison would ever lie together like this, savoring the intimacy of their lovemaking.

What made that probability even more difficult to bear was the fact that Nick loved her.

He wasn't sure when he'd started loving Allison. From the moment he'd met her he'd known she was special. With each passing hour of their acquaintance, she'd endeared herself more to him, with her caring, her warmth, her sense of humor.

And now, when he was no longer frantic with worry about Danny's illness, he had a chance to realize that somewhere along the way, she'd become a vital part of his life.

If only there were some way to fit her into his future....

It was no use. Trying to imagine a life with Allison was like trying to put together a jigsaw puzzle where none of the pieces fit.

Nick and Danny had no choice but to continue their unsettled life on the run. But how could Nick ask Allison to give up her family, her friends, her business? Because that's what she would have to do if she came with them. Nick's number-one priority was still protecting his son. And no matter how much he loved her, he couldn't allow her to leave a trail for their pursuers to follow.

Nick flung an arm across his eyes. Why would Allison want to stay with them, anyway? What did he have to offer her besides a series of hastily rented and hastily vacated apartments? One temporary job after another... would-be friends to keep at a distance so they didn't learn the truth. And how could he and Allison ever have children together? What if Kellogg caught up with them just as Allison was going into labor? What if... what if... what if? Nick had no trouble dreaming up dozens of disastrous scenarios.

"Nick? Is something the matter?"

Allison's worried voice interrupted his depressing thoughts. Removing his arm from his face, he managed a reassuring smile. "Nothing's wrong."

"You seemed a million miles away for a minute."

Nick smothered a sigh. If only they *could* be a million miles away, in some happy place where they didn't have to worry about detectives and ex-wives, or about little boys getting dangerously ill.

He laid his hand against Allison's face, kissing her gently. She opened her eyes as he drew back, and Nick saw her look of uncertainty. He longed to tell her that everything would be all right, that they had just started a joyful new life together.

But it wasn't true. And Allison knew that as well as he did.

Nick rolled on top of her, careful not to crush her with his full weight. They lay that way for a moment, locked in each other's arms, lost in their own thoughts. She smelled like flowers, and he inhaled deeply, savoring the delightful softness of her body, the sweet silkiness of her skin.

Reluctantly he levered himself off the bed. His frank, appreciative gaze traveled from the top of Allison's head to the tips of her toes. Blushing, she pulled a sheet across her breasts.

Nick threw her a rakish grin. "It's too late to be shy with me now," he said. "I know all your deepest, darkest secrets."

She rose to the bait. "Oh? Such as?"

"I know what a wanton wench you really are." He tugged on his jeans.

"Wanton wench? What have you been doing, reading nineteenth-century novels on the sly? Wanton wench, indeed." She threw a pillow at him.

Nick dodged it, nearly toppling off balance as he stuck his other leg into his jeans. "See what I mean?" he said. "Totally wanton."

"Hmph." Allison folded her arms across her chest. She watched him as he buttoned his shirt.

Nick leaned over to kiss her, and she grabbed his collar and pulled him down onto the bed. "Why, you little..."

He imprisoned her in a bear hug, but somehow she managed to wriggle free. They tussled for a few moments, pillows flying, bedclothes tangling. At last Nick captured her wrists and pinned her to the mattress, both of them red-faced and panting with laughter.

As they stared into each other's eyes, their breathing slowed, their smiles faded. Nick swallowed. "Allison, I—"

"Yes?" She watched him expectantly.

Words of love filled his chest, pushing up into his throat. How he longed to speak them, to tell Allison that he loved her! But confessing his true feelings would only complicate matters. And matters were complicated enough.

He choked back his words, running his hand through his hair. "Nothing," he mumbled.

The hopeful gleam in Allison's eyes faded.

Nick kissed her with a playful smack, then pushed himself off the bed. "I'm going to check on Danny." He left her lying alone in bed, sheets, pillow and blankets strewn in disarray around her.

After he'd gone, Allison remained where she was for a moment. Her hand wandered across the mattress. It was still warm where Nick had lain. But it would soon grow cold, like the warm radiance of her skin where he'd touched her, like the heated memory of their lovemaking.

Then one day soon she would have to say goodbye to Nick, and the blazing love she felt for him would begin to flicker and die, leaving her nothing but cold embers and bitter ashes of remembrance.

Fighting back tears, Allison rose from the bed they'd shared, and started to get dressed.

Danny made a remarkably fast recovery over the next few days, but by that time, Allison was climbing the walls with boredom and frustration.

By unspoken agreement, her departure had been delayed until Danny was well again. Nick left early each morning, having found a short-term construction job that left him physically drained, muscles aching and eyelids drooping by the end of the day. But the pay was decent, and Nick refused Allison's suggestion that he find less exhausting employment.

During the day, then, she was alone with Danny, feeding him, giving him his medicine, changing the TV channel for him. When he started feeling better, Danny's antagonism toward Allison returned, although at least he consented to speak to her occasionally. Whether this was a result of Nick's admonition, or whether Danny simply realized Allison couldn't wait on him hand and foot without at least minimal communication, she didn't know.

What she did know was that Danny's barely concealed hostility, combined with the normal grouchiness and impatience of a recovering invalid, was driving her crazy.

When Nick trudged in the door each evening, Danny's pent-up chatter exploded, and he peppered Nick with questions, complaints and a recap of what he'd seen on television that day. Exhausted, Nick responded patiently, but Allison could tell that Danny's constant demands for attention wore him down.

The tension between the three of them piled up as the days went by.

Allison hadn't expected Nick to make love to her again—not with Danny so close by, not with Nick so tired all the time. It was probably just as well. Making love with Nick would be a tough habit to break.

But Allison couldn't help feeling . . . well, a little hurt and neglected. She waited eagerly for Nick's return every day, anticipating a tender touch, a meaningful glance—

something to show her that he hadn't forgotten about the wonderful, enchanted interlude they'd shared.

But Nick treated her casually, as if he were trying to keep her at a distance. Oh, sure, on occasion he'd pat her affectionately on the shoulder, or cast her a weary smile. But the sexy, suggestive gleam in his eye, the secret squeeze of her hand . . . were missing.

By the time the weekend rolled around, Allison felt like the walls were closing in on her. It seemed she'd always lived here, stuck in these two clean but character-less rooms, with only an occasional trip for takeout food to relieve the monotony.

On Sunday, Nick had the day off.

He lay on top of the bed in his and Danny's room, watching the television with a zombie-like expression. Allison plopped down next to him.

"Let's go to Fisherman's Wharf," she said.

"Hmm?" Nick shifted his gaze to her. "I'm sorry— what did you say?"

Patience, Allison, she warned herself. She smoothed the bedspread. "I said, let's go to Fisherman's Wharf."

Nick looked puzzled. "You mean today?"

"Today. Right now. This very second."

Nick shot a glance at Danny, who was sitting cross-legged in his pajamas, playing on the floor with a pair of toy cars Nick had brought home earlier in the week. He frowned. "I don't know if Danny's up to it."

"Vroom! Vroom!" Danny said.

"It'll be good for him," Allison pointed out. "Fresh air, exercise, a change of scenery. It'll do us all some good."

Nick winced. "I've had all the exercise I need, thank you."

"You know what I mean." She tugged on his hand. "Come on. If I don't get out of here soon, I'm going to go insane like one of those isolated prairie women, and start chasing you and Danny around with a butcher knife."

Nick chuckled. "Well, if that's the alternative, by all means, let's go to Fisherman's Wharf. Danny?"

"Yeah, Dad? Vroom!"

"How'd you like to go to Fisherman's Wharf?"

Danny wrinkled his nose. "What's that?" he asked suspiciously.

Allison jumped to her feet. "It's a really fun place with lots of people and lots of things to do and lots of yummy food to eat."

Danny continued to eye her mistrustfully.

"Come on, Shortstop. Get dressed. Let's go," said Nick.

What a good idea this was, Allison thought a couple of hours later as she strolled along the waterfront, spooning shrimp cocktail out of a plastic container. Danny bounded ahead of them, leaning over the railing to peer at the water below, pausing to gawk at one of the colorful habitués of Fisherman's Wharf.

It was a gorgeous day, warm with a clear blue sky. The breeze gusting off San Francisco Bay blew away Allison's depression and the sense of oppressiveness that had clung to her for days, weighing her spirit down. Even Nick was having a good time.

Allison inhaled deeply, filling her lungs with the piquant smells of seafood and brine. The wharf area was teeming with tourists and locals, pausing in their Sunday strolls to watch a juggling clown or listen to an impromptu concert by a Dixieland band.

Danny's misgivings about their expedition had evaporated the minute they climbed onto the cable car two blocks from their hotel. By the time they arrived at Fisherman's Wharf, the sickly pallor had vanished from his face, and his lingering cough had subsided.

He hadn't stopped running, either, except when Nick had challenged him to a game of Space Invaders in a video arcade. It was as if Danny had been storing up energy during his illness, and now that the dam had burst, he couldn't keep his feet still. Just watching him dart back and forth across the sidewalk, bouncing up and down like a beach ball, was exhausting.

"What a dynamo," Allison said, glancing up at Nick.

"Yeah," he said, beaming at her. "Isn't it great?"

Allison smiled and leaned her head against his shoulder. Nick took her hand in his, and suddenly the day was perfect.

"Danny!" Nick called. "Don't get too far ahead of us!"

They caught up with him next to a cluster of people watching a white-faced mime trying to escape from an invisible box. Danny watched in fascination, his mouth hanging open. Allison smiled with amusement and leaned against Nick, letting her gaze stray over the crowd.

She loved to people-watch. It was fun to try to guess things about other people. That young couple over there, for example. Were they engaged? Married? On their honeymoon, maybe?

Or what about that plump, elderly woman who kept smoothing down her dress as the wind whipped up her skirts? That little girl next to her, clutching a red balloon in her fist, must be her granddaughter.

Allison's eyes swept across the panorama of humanity congregated there that afternoon. Tourists shopping for souvenirs, enjoying the street theater, collapsing on benches to rest their aching feet. Some people were basking in the sun, or reading newspapers, or just watching people go by— Allison's gaze snapped back to the bench about thirty feet away, beyond the crowd gathered around the mime. The hair prickled on the back of her neck, and her stomach swooped a little. Something she'd seen set off warning alarms in her brain. Something familiar, something dreaded . . .

A family with three small children occupied most of the bench, the kids scrambling and swirling between their parents' feet. At the far end of the bench a man was reading a newspaper. As Allison watched, he crossed one leg over the other, and she noticed the neat crease in his brown trousers.

Then he lowered the newspaper for an instant before retreating behind it again.

But that instant was long enough. Allison gasped and clutched Nick's arm. Her heart hammered painfully in her chest and thundered in her ears.

Through the din, she heard Nick ask, "What is it?" in a worried voice.

She swung him around so they were both facing away from the man with the newspaper.

"Nick, it's him! Over on that bench. No, don't look!" Allison choked back the fear rising in her throat. "It's Kellogg—the detective! He's sitting less than ten yards from us!"

Chapter Twelve

Ice water poured through Nick's veins.

"Are you sure it's Kellogg?" he said quietly, barely moving his lips.

Allison's eyes were enormous. Her rosy cheeks had turned pale. "I'm positive," she whispered. "I saw him watching us."

"Come on." Nick grabbed Danny's hand and started to walk rapidly away from the group of people watching the mime perform.

"Hey, Dad, can't we stay a little longer?"

Allison hurried after them.

"Just keep walking," Nick said from the side of his mouth. "Don't look back. Maybe he won't see us leaving."

Danny was scuffling his feet, unhappy at being so abruptly dragged away from the entertainment. Nick gripped his arm securely and pulled his son along, practically lifting him off the sidewalk.

"Ow, Dad, that hurts!"

Nick's eyes darted from left to right, searching for the best escape route. He prayed that Kellogg wouldn't notice their disappearance right away, so they would have at least a small head start.

Allison strode beside him, looking straight ahead. She was breathing rapidly, and her face had a pinched, scared look. Nick was struck by a flash of regret. It was his fault Allison was in this desperate situation, fleeing like an escaped criminal. Nick knew he was responsible for that haunted, panicky expression, and he hated himself for it.

But he didn't have time to indulge in remorse. He had a more urgent priority at the moment. He glanced quickly over his shoulder, just in time to see Kellogg throw down his newspaper and push his way through the mob of tourists.

Dread filled Nick's chest. "He's seen us," he warned Allison. "Run for it!"

Nick swung Danny up into his arms and took off, trusting Allison to follow in his wake. Shoving people aside, he forced his way through the crowd like a football player dodging would-be tacklers.

He dashed into the street, crossing against the traffic signal. Horns honked, brakes screeched, but the three of them somehow managed to make it to the other side.

Nick didn't dare waste precious seconds by glancing back to see if Kellogg had made it across, too. Besides, he figured it was a safe bet the detective was still right behind them.

As Nick pounded up the sidewalk, Danny bounced against his shoulder like a sack of flour. Nick could hear Allison's footsteps right behind him.

What nearly drove him over the brink of panic was the horrible familiarity of their desperate predicament. How many nights had Nick suffered through terrifying dreams of exactly this situation? The dreams were always the same—running, running with Danny in his arms, running with legs that felt like rubber and wouldn't cooperate and move fast enough. Sensing their pursuer closing in on them, getting nearer and nearer, so close that Nick could hear footsteps pounding and feel the man's breath hot on the back of his neck.

And now Nick's worst nightmare was coming true. Only this time he wouldn't wake up at the last second with a hoarse cry, his body drenched in sweat and his heart pounding a mile a minute.

Because this time the nightmare was really happening.

Nick scanned their surroundings frantically for an alley or building entrance they could duck into. But they'd never escape that way, not with Kellogg right behind them.

Up ahead Nick spotted a line of people boarding the cable car. And suddenly he knew that was their only chance.

A surge of adrenaline coursed through his body, like the last-minute spurt of a long-distance runner. He only hoped Allison could keep up.

She did. Nick heard her harsh, even gasps as she chased after him. They were less than half a block away when the last passenger boarded and the cable car started to move.

Nick nearly stumbled with despair, but Allison kept right on running. She caught up with the cable car and leaped aboard. Hanging on to a pole, she leaned out. "Give me Danny!" she shouted.

Nick's muscles screamed in protest as he pushed them to run faster. "Go with Allison!" he gasped, hoping Danny would let go of his neck in time.

Allison circled Danny with her arm and pulled him onto the accelerating cable car. With a last desperate burst of energy, Nick grabbed for the pole and pulled himself aboard. He lost his balance and nearly toppled off backwards, but regained his equilibrium at the last second.

He turned around and saw the puffing detective pull up short as the cable car sped up and outdistanced him. Kellogg angrily punched his fist into the air.

Allison, hugging an ashen-faced Danny against her, gave Nick a wobbly look of relief, just as the conductor shoved his way past the other passengers.

"Are you crazy?" he yelled at Nick. "You could get killed that way! It's illegal to jump aboard a moving cable car." He glared at Allison, then held out his hand. "That'll be a dollar fifty each, and seventy-five cents for the kid."

They arrived back at their hotel exhausted. Nick had herded them off the cable car three stops after they got on, in case Kellogg had retrieved his car so he could follow. They'd walked the rest of the way back, taking a roundabout route just to be on the safe side.

The minute they entered the room, Nick started throwing things into the shopping bag that had replaced his stolen suitcase. It nearly broke Allison's heart, the way Danny followed suit without saying a word. He simply started stuffing things into his backpack, so accustomed was he to these frantic, hasty departures.

"Where are we going?" she asked.

Nick looked up, then glanced at Danny, then took Allison by the hand and led her into the other room. He raked his fingers through his hair, and she couldn't help noticing that his hands were trembling a little.

"Look," he said, swallowing, "maybe this is a good time for us to say goodbye."

There could never be a good time for that, Allison thought. But all she said was, "I'm coming with you."

Nick's eyes roamed her face. "Sweetheart, I've gotten you into a big enough mess already. I don't want to cause you any more trouble."

"You're wasting time," she said, her chin jutting forward. "We should be packing, instead of standing here gabbing."

Nick stared at her intently for a moment, his dark brows drawn together. Then a grin spread across his face. He cupped Allison's face in his hands and planted a quick, hard kiss on her mouth.

"I love you," he said. "Now come on, scoot! We've got to get out of here."

The next few hours passed in a daze for Allison. As Nick drove through the flat farmland of California's Central Valley, one question kept spinning through her mind. Had Nick meant what he said when he'd told her he loved her?

Or was it only a figure of speech, spoken on the spur of the moment because she was being a good sport?

Well, she wasn't likely to have a chance to find out for a while. If Nick's determined expression was any indication, he intended to keep driving for at least the next week without stopping.

But stop they did, several hours after dusk, in the city of Fresno—the Raisin Capital of the World, if you believed the billboards outside of town.

"Why Fresno?" Allison asked the next morning, as they sipped instant coffee in plastic cups that Nick had brought back to the room from the motel office.

He shrugged. "The obvious place for us to head next would have been Sacramento. Hopefully that's where Kellogg will head, too."

"But if that's the obvious place, wouldn't he figure out that we'd have gone somewhere else?"

Nick leaned back in his chair and swallowed a huge gulp of the bitter coffee. "You seem to be under the impression that I have some kind of master plan, some ultimate destination in mind where we'll be safe."

Allison frowned into her coffee. "Don't you?"

"Nope." Nick drained the contents of his cup and set it on the table with a bang. "My only goal is to put as much distance as possible between that detective and us."

"But where were you heading before he found us in San Francisco?"

"No place in particular."

Allison stared at him. "You mean all this time, you didn't even know where we were going?"

"That's right." The amusement in Nick's face died away. His eyes were a deep, smoky blue as he leaned forward across the table and took one of her hands in his.

"This is what our life is like, Allison—Danny's and mine. Always on the run, never knowing where we'll end up or how long we'll stay there. Every single day for the last two years I've lived with uncertainty and fear. This is what it would be like if you—well, you know."

"No," she said deliberately. "I don't know. What do you mean?"

They stared at each other for a moment. *Say it*, Allison thought. *Say, this is what it would be like if you stayed with us. Ask me to stay with you, Nick. Ask me.*

In his narrowed eyes, his sharply chiseled features, she sought some sign, the faintest indication that he'd meant what he said when he'd told her he loved her.

Whatever Nick was feeling, he hid it well. He squeezed Allison's hand tightly, then rose to his feet. "We'll stay here a couple of days," he said. "I have to earn some more money before I can make any definite plans."

He kissed the top of Allison's head. "See you this evening." Then he left her alone with Danny, who was still sleeping—worn out by yesterday's excitement.

An hour later the phone rang. Allison jumped, and the book she was reading fell to the floor. She approached the phone cautiously, as if it were a coiled rattlesnake. What if it was Kellogg?

Well, he could hardly have tracked them down this fast. She lifted the receiver gingerly. "Yes?"

"Hi, it's me." Nick's voice filled her with relief. "I found a job, but it's going to be an all-nighter."

"What does that mean?"

"It means I won't get back to the motel until tomorrow morning."

"Tomorrow morning?" Allison exclaimed, casting a worried glance at Danny. He'd been pretty reasonably behaved this morning, but she was afraid he would throw a temper tantrum when he found out his father wouldn't be back till tomorrow.

"They're driving a bunch of us out to do some construction work on a big farm about forty miles from here," Nick said. "Let me talk to Danny, will you?"

Allison held out the receiver. "Danny, it's your dad."

Danny's eyes lit up. He scrambled to his feet and snatched the phone. "Dad? Uh-huh. Yeah. Okay. Sure. Bye."

When he hung up, that dull resentment Allison had come to know so well had returned. He spent the rest of the day resisting her attempts to cheer him up.

By the time bedtime arrived, Allison could have used some cheering up herself. It was strange, but this would be the first time in more than a week that she wouldn't be sleeping close to Nick.

Better get used to it, she warned herself as she tucked Danny into bed. *You've got a whole lifetime of lonely nights ahead of you.*

Allison had expected to have trouble falling asleep, but she lost consciousness almost as soon as her head hit the pillow. The next thing she knew, someone was screaming.

Not really screaming, more like wailing or crying. The heartbreaking noise penetrated her dream and became a part of it. She rolled over, hiding her head under the pillow, trying to escape that mournful sound.

All at once she realized she was awake and the sound was coming from the next bed. In an instant Allison had flung off the covers and flown across the room.

"Danny, what is it? Danny, hush, it's okay, I'm here...."

In the faint illumination seeping through the curtains, Allison could see that the boy's eyes were squinched shut, his thin body curled into a fetal position as he emitted one terrified howl after another. He was quivering so hard he shook the bed.

Allison bent over and pulled him against her body, cradling him in her arms, stroking his hair. "Shh, shh, it's okay honey...don't be scared...I'm here. It was just a bad dream, Danny, just a dream."

His body, rigid with fear, gradually relaxed as his howls subsided into steady sobs. His arms slid up and encircled her neck, and she hugged him tighter. Soon his tears had soaked the front of her nightgown, but Allison didn't care.

"Hush, sweetie...don't be scared." She crooned softly for a few minutes, until his sobs had dribbled into a series of wet hiccups.

"There, that's better. That's my boy," she said, patting his back.

She stretched out her arm and managed to turn on the bedside lamp. It cast a golden glow on Danny's tear-streaked face when he finally lifted his head from her shoulder. Allison smiled and ruffled his hair. "See? Everything's all right. Do you want to tell me about your dream?"

Danny's lower lip quivered, and his breath came out in little gulps. "He was chasing us," he said in a thin, quavering voice.

"Who was chasing us, Danny?" Allison asked. But she already knew the answer.

"That man! That bad man who's always chasing us! It was like yesterday, when we were running away and he almost caught us! Only this time—in the dream—he *did* catch us, and he took me away from my daddy and back to this cave where he lives, and it was dark and I couldn't see anything but he was going to kill me!"

Danny's eyes had expanded with fear as he related his nightmare, and by the end of his story they nearly filled his face. Allison smoothed his hair back and studied those eyes, so like Nick's. Her sympathy for Danny was mixed with anger—not at him, but at all the adults in his life who were responsible for this nightmare and all his other nightmares...the ones Danny had while asleep and the ones he lived through while awake.

She tucked the covers around him again. "Feeling better now?" she asked, smiling.

He nodded up at her.

"Do you want me to leave the light on until you go back to sleep?"

He hesitated. "No, that's okay. You can turn it off," he said, rubbing his face with his pajama sleeve.

Allison bent forward and kissed him on the forehead, and this time, Danny didn't turn away. She turned off the light and crawled back into bed. A minute or two later he called her name.

"Yes, Danny?"

First there was silence. Then, in a small voice he asked, "Could I sleep with you tonight?"

Allison swallowed the lump in her throat. "Sure." She threw back one side of the covers. "Climb on in."

Nick let himself into the motel room, struggling to keep his eyes open. His hands were sore and throbbing from wielding a shovel all night long. His back ached.

After locking the door behind him, he halted in surprise. As he tiptoed toward Allison's bed, a tired, puzzled smile crept over his face.

Danny lay next to Allison, his hand tucked into hers. Their heads were bent together, almost touching. They were both asleep.

What on earth could have happened during the last twenty-four hours to bring about this unexpected turn of events? Nick stripped off his clothes and crawled between the sheets of the other bed. He didn't believe for a minute that his recent talk with Danny had brought about this change of heart. Yet somehow Allison had finally managed to win Danny over....

The next thing Nick knew, sunlight was blinding him and the smell of food was making his mouth water. He lifted his head, bleary-eyed, from the pillow and saw Allison and Danny sitting at the table, eating breakfast. Or was it lunch by now?

Danny noticed him first. "Dad's awake," he announced to Allison.

She smiled at Danny as if they were involved in a secret conspiracy. "Hungry?" she said to Nick.

"Famished." He propped himself up on one elbow and rubbed his eyes. "What time is it, anyway?"

"Almost noon. Danny and I went out and brought back lunch."

Nick climbed out of bed, wearing only his underwear. Allison arched one eyebrow, but didn't say anything. "What are we eating?" Nick asked.

"Pizza!" Danny said happily.

Nick groaned. "Pizza? For breakfast?"

"I beg your pardon," said Allison. "I'll have you know this pizza is delicious. Danny picked out the toppings himself. Garlic and anchovies."

"Ugh. No wonder the smell woke me up."

"It's your own fault for sleeping in so late. You missed bacon and eggs earlier."

Danny giggled at Allison's remark, and she tugged down the brim of his baseball cap so it covered his eyes. Nick looked back and forth between the two of them. He was dying to find out the reason for their newfound friendship, but he didn't want to ask in front of Danny.

He settled himself into a chair and grabbed a slice of pizza. The first bite assaulted his taste buds and nearly brought tears to his eyes, but after another bite or two, he discovered he was ravenous. "You know," he said, his voice muffled, "this stuff's not so bad after all."

The other two looked at each other with smug expressions.

Danny and Allison might have formed a new alliance, but for some reason, Nick and Allison's relationship had taken on cold war overtones. As the day slipped by, he couldn't figure out what was the matter with her.

Allison wasn't unfriendly, exactly—just so...aloof. She refused to meet his eyes; when he reached out to touch her she casually drew away as if she hadn't noticed. She never initiated any conversation with him, and when Nick spoke first, she replied with abrupt one- or two-word answers. Once or twice Nick caught her watching him with a thoughtful expression, but the minute his eyes met hers, she glanced quickly away.

This unexplained behavior was all the more distressing, because for the first time, the three of them had a chance to live like a real family. Now that Danny and Allison were pals, Nick saw what a good mother she would be for his son...and for any other children she and Nick might have.

He shook his head, impatient with himself. Why did his thoughts keep returning to these same lines, like a record stuck in the same groove?

But it was impossible to resist speculating about the life they might have had together...if only circumstances had been different. Danny plainly worshipped Allison, and she was equally fond of him. The three of them could be an unbeatable team...if only Nick could figure out why Allison was giving him the cold shoulder.

He scanned his memory, searching for something he might have said, something he'd done—or forgotten to do—that might have upset her. He couldn't think of a thing. After all, he hadn't even been near Allison for most of the last twenty-four hours.

By evening Nick was going crazy. Earlier he'd volunteered to take Danny to a nearby park for a game of catch, thinking that maybe Allison wanted some time alone. But when Danny had begged her to come along, Allison had readily agreed. The three of them had spent an enjoyable afternoon in the park, eating dinner in a coffee shop across the street from the motel.

The whole time, Allison had practically ignored Nick, focusing most of her attention on Danny.

Good grief, could I be jealous of my own son? Nick wondered. He'd been so anxious for Allison and Danny to become friends, but now he couldn't help begrudging the special twinkle in Allison's eye, the secret smiles that she reserved only for Danny.

Nick craved some of Allison's attention for himself. But he knew that Allison's coolness toward him wasn't because she was spending all her affection on Danny. Allison had plenty of love to share, and she wasn't the kind of person to hoard it. That was one of the things Nick loved about her.

But his attempts to break through her shell were in vain.

She sat on the floor with Danny that evening, watching a baseball game on television. Nick couldn't help smiling. Allison was as caught up in the game as Danny.

"Out? What d'ya mean, out? He was safe by a mile. That referee's blind."

"Umpire," Danny corrected. "In baseball it's called an umpire."

Nick winked at his son. "Girls," he said, shrugging.

"Girls," Danny echoed, rolling his eyes in agreement. Then he scooted closer to Allison.

As soon as the game ended, Nick said, "Okay, Shortstop, it's past your bedtime."

"Can I have one bedtime story first, Dad?"

"Well..."

"Just one? Please?"

"All right. Which one do you want to hear?"

Danny tugged on Allison's sleeve. "I want Allison to tell me a story."

With a sheepish glance at Nick, Allison sat down on the bed and tucked Danny in. "Let's see, once upon a time there was this famous baseball player named Danny. And one day, he..."

After Danny drifted off to sleep, Nick took Allison's hand. "Let's go outside for a while," he whispered. "It's a beautiful warm evening."

She seemed to resist him at first, then, with a sigh, followed him outside. They strolled over to the motel's swimming pool, a short distance from their room, and lowered themselves onto lounge chairs. Aside from them, the place was deserted.

"You and Danny are sure getting along well."

A faint smile danced across Allison's lips. "He's a great kid, Nick."

"I can tell he feels the same way about you."

Silence descended as they gazed up at the dark, star-strewn sky, avoiding each other's eyes. A huge truck lumbered down the highway. As the roar died away, the awkwardness between them became almost painful.

Nick watched Allison from the corner of his eye. She twisted her fingers in her lap, studying her hands as if she'd never seen them before.

"How did you manage to win Danny over so completely?" Nick asked. His voice sounded unnaturally loud.

Allison shrugged. After a moment, she said, "He had a nightmare last night. I was there to comfort him. I guess after that, he realized I wasn't such a monster after all."

"A nightmare?" Nick frowned. "What kind of nightmare?"

"Oh, you know...a nightmare."

Nick couldn't stand it any longer. "Allison, what's wrong? Have I done or said something to offend you?"

She bowed her head. "No. Nothing like that."

"Then *what*, for God's sake?" Nick took her hands in his, turning her to face him. "Why have you been acting as if you—as if you're mad at me or something?"

She squeezed his hands, looked away and sighed deeply. "We need to have a talk, Nick. About Danny's nightmare."

"Danny's nightmare?" Nick arched his eyebrows, confused.

"His nightmare . . . and other things." She stood and walked to the edge of the pool. Suddenly she whirled and faced him. "Nick, I think you should take Danny back to Boston."

He felt as if she'd slapped him in the face. "So we're back to this again," he said stiffly. "I thought I'd made myself clear. There's no way in hell I'm giving Danny up."

"Nick, maybe you wouldn't have to! Maybe things have changed—maybe Sheila will let him stay with you."

"If that were true, she'd have called off her bloodhounds now."

"Not necessarily. Even if she realized that Danny's better off with you, she'd still want to see him."

A cold anger prickled Nick's skin. "I can't take the chance that Sheila's had a change of heart. The risk is too great."

"Then maybe you could find another judge—someone who'd believe that Sheila abused Danny." She stepped toward Nick, a pleading expression on her face. "Maybe Sheila's better. Maybe she's stopped drinking and gotten some help. Even if the court turned Danny over to her, he's two years older now. A judge or a social worker would be more likely to listen to him. And when Danny's older, surely the court will allow him to live with you, if that's what he wants."

She touched his shoulder, and Nick jerked away. "I'm going to say this one more time," he said, gritting his teeth. "I will never surrender Danny willingly. I saw how that woman mistreated him—you didn't."

"But I've seen the price he pays for staying with you!" Allison cried.

Nick froze. "What are you talking about?"

"I'm talking about last night, about his nightmare. He was dreaming that Kellogg was chasing us. Only it wasn't like most nightmares, Nick, because it really happened. And it'll happen again!"

Allison knotted her fists at her side. If only she could make him see the truth! But that stubborn, closed expression on his face told her she was banging her head uselessly against a wall.

"It's not just the nightmares," she said, trying to stay calm. "It's that nervous, worried look that's always on his face. You don't notice it, Nick, but I do! It's the way he jumps every time a door slams or a car backfires. It's the terror in his eyes whenever it's time to run again."

Allison grasped Nick's shoulders, wanting to shake some sense into him. "That poor little kid is scared of his own shadow, Nick! He has no sense of security, no peace of mind. This life you're leading is destroying him!"

The moonlight reflected coldly in Nick's eyes. He studied her for a moment, and just when Allison was starting to hope that maybe she'd gotten through that thick skull of his, he said, "I guess I have to start worrying again that you're going to sneak off and call Kellogg."

Allison jumped back as if his words had scalded her. "What do you mean?" she asked. Her lips felt numb.

"I mean that I finally trusted you, Allison. I thought you were on my side—on Danny's side. I see now that I misjudged you."

His words were like the cruel lash of a whip. "How can you say that?" she breathed. "After what we've shared . . . after what we've meant to each other?"

Nick shrugged. "I know how you feel," he said. "I thought we had something special, you and I. Now I find out you're ready to turn me over to Kellogg."

"I never said that!" she protested. "I only said that Danny would be better off back in Boston."

"It's the same thing," Nick said. "Either way, you don't trust me. You don't believe in me."

"That's not true. I *do* trust you, Nick. But I think you're making the wrong decision."

"But it's *my* decision, isn't it?" His voice was flat, emotionless.

She gazed at him in despair. Then a spark of anger flared inside her. "You accuse me of not trusting you. But *you're* the one who doesn't trust *me*. How could you think I'd betray you, after all we've lived through? Didn't I sound the alarm when I saw Kellogg yesterday? If it hadn't been for me, Danny might be back in Sheila's clutches by now."

Nick's cold, stern expression melted a little. "Allison, I didn't mean—"

"Your meaning's perfectly clear," she said, her indignation rising. "You're glad enough to use my car, to borrow money from me, to have me babysit Danny. But if I dare to open my mouth and express an opinion, suddenly I'm the enemy."

Nick flinched under her words. Allison knew she was being unfair, but she was past caring. Nick had hurt her deeply, and in her pain, she lashed out instinctively.

He reached for her, but she shrugged off his hand. "What a fool I've been," she said. "I thought you cared for me. I thought our lovemaking meant something. But I see I was wrong. Without trust, without respect, our relationship is nothing but a hollow sham."

With that, Allison turned her back and strode away. With each step, her heart cried out for him; her ears strained for the sound of his voice calling her back. But the only sound was the beat of her own footsteps, walking across the motel parking lot, taking her farther and farther away from the man she loved.

Allison sat in the coffee shop across the street for nearly two hours, staring morosely into her cup of decaffeinated coffee. Each time the door swung open, she looked up eagerly, hoping to see Nick enter, his eyes searching the restaurant for her.

After a while she went into the ladies' room and cried into a handful of paper towels. Then she walked slowly back to the motel, dreading the reception that awaited her. Allison had said a lot of things she regretted, but Nick's words still stung. Could they ever repair the rift in their relationship? Or had the hurtful accusations they'd hurled at each other opened a breach of trust it would be impossible to mend?

Maybe their argument was for the best. Surely it would be easier to leave Nick and Danny now, while she and Nick weren't on such friendly terms.

Yet Allison couldn't bear the thought that they would end their relationship on such a bitter, angry note. By the time she reached the motel room, she still hadn't decided how to act toward Nick. Apologetic? Forgiving? Perfectly normal, pretending nothing had happened?

She pasted a bright smile on her face as she opened the door.

But the room was dark, and she could hear the slow, even breathing of sleep. Fumbling in the darkness for her nightgown, Allison crawled into bed and lay huddled beneath the covers. She stared miserably at the ceiling for a long time before sleep claimed her.

When she awoke, sunshine filtered into the room through the thick draperies. She lay there with her eyes closed, trying to figure out what to do about Nick, no closer to an answer than she'd been last night.

With a sigh, Allison finally rolled over and opened her eyes. Then she sat bolt upright. Rubbing her eyes, she looked around the room again. She flung back the covers and dashed into the bathroom.

Fighting back panic, Allison hurried back to the front room and ran to the window overlooking the parking lot. She threw back the curtain and peered outside. Her car was still there.

But Nick and Danny and all their possessions were gone.

Chapter Thirteen

Aren't you ready yet? You're supposed to be at the Dunbars' in half an hour!''

Allison brushed a damp lock of hair out of her eyes with the back of her wrist. Scowling in concentration, she squeezed the last dab of whipped cream on top of the rum-chocolate torte. "There. All finished."

"But *you* aren't.'' Marilyn Grant grabbed her partner's sleeve and dragged her into the cluttered office next to the kitchen. "Here.'' She handed Allison a silk dress the color of lime sherbet. "Put this on.''

"Why can't I go to the Dunbars' party like this?'' Allison asked. "I'll be working in the kitchen all night anyway. The guests won't even see me.''

Marilyn propped her hands on her hips. "For one thing, you've got a really unattractive guacamole stain on your blouse. And I believe that's hollandaise sauce dripped all over your shoes.'' Marilyn snatched the dress back and started undoing the row of tiny buttons running down the back. "And for another thing, you're representing Incredible Edibles. You don't want all those potential customers thinking we're a couple of slobs, do you?"

"No, I guess not," Allison sighed as Marilyn pulled the dress down over her head. She kicked off her shoes.

Marilyn handed Allison a pair of high-heeled sandals the same shade as the dress. Then she stepped back and scrutinized her friend. "Allison, do you want me to work the party tonight? You don't look like you're up to it."

"No, tonight's my turn. Thanks anyway. I'll be fine." Allison morosely studied her reflection in the mirror on the wall. "What am I going to do with this hair?" she muttered.

"Here, I'll pin it up for you." Marilyn grabbed a comb and went to work on Allison's unruly locks. Through a mouthful of bobby pins, she said, "I'm worried about you, Allison. You've been so down in the dumps lately. Ever since—well, ever since you came back from that crazy escapade two months ago."

Allison smiled in spite of herself. After returning to Los Angeles, she'd outlined for Marilyn a rough sketch of her journey with the Caldwells. She'd left out some of the details, of course, feeling somehow that she owed it to Nick and Danny not to reveal too much. And she'd glossed over her romance with Nick.

But Allison could tell that Marilyn had her suspicions about what had happened between them. And every time the subject came up, Marilyn referred to it as "that crazy escapade of yours," as if Allison had suffered a bout of temporary insanity. Well, maybe she had.

"I *have* been a little depressed lately," she admitted. "But don't worry about me. I'll get over it."

"Get over what?" Marilyn jabbed the last bobby pin in place. "Allison, what exactly happened during that crazy escapade of yours that's had you moping around with your chin dragging on the floor for the past two months?"

Allison gingerly patted her upswept hairdo. "We've gone over this before, Marilyn. *Nothing* happened. Absolutely nothing."

"You're a terrible liar, you know." Marilyn folded her arms. Then her stern expression softened, and she rested her hand on Allison's arm. "But if you ever *do* feel like talking about it, I'm here, kid."

Tears pricked Allison's eyes. "Thanks," she said. "That means a lot to me." She hugged Marilyn.

"Come on now, enough of this. You'll wrinkle that gorgeous dress. Here, I've got a present for you. Well, a loan, actually."

Allison opened the narrow white box Marilyn handed her. "Your pearls!" she exclaimed. "Oh, Marilyn, I know how much these mean to you. I couldn't possibly borrow—"

"Yes, you could," Marilyn insisted, fastening the strand of pearls around Allison's neck. "They go perfectly with that dress. Besides, I thought they might cheer you up."

Allison forced herself to smile. "They're lovely. And I *do* feel better, Marilyn. Scout's honor!"

Marilyn studied her doubtfully. "Well, if you say so. You certainly *look* fabulous." She checked her watch. "Yikes, you've got to get out of here! I'll help you carry the rest of the stuff out to the van."

It was a good thing Marilyn had made her get dressed up, Allison thought later that evening. Mrs. Dunbar had decided to set up a buffet in the ballroom instead of having her maid serve the food from the kitchen. So Allison wound up tending the buffet table in full view of the hundred or so guests invited to celebrate the Dunbars' golden wedding anniversary.

She had to admit, being out here watching the party was a lot more interesting than being stuck in the kitchen, loading up trays of food for Consuelo to serve. Mrs. Dunbar's last-minute change of plan had thrown Allison for a loop at first, but as always, she'd managed to cope with her client's sudden whim.

One thing she had to say for the Dunbars—they really knew how to throw a party. Besides hiring the best caterers on the Westside, they'd brought in a ten-piece orchestra to provide music for dancing, and three bartenders to provide liquid refreshment for thirsty guests.

The ballroom of the Dunbars' Beverly Hills mansion was redolent with the scent of a dozen flower arrangements, and light from the crystal chandeliers sparkled off gilt-edged mirrors like an explosion of fireworks.

Couples danced around the potted palms to the pleasant strains of a waltz; the clink of champagne glasses and a lively chorus of conversation and laughter filled the air.

Everyone was having a perfectly marvelous time.

Everyone, that is, except Allison.

Her earlier conversation with Marilyn had started her thinking about Nick again, remembering those wild, frantic, passionate days in May.

Not that an hour didn't go by when Allison didn't think of Nick anyway. But Marilyn's concern made her realize that she wasn't getting over Nick the way she'd planned.

With an unpleasant shiver, she recalled that last morning in the Fresno motel room, when she'd woken to find that Nick and Danny had vanished. The only explanation for their disappearance was a brief note in Nick's bold, masculine scrawl: "A. I have to do what's best for all three of us. N." Throwing on her clothes, she'd hopped in the car and started searching for them, checking the bus station, the train station, the local airfield.

She'd found no trace of the Caldwells.

Allison was no detective, and she knew how well Nick could cover his tracks. She didn't have a snowball's chance in hell of finding them.

With a weary heart, she'd returned to Los Angeles, determined to forget Nick, to blot out of her memory all the tender moments they'd shared. She'd had to do some fast talking at the Department of Motor Vehicles to convince them that some prankster must have switched her license plates with that station wagon in San Ysidro.

Once Allison had taken care of this detail, there were no more loose ends, no more reminders that Nick and Danny had ever passed through her life. It should have been easy to pretend that Nick had never existed. Instead, it had proven to be an impossible task. Allison discovered it wasn't easy to stop loving Nick, to stop wondering every single day where he and Danny could be right now.

Had they found sanctuary in some remote mountain town in the wilds of Montana? Or maybe they'd concealed themselves in the crowds of Chicago....

One of the hardest facts for Allison to accept was that she would never know. By clashing with Nick over the issue of Danny's welfare, Allison had driven them both out of her life forever.

Allison dragged into the kitchen to replenish the ice beneath the shrimp tray. Why did even the slightest chore seem like such an effort these days? Her melancholy was like a leaden cloak around her shoulders, slowing her down, wearing her out, making Allison wonder if she would ever again walk with a light step, her head held high, ready to take on the world.

When she returned to the buffet table, the Dunbars' maid, Consuelo, was sneaking a cheese ball. "Oops, you caught me!" she said, licking her fingers. "Promise you won't report me to Mrs. D." Her dark eyes sparkled mischievously.

Allison smiled. She'd met Consuelo at one of Mrs. Dunbar's previous parties, and liked the woman immensely. "I promise I won't tell on you, if you'll sneak over and bring me a club soda from the bar. I'm dying of thirst."

"Club soda? How boring." Consuelo leaned closer and whispered, "How about some champagne?"

"I don't drink on the job. Just like a policeman. Policewoman. Whatever."

Consuelo wagged her finger. "Afraid you'll get mixed up and put salt in the sugar bowl, eh? I understand. Be right back."

Allison watched Consuelo navigate through the guests, her waist-length black hair dancing merrily behind her as she headed toward the bar. In a moment she returned with Allison's drink. "Lots of good-looking men at this party," she observed with enthusiasm.

Allison sipped her club soda. "Are there? I hadn't noticed."

Consuelo looked shocked. "Didn't notice? What's the matter with you? Are you blind? Of course, most of them are older, but still . . . I bet they're rich."

Allison laughed. "You're terrible, Consuelo. Don't you think there are more important qualities to consider than the size of a man's bank account?"

Consuelo shrugged. "Oh, sure. But being rich sure doesn't hurt, eh? Or being handsome, either." Suddenly her eyes lit up. "Speaking of handsome, check this guy out. Mmm, *qué guapo!*"

Allison was too busy rearranging the stuffed mushrooms to "check out" the object of Consuelo's latest infatuation.

"Oh, my God, he's coming this way! How do I look?" Hastily she smoothed her frilly white apron.

"You look gorgeous, as usual," Allison said without glancing up.

"Here he comes!" Consuelo whispered.

"Hi, there," said a deep, strangely familiar male voice. "Those look delicious. Mind if I try one?"

Unable to believe her ears, Allison raised her eyes slowly from the tray of mushrooms, taking in the man's silver belt buckle, his well-tailored gray sport coat, his broad shoulders, his face.

"Nick," she breathed.

"Allison," he said softly. They stood staring at each other for a long moment.

"Hey, you two know each other?" Consuelo asked.

Nick nodded slowly without taking his eyes from Allison. "Oh, yes," he said, "we know each other."

Then Allison grew flustered. "Nick, what are you doing here? How did you find me? Where have you been?" She swallowed. "Is—is Danny okay?"

"He's fine," Nick assured her. He glanced around the room. "Is there someplace private we can talk?"

"Nick, I—I'm working right now, I don't know if I can take time to—"

"Sure you can." Consuelo put her hands on Allison's back and gave her a gentle shove. "You can sneak out through the kitchen. Don't worry, don't worry, I'll keep an eye on your precious food. And if Mrs. D. asks where you are, I'll tell her you went to the powder room." Consuelo gave Allison a sly wink.

"Thanks," Nick told her. "I really appreciate this."

"Oh, you're *very* welcome," Consuelo replied, batting her eyelashes and giving Nick a dazzling smile.

Allison stumbled through the kitchen and into the backyard, scarcely aware of where she was going. Her mind reeled with surprise and confusion and happiness. A thousand times she'd imagined Nick's reappearance, never believing her dreams would actually come true. Now that he was really here, she didn't know how to act, didn't know what to say.

Nick slipped his hand over Allison's and led her into the rose garden. Their footsteps echoed on the stone pathway, matching the excited rhythm of Allison's heart.

At the far side of the garden Nick stopped beside a wrought-iron bench. He stepped back to get a better view of Allison.

"Let me look at you," he said. "Turn around." He made a spinning motion with his hand.

Allison turned, slightly self-conscious, but welcoming the admiring gleam in Nick's eyes. The silken folds of her dress rippled seductively, clinging to her legs when she stopped.

"Wow. You look sensational," Nick said.

"You're not so bad yourself," she said almost breathlessly. Even in the shadows, Allison could see that Nick looked ten years younger than when she'd last seen him. Something had erased the lines of anxiety and suffering etched in his face. He was even more handsome, with an almost boyish cast to his features, now that he no longer wore that grim, determined expression. He walked with a bounce in his step that Allison had never seen before.

She had so many questions tumbling through her mind, she scarcely knew which to ask first. She started with the safest one. "How on earth did you find me here?"

"When you weren't at home, I called your partner and asked if she knew where you were. Whew!" Nick rubbed his chin. "She's a dragon lady."

Allison giggled. "She is not! She's just kind of protective about me, that's all."

"You can say that again." Nick grinned ruefully. "It took me nearly fifteen minutes to convince her that I wasn't a dangerous criminal or something. It was kind of hard to explain who I was. I didn't know how much you'd told her about—well, about us."

"Not much."

"Hmm." He gave her an uncertain look. "Well, anyway, I finally wore her down, and she told me you were here. I'm sorry to interrupt you while you're working, but the truth is, I just couldn't wait any longer to see you."

His words filled Allison with joy. She sank onto the bench. "Come sit next to me," she said, "and tell me about Danny."

Nick's shoulders brushed against her as he lowered himself onto the narrow bench. "I guess I should start with that last night, when you and I had that discussion."

"It was a fight, Nick."

"Okay, when we had that fight." He combed his fingers through his hair, leaving a stray lock curled across his forehead. "After you walked off, I did some serious thinking. You'd planted doubts in my mind, Allison. For the first time in two years, I began to wonder if Danny *would* be better off back in Boston."

"Nick, why didn't you tell me? Why did you run out on me that way? Do you have any idea how frantic with worry I've been?"

"Didn't you find my note?" he asked in surprise.

"Your note? You mean that cryptic, one-sentence scribble? 'I have to do what's best for all three of us.' Is that your idea of an explanation?"

A sheepish expression crept over Nick's face. "I guess that wasn't very clear, was it?"

"Clear as mud."

"Sweetheart, I'm sorry—but it was pitch dark when I wrote that note, and I was in an awful hurry."

"Nick, I thought you'd gone on the run again, that you meant all three of us would be better off if we parted company forever."

He took her hand in his. "I'm terribly sorry for what I put you through, Allison. You see, that last night, our conversation—*fight*—made it all too plain to me that the three of us—you, Danny and I—could never have a future together as long as we kept on running. Also..." He stroked Allison's fingers. She noticed his calluses had faded a little.

"I guess I was worried you might want to come back to Boston with me," Nick continued. "But taking Danny home was something he and I had to do by ourselves. Besides, I didn't want to involve you in the legal and emotional mess I knew was waiting for me."

"What happened?" she asked quietly.

Nick took a deep breath. "Well, you were right. A lot of things had changed while Danny and I were away."

"Such as?"

"For one thing, Sheila's been getting professional help to deal with her problems. She's been going to Alcoholics Anonymous, and making good progress. She's gotten her drinking under control."

"Nick, that's wonderful!"

He nodded. "I don't know if I can ever forgive Sheila for the way she treated Danny in the past. But I'm glad

she's pulling her life together. And now her father real-
izes that Sheila wasn't the innocent victim in the breakup
of our marriage. I don't know if Sheila confessed the
way she abused Danny, but I'm fairly certain her father
suspects the truth. He's certainly changed his attitude
toward me.''

"How so?"

Nick chuckled. "Well, for one thing, he didn't have
me thrown in jail the minute I set foot in Boston."

Allison couldn't stand the suspense anymore. "Tell
me what happened with Danny."

Nick crossed one leg over the other. "Well, I left
Danny with my Aunt Lydia until I could straighten
things out. Then all of us got together with the judge—
Sheila, her father and I. And our lawyers, of course."

"And?"

Nick patted her hand. "Hold your horses! I'm getting there. Anyway, the judge was ready to throw the
book at me at first. But then Sheila's father started talking. He told the judge he and Sheila understood why I'd
taken Danny, and they didn't want me prosecuted on
child-stealing charges. Then he said that they'd had two
years to think the whole matter over, and that if Danny
wanted to keep living with me, they wouldn't fight it."

A radiant smile broke across Allison's face. "Nick, I
can't believe it."

His teeth flashed white as he grinned. "Believe me,
neither could I. Sheila didn't say a word the whole time.
I think she was hoping if she kept her mouth shut, her
drinking problem and the subject of child abuse
wouldn't come up. I suspect that over the past couple of
years, Lawrence Hammond finally came to realize that
Sheila might not be the best person in the world to raise
his only grandchild."

Allison was fidgeting with impatience. "So?" she exclaimed.

Nick gripped her hands between his. "So the judge set up a visitation schedule for Sheila. And he awarded Danny's custody to me."

"Oh, Nick!" Allison threw her arms around his neck.

He hugged her close, his head bent over hers, his strong arms wrapped tightly around her. "Hey, hey, what's this?" he said a moment later. "You're not crying, are you?"

"Of course not," Allison mumbled, wiping away the tears on the lapel of his coat. "I'm just so happy for you, that's all. Can you blame me for getting a little emotional?"

Nick gazed at her with a tender, understanding expression. "No. Of course not."

Relief and happiness welled up inside her, filling her to the brim, making her want to fling out her arms and sing to the sky. She jumped to her feet, unable to sit still. In light of Nick's return and his wonderful news, the universe was suddenly a terrific place again. Allison strolled a few steps down the path, inhaling deeply, drawing in the sweet, strong fragrance of roses. The warm night air was like velvet against her skin.

Nick followed, catching her hand and turning Allison to face him. As she looked up at him, a backdrop of stars glittered like sequins on the black satin of the sky.

"Allison." Nick swallowed. "I didn't come all this way just to tell you about Danny."

"No?" She fought down the hope rising in her heart. This couldn't be happening. She was dreaming, and any minute she would wake up to bitter disappointment.

"No." Nick folded her hands between his and searched her eyes with a half-loving, half-anxious expression. "Allison, I came to ask you to come back to

Boston with me. To be a family with Danny and me."
He cleared his throat. "Allison, I love you. Will you
marry me?"

She fell back a step. Oh, what a cruel dream this was!
To taunt her with the one thing she wanted more than
anything else in the world...

"Allison?" Nick said anxiously. "Are you all right?
You look sort of...stunned."

She raised a hand to her forehead. "I guess I am," she
admitted. "This is all happening so fast—your showing
up here tonight, telling me about Danny, and now asking me to marry you." She bit her lower lip. "Nick, I'm
so afraid I'm going to wake up and this will all be a
dream!"

Then he laughed, and pulled her into his arms. "If this
is a dream," he said, "then we're both in it. And I hope
we never wake up."

"Me, neither," she said, snuggling against him.

"Does that mean your answer's yes?"

Allison slid her arms from around his waist. "Nick,
there's something I have to tell you."

His face clouded with uncertainty. "You—you hav-
en't gotten married in the past two months, have you?"

"No, of course not. Although it would serve you
right, deserting me in that motel room, not telling me
where you'd gone...."

Nick tilted her head close to his and brushed his lips
against her cheek. "I'm sorry. Please give me the rest of
our lives to make it up to you."

Allison bowed her head. "Nick, remember when you
first came to my house that night, looking for your
keys?"

"Sure, I remember."

"Well, uh, you see..." Allison fiddled with her necklace. "The truth is, that I, uh, I *did* have your keys. I had them all along."

"I know."

Her eyes flew to his face in amazement. "You *knew*?"

Nick shrugged. "Well, I didn't know for certain. But I was pretty sure I'd lost my keys in your van. Where else could they be, if you didn't have them?"

Allison's jaw dropped. "Then why didn't you say so? Why didn't you put up more of a fight and demand I return them? If you'd pressured me, I probably would have surrendered and given them back to you."

Nick lowered his head and nuzzled the soft curve of her neck. "Aren't you glad I didn't?" he said.

"Nick Caldwell!" Allison slapped his chest. "You knew I had those keys, and you let me keep them and used that as an excuse for dragging me along...." Her voice trailed off. "Hmm. Maybe you made the right decision." Her head rolled to one side, allowing Nick easier access to her throat. His kisses sent thrills of pleasure up and down her spine, making her knees weak.

"You still haven't answered my question," Nick said. He trailed his lips along her jaw, her cheek, her chin...finally capturing her mouth with his.

She clung to him, reveling in the delightful sensations he was arousing in her. "Mmm, um, what question?" she murmured.

Nick raised his lips the barest millimeter above hers. "Will you marry me?" His breath was warm against her lips.

"What do you think?" she replied in a dreamy whisper. "I love you, Nick Caldwell. Of course I'll marry you."

"Allison." Her name was trapped between them as he pressed his lips firmly against hers, circling her tightly with his arms, making her dizzy with his ardent embrace.

She slid her hands beneath his coat and across his broad, strong back, reacquainting herself with every bone, every muscle...knowing that she had a lifetime to explore every single aspect of Nick Caldwell. And what a delightful project that would be.

At last Nick lifted his mouth from hers, leaving Allison breathless and dazed with happiness. "I guess I'd better let you get back to work," he said with a lazy smile. "*Someone* in this family has to earn a living, until I can build up my architecture business again."

"So you're only after me for my money?"

"Of course." Nick kissed the tip of her nose. "What other attraction could you possibly hold for me? Your caring, your warmth, your sense of humor, your sexy body..." He skimmed his hands down her waist and over her hips.

"You're as bad as Consuelo," Allison said, swaying close to him again. Then she clapped her hand over her mouth. "Oh, my goodness, I forgot about Consuelo! I've got to rescue her from the buffet table before we both get fired."

She darted around Nick and dashed down the path toward the house.

"Why is it that whenever you and I get together, one of us is always running off someplace?" Nick grumbled, tagging close behind her.

Allison screeched to a halt. Nick bumped into her.

"I just thought of something," she said.

"Good. I thought of the same thing. Come on, let's go. Forget about Consuelo. I know this romantic little inn—"

"Not that," she scolded, her eyes sparkling like emeralds. "I forgot that I can only marry you on one condition, Nick."

His brows drew together in a puzzled frown. "What— oh!" A broad grin spread across his handsome face. Lifting his hand to touch her cheek, he said softly, "Don't worry. Danny approves. I've already spoken to him about it. He's dying for you to come to Boston so we can take you to a baseball game."

Allison breathed a sigh of relief. "Great," she said happily. "Then the wedding's on again." She linked her arm through Nick's, and they strolled side by side toward the house, the sounds of the party growing louder, the lights growing brighter.

"Okay, help me out here," Allison said. "What's the name of Boston's baseball team? Some kind of socks, right?"

*   *   *   *   *

Silhouette Special Edition

COMING NEXT MONTH

#583 TAMING NATASHA—Nora Roberts
Natasha Stanislaski was a pussycat with Spence Kimball's little girl, but to Spence himself she was as ornery as a caged tiger. Would some cautious loving sheath her claws and free her heart from captivity?

#584 WILLING PARTNERS—Tracy Sinclair
Taking up residence in the fabled Dunsmuir mansion, wedding the handsome Dunsmuir heir and assuming instant ''motherhood'' surpassed secretary Jessica Lawrence's wildest dreams. But had Blade Dunsmuir wooed her for money...or love?

#585 PRIVATE WAGERS—Betsy Johnson
Rugged Steven Merrick deemed JoAnna Stowe a mere bit of fluff—until the incredibly close quarters of a grueling motorcycle trek revealed her fortitude *and* her womanly form, severely straining *his* manly stamina!

#586 A GUILTY PASSION—Laurey Bright
Ethan Ryland condemned his stepbrother's widow for her husband's untimely death. Still, he was reluctantly, obsessively drawn to the fragile-looking Celeste...and he feared she shared his damnable passion.

#587 HOOPS—Patricia McLinn
Though urged to give teamwork the old college try, marble-cool professor Carolyn Trent and casual coach C. J. Draper soon collided in a stubborn tug-of-war between duty...and desire.

#588 SUMMER'S FREEDOM—Ruth Wind
Brawny Joel Summer had gently liberated man-shy Maggie Henderson...body and soul. But could her love unchain him from the dark, secret past that shadowed their sunlit days of loving?

AVAILABLE THIS MONTH:

You'll flip . . . your pages won't!
Read paperbacks *hands-free* with

Book Mate · I

The perfect "mate" for all your romance paperbacks

Traveling • Vacationing • At Work • In Bed • Studying
• Cooking • Eating

Perfect size for all standard paperbacks, this wonderful invention makes reading a pure pleasure! Ingenious design holds paperback books OPEN and FLAT so even wind can't ruffle pages — leaves your hands free to do other things. Reinforced, wipe-clean vinyl-covered holder flexes to let you turn pages without undoing the strap . . . supports paperbacks so well, they have the strength of hardcovers!

Pages turn WITHOUT opening the strap

SEE-THROUGH STRAP

Reinforced back stays flat

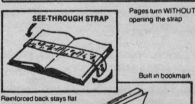

Built in bookmark

BOOK MARK

BACK COVER
HOLDING STRIP

10 x 7¼ opened
Snaps closed for easy carrying, too

At long last, the books you've been waiting for
by one of America's top romance authors!

DIANA PALMER

DUETS

Ten years ago Diana Palmer published her very first
romances. Powerful and dramatic, these gripping tales
of love are everything you have come to expect from
Diana Palmer.

In March, some of these titles will be available again in
DIANA PALMER DUETS—a special three-book collection. Each book will have two wonderful stories plus an
introduction by the author. You won't want to miss them!

Book 1
SWEET ENEMY
LOVE ON TRIAL

Book 2
STORM OVER THE LAKE
TO LOVE AND CHERISH

Book 3
IF WINTER COMES
NOW AND FOREVER

 *Silhouette Books*®

DP-1